Leather Dreams
Lexi Gray

Thank You!

Description

You're a woman stuck in a man's world. You had to fight your way to the top with no legacy to follow.

You've worked to push through your troubled past, putting it behind you.

Of all things you've learned on your road to recovery, you know your self worth. You're hot, you're a motorcycle babe, and you're able to put a bullet between the enemy's eyes without hesitation.

You learn to survive, living day to day.

You move on...but the past is never really gone.

What you didn't expect? Three members of the club waltzing into your life. Enveloping you into a world between pain and pleasure.

The pain can sometimes outweigh the pleasure, but can you survive?

Welcome to Leather Dreams.

Triggers

Blood

Murder/Death

Gore & Blood

Violence

Vulgar Language

Mentions of child sex trafficking (scenes off screen & non-descriptive)

Historical physical abuse of FMC (mentioned on-screen)

On-Screen torture FMC

Consensual-non consensual

MM/MMF/MF

Did I mention blood?

BDSM & torture techniques including, but not limited to:

Blindfolding

Breath Play

Cuckolding

Humiliation/Degradation

Impact Play

Voyeurism/Exhibitionism

Dedication

To my lovely, horny readers...I hope you like a good slow burn,
because you'll burn so damn hot you'll need a skin graft.

Chapter One

LEATHER

Why can't anything go the way I need it to?

"You're a piece of shit!" I snap, smacking him. *Hard.*
He grunts as my hand *whooshes*, his head whipping to the side with the force. Arms tied behind his back, his chest pushed out and begging for me to rip his meek little heart out. "I don't know who you think you are, but you've fucked with the wrong woman."

"Fucking cunt," he spits, blood coated saliva landing on my boot. "You women think you can just jump into a man's world? You're nothing more than breeding bitches!"

"Really?" I pretend to pout and kick a rock under my boot. "That is just too darn bad. This little breeder has been a naughty girl! She hasn't laid on her back for a useless man in a while. Sad face," I taunt, jutting my bottom lips out. He shouts and attempts to break the rope off his wrists again.

He continues to struggle, yet I can only watch in pure fascination. If he manages to get out, then I get another chance at whipping his ass into shape.

"Get on your back like a good bitch does, and maybe you'll finally understand your place in this world." Tilting my head from side to side, I pretend to contemplate my decision.

"Hmmm, nah, I don't think so." His elbow twitches, and I whip my pistol from my holster. "Night night!" With a simple pull of the trigger, a bullet lodges between his eyes.

Blood splatters the wall behind him, brain matter spilling across the bricks. I watch as his body crumples to the ground, legs giving out without the tension in the muscles. His empty brick head slams onto the ground, cracking open from the back. The splatter flies around him and up onto me.

I revel in the way it trickles from his hair, zoning into the droplets falling and splashing onto the concrete. It's almost like I can hear the droplets falling.

Splash.

Splash.

Spla-

The distant sound of engines revving snaps me out of my daze. Glancing down at my body, I watch the red liquid slowly drop down the leather pants. "Ah, fucking hell," I grumble, reaching into my pocket for my phone. "You'd better fucking pick up." Dialing the number, the ring is monotonous as it goes, and it's almost like-

"What?" He barks, his breathing heavy and labored. Yanking the device away from me, I can't help but cringe in disgust.

"First off all, that's fucking gross," I grimace, knowing that my Prez is probably balls deep right now. "Should have just let me go to voicemail. Second, it's done." I don't wait for a response before ending the call since I have zero desire to hear that shit.

It's not like I have an aversion to sex, don't get me wrong, but Prez is like an older brother I never wanted, other than he's not really brother material besides being my biker brother...does that make sense? Probably not because I would fuck him in a heart beat. So, I suppose he's not brotherly at all in any way, shape, or form. Which is a plus because I have seen him with some of the jacket pickers. He's hung.

Eyeing the dude, I take his jacket off and tie it around my waist like I own the fucking thing. I would rather burn it, but it'll make a great souvenir for their men later on. I can see us sending it over to their clubhouse, maybe even add a little memento from this guy to top it all off. Plus, I think this is genuine leather, the good shit. Rolling up his sleeves, I find the tattoo I'm looking for. *Big D Raiders.* Unfortunately, it doesn't mean dick. This dumbass biker gang has been helping use kids for sex trafficking, snatching them off their fucking lawns and sending them across the world for their own benefit.

Anger bubbles in my veins at the outrageous shit they have done. After the shit they have done...I can't pretend I don't have a vendetta of my own.

I grab my switchblade from my pocket, flaying the skin off his arm to remove the piece of garbage ink. The flabby skin dangles from my gloved hand, his arm pouring blood from the open wound, and I make no effort to stop it. Fascinating, really, the amount of work it takes to keep someone from bleeding out, yet it's so easy to just...*slice* right in the throat.

"Serves you right for acting like a dick," I mutter, pulling a small baggie from my other pocket. Stuffing the removed piece in and shoving it away, I eye the guy curiously.

I bet his penis is the size of my pinky.

Scooping a bit of blood, I smear *SRWD* on his forehead. Silent Renegade of Washington District. They will know we're onto them, exactly like we planned. Big D will have to watch their backs, look over their shoulder during every transaction. Every waking minute they will be anticipating when and how SRWD will strike next.

A bead dribbles down his cheek into his open eye, and I watch with utter fascination as it coasts into his ducts. Collecting there, it's like a red waterfall, flowing dramatically down his cheek. A possessive inkling digs into my chest, the longing feeling that I just skinned this man for revenge. While the blood oozes from the wound, my chest grasps for the feeling again. The triumph, the glory of taking the last breath of a man involved in one of the worst things in the world. A vile creature he is, and I want nothing more than to take out the whole fucking gang that tore my brother from me. I will do whatever it takes to get my vengeance.

"That was hot," a deep voice calls from behind me. Jolting, I swing around with my gun aimed right for his head. The barrel points right between his eyes, the middle ground for a quick execution. But, just as I go to pull the trigger, I exhale raggedly.

"Fuck," I bark, swinging my arm down. "Dumbass! You don't just walk up on people like that." Irritation floods my nerves as I turn back to my victim. The shocked expression he wore is still imprinted in my mind, lingering in satisfaction as my work blooms and the blood drips from his other wounds. A perfect, miserable masterpiece.

A sudden weight presses against my back, a knife tilted at my throat. The sharp edge threatens to nick my skin, yet I push into the blade, if only slightly.

"All bark, no bite." Gnashing his teeth, he drags the point of the tip against my jaw and his free hand snakes around my waist. "Maybe you should stay more vigilant. Don't worry, I'm here to save the day. When I said you were hot, I wasn't joking. Can't you tell?" His hips press into me, his hardened bulge pressing into my ass as he releases a strangled groan. Rolling my eyes, I push back against him, rubbing a little. Teasing him a bit.

"And I'm pretty sure I said I only like big cocks," I retort, knowing damn well he's packing more heat in his jeans than I do in my weapons. The knife presses even harder into my throat, the sting in the slice of my skin brings clarity to my brain before he drops it away with a huffed laugh. Red is barely evident on the shiny metal, but I catch it.

I always do.

You can't miss it when blood is your favorite pastime.

"One day you're going to let me fuck that pretty pussy of yours, Leather," he quips, tucking his knife away.

"How do you know my pussy is pretty?" I tease, crossing my arms over my chest. He points a finger at the dead guy.

"That's how I know. If you can kill a guy with finesse, you've got a pretty kitty." Laughing, I dry my gloves off on his shirt. His face pinches slightly before his eyes twinkle with lust again.

"I don't really see how that correlates, but whatever you say, *Onyx*." Gliding past him, I know he always gets his panties in a twist when someone calls the guys by their names when on the clock.

He scoffs, raising his voice an octave. "Okay, Blaine." I swear to God, I feel my fucking eye twitch with the name. Taking a deep breath, I count to ten. Instead of pushing him more, I respect his position in the club. Another executioner. He earned his biker name because he prefers to use his bare fists.

"You going to the clubhouse tonight, Knuckles?" I ask, shoving my key into the starter of my bike.

"Is that where you're going?" Flicking it over, I let my baby purr to life between my thighs. She rumbles and coos while I straddle her. I have had her since my teens, but I will be damned if I give her up. She's an oldie but a goodie. Matte black with a dark blue leather seat, she's got blue underlights that bump to the beat of any music I play.

"I mean, I need my pussy taken care of," I joke, putting rubber to pavement. His laugh drifts behind me as I fly down backroads.

One thing about me? No matter how much I read and see on the news about brains being carved into the roads, I refuse to ride with a helmet. The feeling of wind slapping your face, letting the breeze flow through my hair, it gives the feeling of being free. Growing up in the MC life wasn't as bad as kids might perceive it. Us lifers, who grew up in this world and decided to stay, were given our respective positions based on our talents.

Mine was seduction. They never anticipated little ol' me to be in a biker gang. Well, that was until I got slashed from temple to lip by a rusty, jagged blade. Now I have this wicked scar that nobody finds appealing, so I take an executioner style approach. Makeup can only hide so much. Unfortunately for me, it doesn't hide a shitty personality.

Chapter Two

LEATHER

"Fuck, yes! Harder, daddy," a jacket picker squeals loudly. Sipping my daiquiri, I do my best to tune out the whores getting fucked into oblivion around me. Am I jealous? A little, but I have put myself into a self-imposed dry spell.

Littered around the clubhouse are guys with jacket pickers. Some guys are pounding them into the wall so hard there may be an indent later. Others are bent over tables getting plowed from behind. It's an erotic sight, but it's not really my scene anymore.

Getting railed into by a dude with an anaconda in his jeans is a life mission for some women, but I have had that shit. I have been around the block, been there, done that. I rode guys in the booths while my ass hung out. I have had a dick in my ass and a dick in my pussy in the middle of the club, but I don't want mindless sex anymore. The constant bouncing around, reteaching a man or two how to find a clit, my preferred angles to hit the right spot, everything. It's tiresome, and I just don't want to do that anymore.

The only problem? I also don't want a relationship. Some guys perceive women to be below them. Not women who are affiliated with a biker gang that helps exterminate others, especially those who harm children. I'm not someone who is going to roll over and become a good girl for a man. Men are the weaker species, expecting someone to wait on them hand and foot, waiting for food to be put on the table for them. Not only that, but relationships tend to make people forget their sole purpose. My purpose is with this club and helping innocent people in any way I possibly can.

I have deduced that men are a distraction. Unfortunately for me, I learned the hard way that guys only want two things. Pussy and power. I have been used by others who get promoted up the ranks, and I refuse to do that again. I refuse to *be* that girl again. Women will take over the motorcycle world one day, and I hope that I'm around to see it.

Speaking of women's genitalia, the moans around me seem to get louder and louder. If I were in a lighter mood, I would have thought the sounds were erotic. But right now? They are only making me feel worse.

It's not that I don't enjoy good, wholesome, live porn. In fact, I may dabble a little in it myself, but I'm just feeling particularly...prickly?

No, that's not the feeling. Maybe it's the fact that they are getting laid and I'm not. Do I want to get laid? Absolutely. Do men suck? One hundred fucking percent. Which rounds me back to why I can't have a permanent male in my life, and also takes me to the point that I don't want to have meaningless sex. Contradictory, I know. I don't want a male in my life, but I also don't want to have one-night-stands. It makes perfect sense to me. I live for helping those who can't help themselves, and I will sacrifice myself to do so.

Slugging back the rest of my drink, I stave off a brain freeze by dropping a twenty dollar bill and stalking up to my room. Irritation bubbles through me as I slam the door shut and flop back onto my bed. The only way I will be able to ward off the noises of the women downstairs is to put headphones in, but I will be honest. They are making me a *little* horny. I'm a human, good sex is contagious, I swear.

I'm no better than a man. *Oops?*

Unlacing my studded heel boots, I shimmy out of my leather pants and lay them off to the side. There's still blood on the front, dry and crusty. Flakes fall onto the floor, dark and contrasting with the ugly pale colored carpet. Shaking myself from the momentary trance, I reach to pull my panties out of the way, but that's a solid perk I forgot about. Leather pants means no panties required. Smirking to myself, I roll my jacket off my body and toss it over the chair in the corner with my shirt and bra following closely behind.

I reach into my night stand, grabbing my pretty blue rechargeable wand. She's got several settings, but I prefer the last one. The one that has solid vibration at a high power. Flicking the bottom on, the familiar buzz courses to life. Dropping onto my bed, my thighs fall open on their own accord. My core pulses with need, waiting ever-so impatiently for friction.

"Shit," I hiss as the cold tip presses against my clit. My hips jerk in reaction, already building to my favorite feeling. Distant moans from the main clubhouse spur me on, the wand dancing over my sensitive bundle as the knot gets tighter and tighter. "O-oh god," I stutter, teetering closer to the edge as I rim my cunt.

Pushing a single finger in, my eyes flutter closed, immediately imagining two huge guys. I recognize their faces as the two guys that I owe my life to. Prez's handsome features pop into my brain, weaving through my mental barricade. With his black hair and deep eyes, that man could lure a woman to her death like a siren. No wonder he's now the president. The man is a fucking monster.

Walking behind Prez, is Knuckles. His bloody fist lands on his president's shoulder with a cocky smirk covering only half his face. He's been vying for a taste of me since we were teens, yet I haven't been able to do it. I never wanted to sway into a world where he didn't exist, so there was a wall built to keep us both safe. His deep hazel eyes scour my naked lower half as I swear I put on a show for them. My hips wiggle in front of their hungry eyes, their cocks sitting in their hands as they stroke them. My moans call out to the two men in my imagination, waiting for them to just touch me.

Please me.

Own me.

The solid edge I'm riding gets closer and closer, my stomach clenching in absolute desire as they stalk over to me, hands whispering over my heated skin. Prez keeps his gaze solely on my eyes, forcing me to look at the ghost of him as I cusp my orgasm. I need him to touch me, fuck me.

"Please, Prez–"

"Leather, can you– Oh shit!" My eyes slam open, the vibrator fumbling onto the bed with a loud *buzz*. One of the men from my imagination decided *now* was the time to come see me?

"Fuck, Prez!" I shriek, grabbing the blanket to cover myself. The high vibrations on the blue piece sputter mutedly on the sheets. Embarrassment and irritation continue to bite at me as I reach for the vibrator, only for it to be snatched away just as my fingers brush it. My mouth gawks open in surprise. "Hey! Give it back!"

"You were just...getting off by yourself?" He asks, letting the vibrations sound through the room. A hungry gaze stays on the wand, almost like he's envious of the thing.

"Turn the damn thing off, at least," I grumble, holding out my hand. "You're going to drain the battery."

"Isn't that what you were just doing?" He teases, turning it off. "I don't see porn pulled up or anything," he muses, walking closer while holding the damn thing captive. Scowling, I keep myself covered.

"Did you need something?" I sneer. "I was in the middle of something." He tosses the wand onto the bed before sitting on the end.

"I did come in with a job, but I think that can wait." He slowly crawls up my body, forcing me to lay back.

"What are you doing?" I gasp, my body shuddering with need. I have wanted to screw this man for as long as I can remember, even before he became Prez of the MC.

What I don't understand, is why the fuck he's in my room, watching me like he wants to eat me for breakfast, lunch, and dinner.

Chapter Three

PREZ

Banging my fist on the table, I push out of my chair. The cheap plastic topples effortlessly behind me, flying out of the way as I stand. "I don't care what you have to say. We're going to figure out a way to fucking remove them from society. Do you understand me?" I seethe through my teeth and into the small phone, barely holding onto my temper as I white-knuckle grip the desk. My red-hot anger won't cool.

As calmly as I can muster, I reach down into the drawer and grab a glass. It's not chilled, but there's worse ways to drink whiskey. The crystal decanter opens with a *pop*, the sound soothing my soul for a few moments. It gives me a moment to direct my brain onto something other than the worst type of people getting closer and closer to our territory. *Again*. The worst part is that we've been struggling to track them down. If we think we have a lead, then they derail us by going to a totally different area. Leather's been extremely lucky in finding the few that she has, but finding them in groups? Nearly impossible, even if clubs are considered like packs.

"Boss, I can't find any traces," the prospect meekly defends, obviously too much of a pussy for his own good. Groaning, I stab my fingers through my hair. It's getting too fucking long. Yanking on the strands, I exhale sharply, reminding myself over and over again that he's just a prospect. They don't know the shit we do.

"I'm telling you, Bear," I stress, picking up my phone and taking it off speaker. "Leather just de-patched a guy off Seventh Ave. They are here, you're just not looking close enough."

"They have no traces though," he argues, obviously starting to get flustered himself. Growling, I take those deep breaths Knuckles always tells me about.

"Ya know what? I will just send Leather to do it. It's her job anyway." Cutting off the kid, I end the damn call. Running a hand down my face, I scratch the scruff on my neck. This shit needs to be trimmed too.

"You still need something?" Jacket picker Janet asks, squeezing herself between myself and my desk. Her ass bumps against the wood and forces it away with a harsh shriek. Pushing away from the desk, my hands firmly plant themselves on the arms of the chair.

As the Prez, jacket pickers are unavoidable. In club life, they make the world go round. If the men aren't killing, their fucking. Jacket pickers grab hold of anyone with a cut, sucking them dry before moving onto the next man. That, or they end up becoming an ol' lady. Which is exactly what Janet is trying to do, and I'm very much not interested.

"Nah, that dumbass killed my boner," I huff, raising the glass and swigging back the liquid in one foul swoop. The harsh burn soothes me, subduing the aching anger buried deep in my soul.

"I could try to cheer you up," she purrs, rubbing her hands along my shoulders. Her nails drag along with leather material while she sucks on her bottom lip like she hasn't eaten dinner in a couple days. She's generally a good fuck, her pussy is wet enough to flood the place, but she's too damn loud. She's always willing to tell everyone that we fucked, another time to spread her legs for the leading man. Normally I don't care, let it roll off my back. Right now, though? I'm just not feeling it.

Talking about kids being hurt tends to stop sexual advances in their tracks, perhaps that's just me. Either way, I'm not about to go thinking of them in the same sentence, let alone the same thought process.

Pushing her hands off, I shake my head. "Nah, I got some shit I need to do. I need to chat with Leather." She visibly bristles when I mention my female lead. Leather tends to...rub people the wrong way. She's fucking boner popping hot but isn't the nicest person to be around. She's got issues.

Just like the rest of us.

Janet grabs her fake leather jacket off the back of the couch and shrugs it on angrily then storms out. I'm half tempted to ask her why she's willing to ruin her jacket over being mad, but I realize it's pleather and only about sixty bucks at the local store. She's waiting for a leather cut for being an old lady. One thing that she mentions almost every single time we're together. When I told her that it'd never happen, I meant it. It's something she will never get. That ship sailed when a two-faced bitch decided to tear my heart in two all those years ago.

Locking the office behind me, I go to the bar, which is one of the three places she would be. Moans and groans of pleasure echo around the club as I move. It definitely sounds like home. If it were quiet, I would ask if another case of herpes was going around in the club. It happened once when I was a prospect, but I love to bring it up to this day. They are never going to live it down, and I have no intentions of keeping it to myself.

Glancing down the bar both ways, her wild auburn mane doesn't pop out. The waitress of the night steps over, ready to serve with her tits pushed high and her smile fake as fuck.

"Where'd Leather go?" I ask instead, watching her face visibly wilt in disappointment.

"Upstairs," she says shortly before moving back down to the paying customers in the club. Rolling my eyes, I take the stairs two at a time. She could either be in her office or in her bedroom. Swinging on the stairs, I try her office first. *Empty.* So, that leaves her bedroom.

I slam my fist on the flimsy wood, waiting to hear from the other side. All I can catch is distant moaning, and I'm pretty sure she said for me to come in. "Leather, can you– Oh shit!" I stop in my tracks, my eyes bugging from my head. *Holy shit.*

Holy. Shit.

"Fuck, Prez!" She shrieks, grabbing the blanket to cover herself, and her full breasts are covered, much to my dismay. Those twins are two that I have been dying to meet. Something in my stomach twists at the thought that someone else could have walked in and saw them. Someone could have seen her entirely naked. A bubbling heat races through my veins at the mere thought. Reaching forward, I snatch the wand from its discarded place. "Hey! Give it back!"

"You were just...getting off by yourself?" I question, feeling the weight of it between my fingers like a knife. It's off balance, the plastic unsure of being held by me as much as I'm put off by it. The only thing this toy and I have in common is the mutual ability to make a woman cum.

"Turn the damn thing off at least," she snaps, holding out her hand. "You're going to drain the battery." Muttering an apology, I flick it off.

"Isn't that what you were just doing, hmm? I don't see porn pulled up or anything," I muse, pretending to look around while walking closer, keeping the vibrator to out of her reach. She shoots me a wicked look, one that would zap me if I were a weaker man. Instead, I hold it up to the light. It's on the smaller side, not a pluggable one like you see in the porn shows or when you're playing in scenes.

She sneers, "did you actually need something?" The blanket is pulled higher up on her body, the soft pale swells of her breasts getting covered even more. "I was in the middle of something."

Shrugging, I toss the vibrator onto the bed and plant myself on the end. I know I shouldn't be here and there's warning alarms going off in the back of my brain, but I can't seem to stop. If anything, the creamy smoothness I can see from her soft body makes me want to sink my teeth into it. I want people to see that she's owned. By the club.

By me.

Tilting my head from side to side, I decide to go for it. What else could go wrong?

"I did come in with a job, but I think it can wait." Crawling up the bed, she lays her body down while I hover over her.

She's completely shocked, not that I can blame her. I'm astonished with myself. Her full, pouty lips tremble slightly, a slight whimper falling from between them. "What are you doing?" She gasps, goosebumps forming on her sensitive flesh. Ignoring her question, I brush my nose along the column of her throat, a shiver rolling through her body.

"Have you ever thought about this?" I mutter against her skin, placing a gentle kiss in my wake. The urge to collapse on top of her, gnash my teeth and mark her is overwhelming, but I hold back.

I have always felt a need toward her, one that I was never able to understand. That is until I see how good she looks underneath me, gasping with blown pupils. She may not know it yet, but I own her.

She will just need time to adjust to her newest title.

Mine.

A small mewl cascades from her, her legs suddenly wrapping around my lower half.

My half hard dick springs to attention and rushes itself to full mass as she grinds her blanket covered pussy against me. The voice in my head is telling me to abort mission and get the hell out of there because it could ruin everything. On the other hand, I have a feeling this is going to be the best tasting cunt I have ever had.

Where's the adventure if there's no thrill?

"Yes," she whimpers, her eyes watching me. Meeting my gaze, she sucks her lower lip between her teeth. I swear this is a fucking dream. My hands form to her sides, squeezing the soft flesh.

Groaning, I start pulling the blanket away, but she stops me, shaking her head slightly before exposing her breasts. The blanket lay down the center of her body. Her stomach comes into view. Her glistening pussy also peeks through, swollen from its previous manipulation. "Fuck, you're already soaked." It's not toned like I would have expected, but that makes it even more perfect. "The things I want to do to you." Without warning, I suck a sweet peeked nipple into my mouth. She pushes her chest closer to me, her hands raking through my hair to keep me close. My tongue flicks over her nipple repeatedly, her moans echoing around us.

"Tell me," she taunts, her hands dragging down my back, slipping into my shirt, and clawing at the skin. Hissing, I bow into her just a bit. The sting of her nails pulses in my cock. If I could just slide into her...

Releasing her nipple with a pop, I grin down at her. "I want to devour this sweet pussy until you pass out." My fingers reach between her thighs, circling her swollen bud. Her hips jerk with the touch.

"Yes," she exhales, yanking on my hair.

Grunting, I can't help the small curse that drops from my lips, "fuck."

"Eat this fucking pussy," she demands, pushing on my shoulders suddenly. Smirking, I trail kisses down her body as slowly as I can.

"Yes ma'am." I bite into small bits of her skin as I go. Her fingers dig into my shoulders, probably to keep from slapping me. Right before I get to her sweetness, I pull back. "Sit on my face." Flopping next to her, her hesitation forces me to take matters into my own hands. I hoist her tiny ass over my face, a small shriek escaping her. Slanting my hands onto her hips, her pussy meets my face without a bit of finesse. She drops onto me and I get to work.

"Fuck, *yes.*" My hands dance up her body as I keep my eyes locked on her. Her head is tilted backward, hips stiff. Reaching a hand back, I toy with her asshole. This seems to pop her out of her stupor as she jerks her attention to my face. I wiggle my brows, sucking her bundle harshly while rimming her.

Her back bows aggressively, her hands tugging on my hair as she grinds down onto me.

"You taste so good," I growl, knowing the vibrations would make it better. She rasps incoherent words, her legs shaking and shuddering above me. She tastes like fucking heaven, which I definitely never thought of before.

She's been on my radar for a while, yet she never appeared to be interested in others. Her only focus was the club. That, and sex. But mostly the club. Now that I have caught her in a...precarious situation, I have every intention of making her my last meal.

She begins to unravel, hips rotating against my face, taking what she wants.

"Take it," I growl, smacking my palm on her ass. Jolting, she rocks harder into my face as I continue to flick and suck on her clit. The little bud is swollen and hard as I make out with it.

"Just like that!" Her body goes still, hands slamming to grasp the headboard as her legs violently start to shake. "*Oh god!*" She screams, wetness pouring from her as she explodes over me. I take it all, devouring and consuming her as she squirms with oversensitivity. Her shocked face meets mine as we simply stare at one another.

It's like something just...clicked. She scrambles off of me, covering herself with her duvet once more. I don't know what came over us, but it wasn't like anything else I would ever experience. I hate repeated sex because that means feelings, but with her...

"Leather," I start. Just as I'm about to try and tie words together, there's a knock on the door.

We both go still, silencing our breaths as much as possible. Scrambling, we both start getting our clothes back on. I slam my pinky toe into the bottom of the bed, a silent curse leaving my lips while I straighten myself.

"Leather?" A deep voice calls from the other side, causing us both to stare in disbelief.

Shit.

Chapter Four

KNUCKLES

"**P**rez is going to fucking kill me," the prospect sighs, running his hand through his hair. Clapping him on the back, I chug the rest of my beer.

"Nah," I deny, squeezing his shoulder before letting go. "It's not your job. We're executioners for a reason. Don't sweat it. He probably hasn't gotten laid in a few hours." The prospect barks a stressed laugh before nodding.

"Maybe. He said he was going to find Leather. I have not been able to find anything on this damn gang, yet she's been on a roll." He waves the bartender down, swishing his cup for a refill.

"*Again*, it's not your job. You don't have the resources nor bargaining chips that we do. We've got leverage, you don't. Don't stuff your cock up your ass about it." I get up, deciding to go find the man of the hour. Gliding by his office, I'm stopped by the annoying voice right as I prepare to knock.

"He's not in there," Janet sneers, glancing down at her nails. "He went to find Pleather."

"You know *Pleather* would kill you for that, right? Disrespect is a big thing with members," I retort, crossing my arms over my chest. Leather doesn't take shit from jacket pickers, only because she's been burned by them before. Leather used to be more smiley, her excitement for life used to be palpable and contagious. Now, it was like she couldn't care less about life. She only cared for the wellbeing of the club and its members, becoming an executioner for that reason alone. Everyone knows Leather doesn't give a fuck now. She's practically ruthless. Everyone knows she will gladly burn in hell just to enact revenge.

Janet pales for a minute before her mask falls back in place, her beady eyes narrowing on me and a sneer on her face.

"Well, tell your Prez to make me a cutter then. I would look better in a cut than she does, and I dare her to try and kill me." She squints before shrugging, twirling a piece of hair between her fingers. "Either way, he went to *her*. So, they are probably boning while they give each other whatever diseases."

"The only one giving 'diseases' is you. She earned her spot in the club with blood and sweat while you fucked your way in. There's a difference so don't get confused. Be glad to be a jacket picker. You were one and done, Jenny. Get over it."

"It's Janet," she snaps, slamming a manicured hand on the wall.

"Shows how much I care," I retort. "She's not a whore, but I can tell that you're projecting." Turning on my heel and walking off before she can say anything else, I hide a smug cackle. I'm honestly surprised she hasn't been killed yet. Debating between his office or her room, I decide hers. That's her comfort zone, one that she only lets select people into.

She's not one to just let people wander in. I know Leather gets overwhelmed with the amount of people that come around the bar but understands that we need the influx of customers. Unfortunately for her, that means the constant noise.

We tried getting her to move out and into a house that the gang rallied up. She wasn't having it, though. She wanted to be near the club in the event that something happened. By that, I mean she gets a tip off and can't sneak out without someone catching her. You'd think that would be a prime reason to be on her own. She's got this thing where she really has no sight on her will to live. When we go into guards or hunts, she will dive in head first. No matter the circumstances, she would die for her club. It's a great quality to have, but it's a bit too much since she's had a few close calls. In all, she understands that her limited will to live isn't exactly right.

So, she stayed here. I have only caught her sneaking out once, which ended with us finding some douchebag attempting to rape a teenager.

Shuddering, I reach my hand up and pause.

"Just like that, *fuck*, yes!" A feminine voice calls, obviously about to orgasm. My mouth drops into an O. "*Oh god!*" She screams. My stomach rolls, thinking about the possibilities. She doesn't swing that way, and I only know that because she experimented a few years ago. It definitely wasn't her thing. Another wild moan, and I immediately registered the voice.

Holy shit, that's Leather. Her moans go on for what feels like hours, ranging from high pitch to needy groans. My cock strains in my pants as she blisses out. If that's Leather, then...

Oh, Jesus fuck. Prez is in there? Apparently, he's rocking her world because holy shit.

The noises get louder and louder, and I can hear the exact moment she falls over the edge. Her sounds mixed with the club is nearly overwhelming, almost enough to have me blow a load in my jeans like a fucking teenager.

Finally, it falls silent on the other side. I hear quick rustling, but it's hard to really make out what's going on due to the noise of the club.

In my hesitation, I catch a couple of guys with their jacket pickers stumbling up the stairs, practically falling over themselves as they rush to find a bedroom. The five of them enter that room, the door slamming shut with another loud thump against it.

Shaking my head, I knock on Leather's door. I swear people would think we were a whorehouse with the amount of shit that goes down here.

Someone on the other side of the door falls heavily and mumbled curse words barely whisper through the door as they clamber around. Sucking my teeth, I clear my throat.

"Leather?" I call, knocking again, followed by another low curse.

"One sec," she calls, her voice so raspy she has to clear her throat. I readjust my cock in my jeans, the mental image of Prez and Leather fucking...

Stop it.

The door swings open, her hair completely messed up and her makeup streaming down her cheeks. "Hi," she huffs, a bright smile plastered across her face. Eyes wide, pupils blown, she stares at me with more cheer than I have seen from her in years.

"Uh," I stare, clearing my throat awkwardly. "Is Prez here?" My throat is still clogged, but clearing it again would just be even more awkward. Her face goes crimson, neck heated, and the tips of her ears turn pink.

"He is," she pauses, glancing behind her. I try to peek in, but I don't see anything. "He's using the restroom. Give me a second." When she shuts the door in my face, I do everything in my power to keep from laughing. At the same time, my chest tightens a little. I have watched that woman grow, seen her fill out. It's stupid, really, but the fact that he got between her thighs...

I don't know how to feel about it. Am I not good enough for her? She knows how I feel, yet she's letting him there and keeping me at a ten foot distance? Or maybe she's slowly warming up to the idea of the three of us. Just thinking about his cock sinking into her pussy while I disappear into his ass...

"Come in," she says, pulling the door open for me. Cautiously stepping through the door, I see that nothing looks out of order. Even the bed is partially made, which is pretty standard for her since she's only a perfectionist in her work. I search the room thoroughly and nothing appears out of place. I also have no idea what I'm searching for.

"Who's at the door?" Prez asks as he steps from the bathroom, his shirt slightly wet. *Holy shit.* The material melts to his body perfectly, the curves of his toned abs like valleys across his stomach.

"Hey, Knuckles. What's up?" The material bubbles out as Prez pulls it away from himself. That seems to do the trick to snap me out of my thoughts. Clearing my throat, my face gets heated from embarrassment. I was just checking out my President.

What the fuck's wrong with me?

"Uhm, I talked to the prospect you threatened," I grumble, thumbing over my shoulder. "He's got his dick up his ass about it."

"You threatened a newb?" Leather asks, plopping down onto her bed. Her shapely legs curve perfectly, sloping ever so slightly from her strong muscles as she crosses them. There's no malice in her voice, if anything, she's teasing him.

"He was being an idiot," Prez huffs, propping himself against the wall, one boot crossed over the other. "When I ask for you to find a club, I don't mean to sit on your thumb. I mean for you to find them."

"Dude. You asked him to locate Big D. They have not been around in a while. Leather just got lucky because he tried to get into her pants," I laugh, dive bombing her bed. She shrieks as she moves out of the way, causing another gruff laugh to leave me.

"If you're done acting like children," Prez scolds, leveling us with his stern gaze. I hold his gaze steady, watching him begin to shift uncomfortably. Glancing down, I see a bulge in his pants attempting to rip through the seams. He must not have gotten off himself. That or she tasted him and he can't get enough. Sucking my bottom lip between my teeth, naughty thoughts swirl through my mind about him binding me and Leather together, a toy stuck between us both as he works us toward the edge.

I rip my eyes away from his crotch, casting them back to his face where I know I have been caught. His irises are nearly gone, his pupils blown wide with a dangerous edge.

"Uhm, let's go to my office," Leather says, her eyes shifting between Prez and I, and I can't get out of there fast enough.

Chapter Five

LEATHER

Their dynamic is way too shifty, especially in my space. The same space where Prez just ate my cunt like it was his last fucking meal...my bottom half is still slick thinking about the magical number Prez's mouth did on me. If Knuckles hadn't knocked...I don't think I would've stopped. We would've absolutely kept going; the tent in Prez's jeans says it all.

While they stare at one another, their growing tension builds so thickly it's suffocating. They look like they are about to eat one another. That or kill one another, it could go either way honestly.

As I contemplate whether they have been like this before or not, Knuckles bolts from the room like it's on fire. Prez clears his throat, thumbing over his shoulder awkwardly. His cheeks are tinted above the line of his beard, eyes darting where his brother just booked it. I nod.

"Men," I mutter, shaking my head. I can't believe I just did that, damn near got caught, too. My core throbs with need, but I can't even fathom going further with him. I would be lying if I said I haven't thought of him like that but for it to happen? Did I manifest that shit?

He can eat pussy like a champ, there's no doubt about that, but I can't decipher if it was just because he caught me in the act, or if it's something more. Good head shouldn't be the reason I come back from my self-imposed male cleanse. Plenty of dudes, and women, can make a girl cum without a second thought.

I can't handle anything outside of temporary hook-ups. After the shit I went through...I would rather just avoid it all together. Feelings tend to shake things up and ruin good things instead of making them better.

"Alright, time to go set them straight." Swinging my legs off the bed, I step back into the tight leather pants, lacing up my studded boots before heading down to the office. Reaching the doorway, the two guys are talking in hushed tones, obviously a bit heated. I attempt to listen to them, but it's useless. They are speaking too quietly, much to my chagrin.

Instead of barging in, I lean against the doorframe, arms crossed. When neither one of them even sense me, I clear my throat, making them jump away from one another like they are caught conspiring.

"Were you about to kiss?" I tease, ribbing them for their previously lustful gazes.

"No," Prez clips out, taking several steps backward and putting distance between them. I raise a speculative brow, which causes a scoff from both men. "We were talking about how the Big Dicks managed to get as close as they did." Flicking my gaze between the two, I notice Knuckles looks almost disappointed with Prez's statement.

Interesting.

I'm also very interested in seeing them indulge with one another. Not that I'm a voyeur or anything...

"Why don't I believe you?" I quirk a brow, pushing off the frame and striding behind the desk. Flopping into the janky chair, I kick my boots up on the desk. Knuckles rolls his eyes, shoving my feet off the desk with a thud.

"We're executioners for a reason. I don't keep tabs on them unless I need to, and the orders weren't given until they were already here." Knuckles raps his hand on the desk, irritation bubbling behind his words.

"You can't expect us to know their every move before they have become a threat," I say. They are under the impression that I'm just as clueless as they are. What happened to my brother isn't necessarily a secret, but I would rather it not be broadcast around the club. Also, they rely on us executioners to ensure their safety. What more do they want from us? "Plus, where are the prospects who will be assigned to the team? Why aren't they here?" Prez quirks a brow at my challenge, his nostrils flaring.

"They are probably fucking jacket pickers," Knuckles snorts, shaking his head and crossing his thick arms. The muscles bulge under the material of his shirt, the threads stretching and threatening to give way.

After a long moment of silence, I realize I'm caught staring.

"You like something you see?" He teases, popping his pecs while the veins on his biceps become more visible. I open my mouth to pop off a sarcastic comment when another throat clears. Whipping our heads to the entrance, Janet strolls in like she owns the place.

"Can I help you?" Prez stands, his shoulders squaring.

"I just came to see if you still needed me." She glances around the office, staring each of us in the eyes. "I can see you're still occupied."

"Give me ten," he responds, shooing her back out of the room. Her features light up happily before she prances away, an overexaggerated sway to her hips. Prez stares after her with longing, almost as if he's wishing to be somewhere else.

"Look, Prez," I sigh, running a hand through my tangled locks. "We get that they need to be exterminated, and Knuckles and I are working on it. Their den isn't as big as it was, so they probably fled. We've been talking about putting extra crews on the doors during open-days for the club downstairs, maybe even starting a membership and conducting background checks. I know it's shitty not being able to find a good, free, and clean BDSM club. But I can't risk them infiltrating our ranks. We'll even make a couple bucks off the fees because Phisher can just do his thing."

Prez doesn't say anything, staring off at the cupboard of liquors next to me. It's silent for a little while before he huffs out a quiet laugh.

"Alright," he nods, waving a hand.

Chapter Six

PREZ

"I guess that's not so bad," I sigh, rubbing my beard thoughtfully. The idea of requiring a paperwork fee sucks, and we wouldn't grandfather members in because it's all about safety, but it would help us keep the club clean from shitholes.

"*Backslide* would benefit from it, you'd have to admit," she hums, obviously proud of herself. The stupid name of the club has been around for as long as I can remember. Either way, I know she's right. This could be a good way to weed out bad apples, too. No one wants to pay money for things they don't want, so if they are just coming around to harass members and shit, then they will most likely be gone. That'll make their jobs easier, less time standing as bouncers and more time tracking those fuckers.

"Speaking of the club," Knuckles purrs, trying to make a move on Leather. She's not susceptible to anyone, apparently. She's been dodging him since the start. She was wild and crazy at one point, then the douch-who-shall-not-be-named fucked her over. Big time. After that, she was like an entirely new woman. While none of us know any of the details, we can all agree that she's not the same as she used to be. There's also been talk about her brother who disappeared, but again, we know nothing.

"You know I only scene with Charles," she teases. Her watch chimes, and she looks down at it, her face turning to a shade of crimson before she stands. "Speaking of, I need to get ready. I completely forgot our scene tonight."

"You're on tonight?" Knuckles jumps up from his seat happily, eyes as bright as a kid in a candy store. Leather just rolls her eyes, tucking the chair back into its place under the table and patting the back.

"According to Charles, I am. I will see you two later." Waggling her fingers at us, she saunters out of the room. Knuckles and I practically drool as her ass jiggles, the soft flesh still giving a bit of bounce even in the tight pants. I'm pretty sure he even gnashes his teeth, growling after her. She laughs, shutting the door quietly behind her.

Leather is a known switch, someone who flips between a dominatrix and a submissive. She loves both and has her limits. Charles, on the other hand, is a total submissive. He thrives on being degraded and belittled, slapped around until he's a sputtering mess.

She's gone through hell and back when it comes to being on stage. It was so bad that she didn't want to be involved with BDSM at all, but he's the one who approached her. He agreed to give her complete submission, total domination. The guy has no triggers, no hard limits. At least that's what it looks like from the outside.

That's when she found her love of being a domme. She thrives on the level of control needed.

"You thinking what I'm thinking?" Knuckles asks, wiggling his eyebrows at me. Narrowing my eyes, I debate if he's being serious. Regretfully, I would absolutely say yes to seeing her put a man on his knees. I would love to even see another guy in the mix, bossing them both around...

"What time is her set?" It's already pretty late, and I have a shit ton to do tomorrow. Just thinking about everything that needs to get done and the amount of sleep I will lose...my cock hardens at the thought of our sassy executioner. I know I won't win this debate.

"In like ten minutes," he says, looking back from his watch. "You in?"

Fuck it.

"I'm in."

Soft, sensual music reverberates through the speakers as Knuckles and I wade through the crowded bar. Women in different varieties of undress flit around while members of Silent Renegade take their usual booths. Outsiders bounce around as different scenes are completed, watching intently as they sip their drinks.

I can't help but eye every single person here, debating if they are spies for Big D Raiders. They are known for their undercover work, but no one appears to be...suspicious looking. Stupid, I know, but it's shitty as fuck to constantly be checking over your shoulder in case you miss someone wanting to stab you in the back. They know we're watching them, so they most likely have someone waiting for us to fuck up too. Contracts can be finicky.

Before Leather, the club would overlook females all together, the stupid stigma that women weren't more than baby pushers. While she had to work harder to get patched in, there's no doubt that she's the most driven. Her specialty was always torture, which works because she's also like a fucking siren. She lures in the enemy, then eats them alive.

Just another reason I shouldn't fucking touch her with a ten foot pole. I can't stop thinking about how she tasted in my mouth, her sweet pussy dripping as she rode my face, grasping my hair for dear life.

"Hello?" Knuckles rams his elbow into my rib cage, a rush of air whooshing from me.

"Was that fucking necessary?" I grunt, hunching slightly from the pain. I rub the spot while glaring darkly at him. He just laughs at me.

"Oh, don't be a giant pussy. You've had gunshot wounds worse than that." Knuckles grabs my elbow, dragging me across the platform to our usual table. If it were anyone else I would knock their fucking teeth in. Our guys dip their heads toward me, a silent greeting as we pass.

"She should be getting ready to go on," Knuckles mutters, plopping his ass in the chair next to mine. A waitress swings by, tits testing the strength of the buttons on her blouse. We both order waters, neither of us planning to get fucked up tonight. The thump of the music continues as they chatter, and I can't help staring at the stage with very thin patience.

Right after she bounces away with everyone else's orders, Leather's signature song hums quietly in the background, "*Queen of Pain*" by The Cramps.

Leather struts out on the dais, a complex leather bodice hugs her with ropes that neatly tie into knots over her lengthy limbs, and her signature studded boots on full display.

Wolf whistles blare around the club as she carries a leash in one hand and a riding crop in the other. She's got this deep seated swagger about her, almost as if she's unbothered by the bullshit around her. Charles, her sub, crawls on his hands and knees, his ass swaying while she prances him by the leather rope and bit in his mouth. She taps his bare ass with the end of the leash while walking him around. I can see his red knees from over here, obviously chafed by the carpet. He's practically naked, his toned muscles on display for the crowd, save for the damn leather jockstrap his impressive dick is crammed into.

With a sharp *crack*, she pulls him to the center of the stage. He obeys mindlessly, preening under the attention of the crowd. While on all fours, she whips the end of the leash against his ass and yanks on it, forcing him to kneel backward on his heels. Chest pushing out, he presents as the perfect submissive; open palms up and all. She takes a single step away from him and gives him the chance to soak up the attention of the crowd.

She steps behind him and gets onto her knees behind him. His body covers what she's doing, but after a moment, his cock visibly jumping in his strap. A wicked gleam shines brightly in her eyes as she looks into the crowd. Whatever she's doing, he loves it because the first guttural groan of the night swims through the sea of pleasure.

In this club, you can fuck while they do the show, you just can't be obnoxious about it. We're still respectful fuckers. Either way, they are enjoying this display of feminine power far more than I realized.

"Fuck," Knuckles mutters, shifting slightly in his chair. Daring a glance in his direction, words are caught in my throat. His large hand palms the engorged bulge in his pants. There's two very different, but very appealing, places to look at. A small part of me wishes I was up there, getting the attention she's giving. Another part of me wants to have her dominate Knuckles while I fuck her.

The song fades before *"Dirty Mind"* by Boy Epic starts up. It's a dirty, filthy song. Perfect for this moment exactly.

Zoning back in, I catch Charles swift nod, drool starting to cover his chest from his mouth being spread open for a prolonged period. She unclips the leash, letting the end drag over his pebbled flesh softly. With a quick flick, it wraps around his neck, and she pulls back. His spine hyper extends backward, his chest pushing even further out. If it weren't for the blissed out expression on his face, I would think he was suffocating for real.

"What a good boy," she coos, letting the leash go with one hand. It drags in front of him as ragged breaths pull into his lungs. She curls it into her hand, flicking it over his taut body. He doesn't move, the obvious desire evident in his hardened cock.

She takes a step back, rounding to the side of his body as she drags the leather over his skin. Grabbing the back of his head, she pushes on him. His face lands onto the platform softly, hands splayed out. Stepping a heeled foot on his back, she keeps him firmly in place as his ass juts into the air.

"That's so fucking hot," Knuckles grunts next to me, undoing the button on his jeans. I flick my gaze around the club, realizing that everyone in the audience is already in some state of pleasure. Leather watches the crowd swallow the sight of her submissive, tugging a little harder on the collar.

"Your ass is so pale," she taunts, her voice hauntingly soft as the crop smooths over his naked backside. "I would much prefer it to be red. Don't you?" Charles mumbles a response, the metal bit stopping him from saying anything legible.

A broken moan pushes past me as I look down, realizing my cock is practically on fire. The hardened length presses against my zipper, begging for friction and release.

Stealing another glance over, Knuckles' fist is wrapped tightly around his girth, the damn thing bigger than his hand. His eyes are hooded as his thumb drags over the bulbous tip that shines bright red with need.

"Holy shit," I mutter, watching as his fist picks up the pace. I swear I'm in a trance, watching him palm himself into oblivion as he watches our girl fuck her submissive into submission.

Hold the fucking phone.

The hand that was trailing to my own cock unconsciously comes to a halt.

She's not mine, and she surely isn't ours.

Fuck.

I'm in deep shit.

Chapter Seven

LEATHER

Being on stage makes me feel...alive. It gives me the sense of control I was never allowed. The control that was taken away from me. I have power over myself, over the situations in my life, over everything.

Relief.

Tugging on the leash, he crawls behind me. He licks the back of my boots with each step, thanks dripping from his lips in a plea. He doesn't hesitate to stand when I yank him up and point to the cross. If anything, he's more than ready for it.

We once talked about him being a brat on stage and me teaching him a lesson, but I don't know my limits on it. Therefore, it's been put on the back burner.

I make quick work of strapping him into the cuffs, lopping the rope into an intricate harness around his lanky body. Using the rope, I make a cock and ball ring of sorts, tightening just enough without hurting him.

"Color?" I mutter, standing before him.

"Green," he whimpers, his legs shaking harshly as he lets the restraints hold him. "Please, Mistress," Charles begs, hands extended and legs spread on the St. Andrews cross. Taking a deep breath, I watch his cock jump as I send another swat to his pecs, the flogger smacking his skin tightly as he jolts with a deep groan.

"You like that, little sub?" I purr, dragging the sweaty leather across his welted chest. The mixture of reds against the pale cream flesh is intricate, enticing. *Addicting.*

"Yes, I love it, please give me more Mistress," he sobs. His body stiffens as he waits for the next hit. As I whip down on his erratic chest, he pleads for more. Again, he stiffens up. It hurts a hell of a lot more when you're tense, and it's not particularly safe, so I wait. After several beats, the whoosh of the whip splits the air as it cracks on his chest.

"What do you think, baby boy? Can you handle more?" I mock. He nods frantically, his body shaking and fists clenched. "Sorry, I can't understand you, want to try that again?"

"I love when you whip me, Mistress. Please." He begs on repeat, sticking his tongue out as a sign of submission. I can tell he looks about ready to pass out, so I don't want to go too hard on him. I check him over continuously as we go to ensure he's okay, never missing a beat when I think his breathing is off or he becomes too pale. As his Domme, it's my job to ensure he's safe.

Unlike the Dom I used to have.

"Color?"

"Green," it comes out in short pants. "Please, Mistress, more, Mistress." His pleas are choked as I suddenly reach down, fisting his dick. The whines are like music to my ears, waiting for him to push on.

Moving my leather-covered fist over his swollen head, his body goes absolutely rigid. A rough feeling takes over my back, almost like I'm being watched. Which is unusual because I'm putting on a show. No, this is like a heavy gaze, one that knows they shouldn't be looking. Though, I don't know who it is. Looking into the sea of people, it's hard to even see anyone besides the first three or four rows of people.

Shaking it off, the heavy weight still lingers. Huffing a greedy laugh, I decide that I'm not in the best head space.

"Keep going, Mistress," Charles mutters, looking me dead in the eyes. Usually, that's a solid sign of disrespect. Yet, Charles knows when I'm off. It's like a sixth sense for him.

I raise a single brow, hoping my eyes portray that I'm not exactly stable at the moment.

His own eyes show me that he's ready for the pain.

One wicked smirk later, I'm in the mood to break him.

"What do you want?" I hiss, roughly tugging on him. "You want me to stick your cock in me? Feel my warm pussy wrapped around your tiny cock?" Shallow groans are heard from the audience, but I'm not focused on them. I'm focused solely on Charles. He's definitely not small if anything, he's on the bigger side, but making fun of him seems to turn him on. Who am I to deny him of his wishes? Free pass to be a bitch basically.

Also, it's a heady feeling being able to take back the control I have lost. I have never spun out of control, but I have gotten close before. Thankfully, I keep in tune with myself and him, for both our safety.

"Color?" I mutter, tossing the flogger to the side.

"Green," he grunts back. Dropping to my knees in front of him, I take his hardened length into my mouth.

"You've been such a good boy, I feel like giving you a treat." Taking him in one go, the tip of my nose touches his pelvic bone as I swallow him all the way down. I wrap a single hand around my throat, and his bulge pops from inside my throat as it's shoved down.

"Shit," he hisses, hips bucking off the table. Pulling back, I drop a swift slap to the inside of his thigh. He jerks, a sharp hiss straining through his teeth.

"You do not move unless I say. Do I need to fully restrain your cock, too?" Raising a brow, I stand back to my full height. In my boots, I'm a solid five feet seven inches, but they give me an extra five inches in height. No one is scared of short girls, so even with the *Demonia* boots, I look innocent.

I'm God's gift to men.

Well, If you consider my willingness to chop their dicks off if they look at me the wrong way...either way, God's gift.

"No Mistress, I'm sorry Mistress," he whimpers, his begging adds an additional puff of adrenaline to my already cloudy headspace.

"Beg," I demand. He immediately dives into pleas and groans of needing me. "You're the only one who can make me cum, Mistress. Please let me cum on your feet, be owned by you. I will worship the cum off your boots while you stuff my ass, Mistress."

It's nice to hear, even if it is only for a scene.

Keeping him strapped to the cross, I reach over and grab the plugged wand, placing the suction attachment to it for his pleasure. His whimpers die down to pouts when the buzzing starts up. I turn it on for a moment before shutting it off again.

"Do you think you deserve this?" I tease, grabbing the lube and walking back over.

"I deserve this, Mistress. I'm a needy whore who will worship you. I will eat your pussy and fuck you how ever you need, Mistress. I have been a good boy for you, please let me cum, please let me cum!" His begging ramps up again, muscles taut with tension to keep himself from moving around.

The overwhelming need for more is bearable, but it feels like my ropes are pulling tighter and tighter. Being vulnerable like this isn't meant for everyone. Even then, many Doms abuse their power and take advantage of their subs. I have seen Doms use their submissives and degrade them outside of scenes.

I supposed that's more of a master and slave relationship, but that's not something I thrive in. It's also something that forced me out of being a submissive. Knowing that, I refuse to be one of those Mistresses. He knows what respect and exceptional aftercare is because I refuse to give him anything less.

Flipping on the wand, I drag the outside against his length, his body spasming against the silicone. He's quickly silenced, forcing me to *tsk* and take a step back.

"You're having an ornery streak today," I admonish, watching his face crumble. "I don't remember telling you to stop."

He perks right back up, boosting my ego as he worships me with his words. I don't need to be told twice. Pushing his deflating cock into the rubber entrance, his whines for more get higher in pitch.

"Oh *God!*" He screams, barely able to breathe. "I need to cum, please let me cum. You're the only Mistress who can make me cum, I'm yours Mistress. Please let me cum all over you, I want to worship you on my knees, licking every inch of your perfect body. Please Mistress, please, please..."

It's like a breath of fresh air. Elation runs through my bloodstream, mixing with the hit of adrenaline I feel. Glancing in the audience, I stare into the burning hot lights, catching glimpses of faces screwed up in pleasure.

"You may cum." The demand is quick, but Charles doesn't wait a moment to follow it. He ruptures in the device, his cum flying from him and landing on my boots. I work the cock holder faster over his lengthened shaft. His entire body visibly buzzes on the cross, eyes rolling back as he attempts to mutter his thank yous.

Surveying the room, I'm about to lean in to tease Charles when I stop, ice freezing my veins instead of the heat I was feeling just seconds ago.

"Mistress?" My hearing seizes, a watery whooshing takes over. There's chatter and calls that I can barely register. I can't seem to move. I'm frozen in time, unwilling to move.

I'm staring a snake right in the eyes.

KNUCKLES

It's like she's frozen. One second she was teasing her sub, teasing the fucking crowd. Then the next moment, she's staring into the crowd, but she's not really...there.

I was stroking my cock, watching her get ready to fucking vibe her sub. Ice water metaphorically pours all over me and apparently it does the same thing for Prez.

"Leather?" Prez shouts, jumping from his chair and running to the stunned woman. Her eyes remain glued to the back. Trailing her dark features, I find a dark figure just...standing. I can't really see the person's face, but I can guess what she's looking at. Their arms are crossed along their chest, the obvious bicep muscle giving me the inclination that it's a guy.

Holy shit...is that?

"Leather!" Screams reverberate, my head whipping around from the mystery man to see Leather's body buckling. Standing, I realize my dick's still hanging out, though it's fucking soft now.

Stuffing myself back in, I do a little hop jig as I fasten my belt and race to the woman of the hour.

"Is she okay?"

"What's going on?"

"She just passed out!"

Voices talk all at once.

They all rush to get on the dais, some for Charles and others for her. My heart pounds in my chest as I digest what the fuck is happening.

Glancing back to the edge of the room, the mystery guy is gone. Most likely slipped out during the commotion. Glancing between the empty space and where people are fluttering around Leather, I decide that she's my current priority.

"Everyone get back!" I shout, my voice thick with the demand. Hustling to the stage, Prez is elevating her head. There's a small trickle of blood from where she crashed. Prez jerks his head at me, and I move to Charles.

"I don't know what happened," he panics, his body shaking harshly. "She was fine one second, then glanced back there and lost herself. I have only seen her like that once when..." he trails off, shaking his head and biting his wobbly lip.

Fuck's sake.

Roughly shaking my head, I undo the ropes around his wrists and ankles, helping him down. I blow a short whistle to one of the monitors, who throws a towel our way. Charles quickly covers himself while shaking like a leaf.

"Move," I demand, roughly shoving people aside. They move easily as I shoulder check them out of the way.

A rag quickly replaces the sudden pouring blood from her head, the sleek hardwoods suddenly staining red.

"What the fuck happened?" Prez mutters, putting pressure.

Confusing thoughts spin in my head, different scenarios playing out as I wrack my brain for what could have possibly caused this.

"Charles said something about seeing her like this before," I murmur in return. His head snaps up, eyes narrowing on the male mentioned. Prez catches Charles' eyes, jerking his head to come here. He kneels next to us, placing a gentle hand on her leg.

"What did you mean?" Prez's forehead vein is protruding, his face red with what I'm assuming is anger and worry.

"Her ex, man." He shakes his head, running a sweaty hand through his short hair. "I can't remember his name...Heller? Henchman..." His eyebrows crease with concentration, focusing on the woman before us.

"Heckles," another deep voice adds, stepping up behind us. "His name is Heckles."

Chapter Eight

LEATHER

"*Such a good girl, Blaine. Who knew you'd look so good in leather?*" His voice echoes around my head, the sickly sweet tone like honey wrapping around my heady-mind.

"Thank you, Sir," I purr, my core hot and ready for round two. His wooden paddle drags along my welted and bloody skin. It stings, but I won't cry or whine. That's how you get into more trouble.

He grabs a gleaming knife off the table, holding it to the light as I refrain from struggling against the bindings. My muscles tense all over my body. In quick succession, he drags the knife through my leather top, digging the metal deep into my skin. Slowly as he goes, fire erupts on my sternum, right between my breasts.

Internalizing my pain, my teeth bust through my lip. The tearing of the skin sounds worse than it is, probably because it's so damn close to my head. That or the fact that blood is rushing to my ears, the whitewater sound whooshes through my head.

I definitely don't want to get into trouble again.

"You're just a dirty little blood whore." Whipping the paddle down, he slams it on the open wound, a splatter of blood coming off.

I can't help the shriek that escapes me due to the overwhelming urge to scream gripping at my vocal cords.

Remember the line: Pleasure and pain...

Silence will get me punished, but he doesn't like when I scream. He only likes it when he sees tears. Tears are easy, but silent tears are near impossible.

"Tsk, tsk, Leather." His boots pound around me, the sound near silenced by the scorching pain. "You're mine."

"Leather?"

"No one would ever want you."

"Come on, wake up!"

"How could they when I have marked you so prettily."

"Open your fucking eyes."

"Til' death do us part, princess."

A heaviness slowly evaporates from my body.

"I think she's coming to." Shallow water rushes me, my throat dry, body cold, but I feel as though I'm gurgling water and sweating buckets from overheating.

Cracking open my eyes, the immediate sting of light flashes before me, forcing them to close again. "Shit," I mutter, moving my hand to my head slowly.

"Don't." Squinting, I notice a guy I had never seen before. To say he's attractive is an understatement.

Don't even think about it, Blaine.

A bucket of reality pours over me as the vividness of my dream comes back. The whippings. The scars. His face.

Pushing everyone away, I scramble to sit up and force my gaze around the club. There's no one here.

"Where'd everyone go?" I wheeze, lungs burning.

"You passed out. We cleared the club to give you guys some privacy," the new guy says, kneeling next to me.

Prez clears his throat, gesturing to the new guy. "Leather, that's Tornado. Tornado, Leather." Lifting my hand, I push it out for a respectful handshake. His face screws up in confusion, glancing down before looking back at my face.

"Once you get cleaned up, we can discuss what your next steps are." He doesn't even touch my hand, simply brushing it off with an awkward glance. Nodding, he stands, rolling his shoulders back to his full height and walking away.

"What," I pause, mouth gaping open at the man who is suddenly going to invade my dreams.

"He's new to the club. He came from a sister gang out west. They are dispersing due to the feds."

My blood spikes, my body growing rigid. I don't need the feds up in our business.

"He can't stay," I demand, though it's more of a measly comment.

"Yes, he can and he will. He's the new sergeant at arms. If you would have accepted the offer, you would have moved up in rank."

"I don't want to be a gun runner, you know that," I scoff, shoving Prez's hands off of me. He leans back, dragging a red colored cloth with him.

"You're right. That's why you're staying where you are. I still need the position filled, and what better way than to have someone know what they are actually doing?" Knuckles laughs, cracking his fists on the floor.

"Here," Prez shoves the red cloth into my hands, only to have red drops hit the floor.

"What the fuck?" I hiss, dropping it to the floor with a wet *plop*.

"Ah, that's your blood. You smashed your head pretty good on the edge of the dais when you tumbled." Screwing my face in disgust, I push to my feet, swaying slightly.

"Easy," Charles coos. A strong hand wraps around my elbow, panic immediately seizing my heart. Grabbing the hand, I start to do a wrap spin when I realize they are not *him*.

"Fuck," I hiss, dropping his hand like a hot potato. "Please just...don't touch me right now." Taking a few steps back, all three guys watch me closely. Prez watches me like I'm a fucking flight risk. Knuckles has a mix of worry and anger in his eyes. And Charles...he looks like he's ready to cry. I want to wrap him up in my arms and tell him everything is going to be okay.

I wish I believed that myself.

Nothing is ever okay.

Chapter Nine

TORNADO

"**D**id you see her?" He asks, his voice grating with irritation.

Thinking about the woman lying there, head gashed open, body limp and vulnerable. When her eyes opened, I swear they were electric. She didn't know me, didn't know I was there, but I'm not against seeing her again.

"Yeah," I grumble, walking across the bar and into the conference room.

"That's it? That's all your going to fucking say?" He snaps. Rolling my eyes, I flop back into an executive's chair.

"You need to ask open ended questions to receive an open ended answer," I quip, feeling pretty damn smug with myself.

They call her Leather, and I can see why. She's a fucking knock-out then add the second-skin made of actual Leather, and I swear I'm hard just thinking about it.

"Did she say anything?"

"No," I retort, making him work for the information. He may have been my boss at one point, but I no longer work for him. He's on the run, feds on his tail for a fucking white collar crime.

Dude's killed people in cold blood, and he got caught fucking money laundering.

Idiot.

"Fucking hell, Tornado!" He shouts. He's bloody fuming.

I love it.

The double doors open to the room, Leather walking in with Knuckles. Both stop in their tracks, their conversation halting with my presence.

"Sorry baby, I gotta run. Text you later, yeah?" I make kissy noises, hearing him rant and rave on the other end before hanging up. Chuckling, I watch as the two approach me cautiously, arms crossed over their chests.

They move in sync, one moving similar to the other in a way that can only mean they are close. I can't decipher if it's brother/sister or if it's something more.

Either way, I have to keep an eye out.

There's work to be done.

"What are you doing here?" Leather asks, taking a seat across from me.

"Well, from what I remember, I'm the sergeant at arms of Silent Renegade. I believe that gives me the right to sit here." Spanning my arms out, I gesture to the room around us.

She squints her eyes accusingly, leaning forward on her elbows.

"I don't know who you think you are, but you're messing with the wrong club. Once Prez gets his head out of his ass, he will see that you're a fucking nuisance to this club," she snarls, face twisted in fury.

I can't help the small chuckle that escapes me. She's deadly, that much I know for sure, but she looks more like an angry kitten.

"I can see why they call you the seducer," I crack, crossing my arms over my chest. Smoke practically roils from her head, face bright red as fire takes over.

"Why?" Her teeth clamp down, jaw ticking.

"Because you couldn't look intimidating if you tried." She's out of her seat, knife pressing to my throat before I can even blink.

Fuck. That's hot.

"Feisty," I mutter, pushing into the blade gently. "I like that." Grunting, she jerks it away, a slight sting leaving in its wake.

"Like I said, I don't know where you came from, but I know it's not a sister club." Knuckles looks quickly between the two of us, trying to work *something* out.

"Alright," Knuckles says, laying a hand on my shoulder. "Leather, you have an *appointment* coming up," he hints, jerking his head the other way.

"What are you guys doing?" I ask, deciding now is better than never to actually get to her.

"Nothing for you," she snaps, shrugging off Knuckles' hand.

"Actually, I am your superior." Raising a brow, I watch her face pull up in disgust. Even then, she's a fucking beaut.

"I don't understand how he has anything to do with my *errands*." Her voice grows heavier and huskier, the irritation in her tone is palpable. I could cut the tension with a knife.

"It means that I'm privy to all business in and out of this club," I retort, waiting for her challenge.

"So, you immediately assumed I have no life outside of the club?" Her smug expression is a complete one-eighty from the pissed off one I was getting.

She's onto me. I know she is, she's called me on my shit. Unfortunately, *he* didn't warn me that Leather was intuitive as fuck.

My stomach turns as the thought, unease kicking inside me. When I first heard about Leather, I will admit that I was intrigued. She's unique. A female enforcer is practically unheard of. It just cemented the fact that I don't want her on my bad side.

"I didn't assume anything."

"Oh, so you've been stalking me?" Her body grows darker, looser, more relaxed as she pesters me.

"No," I start.

"Then you don't know me. Like I said, *Alec*. I have eyes and ears everywhere." With that, she stands up, the chair tipping threateningly. She catches it with her boot, righting it down with a slam. As she leans forward onto the small table, I can finally see the reason so many grown men are scared of her.

My heart races, breath catches.

"If we're done here, I have places to be that don't pertain to you. Either you tell Prez about this...little encounter, or I will. And you better tell the truth." Standing roughly, the table screeches as she pushes against it. "I will be watching."

Fuck.

Chapter Ten

KNUCKLES

What in the actual...

"What the fuck was that?" I hiss, coming up behind her after I shook off the shock.

She spoke to our fucking sergeant like that. If anything, he's the one that we should be allied with. Instead, she's making enemies. I don't know what she overheard, but the fact that she name dropped...that's a big sign of disrespect.

Don't get me wrong, I love Leather as an enforcer, but she's pushing this too far. Patch names are *names* in the club. They all come with a story, they are the trick of the trade, essentially. I got my name by using my fists and duster in fights. Before Prez became Prez, he was once known as Skinner. He got the name because he likes to skin his victims alive. Leather got her name...well, we all know that she wears leather like the devil wears sin.

"I don't fucking trust him, Knuckles," she grumbles, walking quickly. "He gives me bad vibes. I don't know how he sold Prez, but I swear, if it's a case of blackmail..." she cuts herself off, turning the corner to see Prez on the phone, obviously in a heated conversation.

"Come on," I mutter, grabbing her elbow gently. She shrugs me off, leaning against the corner of the wall and waiting patiently. I can't contain my eye roll. She's going to get herself fucking kicked out.

"I have a bad feeling about him." Her voice isn't more than a whisper, the exhaustion heavy in her tone.

"You have to have evidence to back it up, though." Laying a gentle hand on her shoulder, she peeks at me over it. There's demons she's been running from, ones that we'll probably never be aware of.

You can see the drastic change in the woman she was before compared to the one she is now. I can't help but feel for the girl. *Woman.* Bloody and beaten, she gained herself back. I have no doubt that she can protect herself, but there's this feeling in my stomach that I have to help her. Stick with her. That's why I asked to be put on the enforcer tasks. We're a partnership now. Maybe not the kind that I would prefer, but something is better than nothing.

"How else are we supposed to gather evidence if we don't gather it ourselves?"

"Well, generally the sergeant helps gather the evidence," I start, realizing where she's going.

"We're not the one-percent, dude. We're a fucking gang for a reason."

"Yeah, but we don't fucking turn on one another," I retort, my blood slowly starting to boil in my veins.

"I'm not suggesting that we turn on one another. I'm suggesting we try and figure out why the fuck he's come in here from an alleged sister branch. I don't trust him. I have this...deep seated feeling that he's here as a spy of sorts." She wears her worry on her sleeve, her eyes like a mirror into the concerns she's having.

"I know, but if Prez trusts him, then we do too," I reason, pulling her around the corner away from our President. "You have to trust that he knows what he's doing and is going to reap the benefits for the club."

Peeking around the corner, her body loses all semblance of tension. She stumbles back into me, her body weight leaning against mine. Her small frame fits perfectly in my arms, her soft body forming delicately to my hard one.

Heat creeps up my neck, into my ears and up onto my cheeks. Thinking back, I don't recall us ever being this close. She's never let me actually touch her, let alone *hug* her.

"It's alright, baby girl," I mutter, playing with the ends of her hair. She nods, silence enveloping us both. Her arms slowly wrap around my torso, clasping at my back as we start to sway.

It's going to sound fucking wimpy, but I could probably hold her here forever. Though I do have a craving for a wanton woman, preferably the auburn-haired, hazel-eyed girl I'm holding.

Another kicker is the sudden slamming of feelings I have had over the last couple weeks. While I have watched her from afar, there was never an opportunity to venture closer to her. She's closed off, like one of those old leather journals that are bound closed with a cord. The only way to get them open would be to cut the string and tear the pages open. I want her and that's not something I will ever doubt again.

"You're going to put me to sleep," she murmurs, her voice muffled by my shirt. I hum, not wanting to ruin the soothing moment between us.

It just feels...right. I can't help but notice how well she fits with me. How well her personality meshes with mine. There's no denying the connection.

It's a matter of getting her to acknowledge it.

Chapter Eleven

LEATHER

"I think we caught a lead in Vancouver," a prospect says, standing from his chair. "We were scouring sightings and followed a few bikers through traffic cams. We lost them once they entered the city. The last known address was a parking garage."

Staring at a spot on the table, I let the conversation move around me. We need to put an end to the Big D Raiders. One of their own took everything from me. It may not be anything physical, but mentally...

I swallow thickly at the thought of *him* being back.

"They probably did a swap," Knuckles mutters, pointing at the prospect. "What's your name, kid?"

"Uhm, I don't have one yet." He looks around nervously, his buddies anxiously waiting to rib him.

"That sucks, what about something technical?"

"Uhm," he mumbles, looking around at everyone else around him. "Sure?" Unsure of himself, we continue to just stare at him. Prospects are usually far too easy to tease.

"I'm thinking Technocrat," Phiser pipes up, a teasing smirk on his face. "Or maybe Technophile?" The prospect pales a little bit, obviously not catching that we're just fucking with him.

"Oh, what about Techno-Wizard?" I ask, barely containing my laugh. We bounce back names, before I crack, laughing loudly at the horror on his face.

"You should see yourself," Knuckles cackles, pointing to the poor kid. After a few moments, he settles down. "Who all was on the task force to run down Big D? Maybe we can get a name together from them?" Knuckles leans his elbows on the table, steepling his fingers. He would look posh if he wasn't wearing his jean cut that looks as if it was run over by a semi-truck in the mud.

"There were about ten of them," Phisher notes, looking back to his laptop. "They are all around here somewhere."

"Shit, I can't think of that many names right now," I huffs, sitting back in my chair. "You got a name in mind?"

"No, ma'am." The prospect wrings his fingers, nervousness pouring out the poor kid.

"First of all, never call me ma'am again, that makes me feel fucking old. Second of all, you have to have something? Haven't you been dreaming about getting your own name?"

"I-I-I mean, yeah, but like, it's. Well, I just..."

"Today kid," I jump in, circling my pointer fingers to try and get him to move along.

"I didn't think about it," he finally admits. Nodding, we all decide to just give the kid a break.

"We'll think about it. Sit down." Out of the corner of my eye, I see Knuckles wave his hand, dismissing the kid.

We've been on the hunt for more Big D's in the area. Unfortunately, I think they may have taken my threats a bit too seriously. If they are near me, that means *he* is near me. Even still, I can't handle the thought of him being so close yet kept so far away. I need him *gone*. Out of my life. Permanently.

"We'll continue to run surveillance and check vehicles coming out," I mumble, picking at a piece of stubborn tape on the table. A knee nudges me from under it, and I glance to the left as Knuckles watches me closely. His eyes bore into me, and I swear I could get swallowed into them.

"We can run point," Phisher announces, giving our main executioner his full attention. A major sign of respect.

"Good. I would want nothing less." I make a tight smirk, trying to force myself back into a happier mood. My closest allies know me best, which includes Phisher. He's been running main surveys for me since I got the gig.

"Anything else?" Knuckles asks, putting the stupid files and stuff back together.

"I would like to keep this under wraps," I announce, pushing back from my chair. A wave of irritation flows through me remembering my conversation with Tornado earlier. He thinks he can come into this club and start running me? I trust Prez, I really do. But I don't trust Tornado. Not as far as I can fucking throw him. "If you're part of this task force, you will be held to a higher standard of confidentiality: patch and blood. I catch any of you gossiping about this shit, your patch is mine. Understood?"

Murmurs of agreement roll through the doors as they head out into the main room.

One-percenter my ass. There's no way this isn't going to meet his ears. He's nosey, hot as sin, wears his fucking jeans like they are glued onto him, and has a mouth like a fucking grump. I can't stand the thought of him being around here, wrapping himself around my missions and just expecting me to go along with it.

His presence just brings bad fucking vibes with it. I can't explain it, can't define why I feel it. I just know that I don't feel fucking safe, not even in my own club.

Chapter Twelve

PREZ

I wish I had a fucking flip phone so I could slam it shut. This has been the longest week in my life, I swear. CJNC has been going back and forth on contract negotiations, keeping us tied up to just save face. If they are going to fucking pick, they need to hurry up. You'd think working in the black market would be less strict, but no. Fucking hell, man. I'm fucking over it.

"Listen here, Tiny," I grunt, leaning my forearm against the wall and putting my head in the bend of my elbow. "You act as if this contract will end us. It won't. Be my fucking guest, but we'll move on to another gang. This slot isn't going to be open forever."

"You act as if you hold the fucking cards, Prez." Pushing off the wall, I shove a hand through my hair. "We're in the middle of mediation right now. If you call me again outside of the lawyers, you'll be forfeiting your spot on scene. Got it?" He hangs up without another word.

I grip the phone so tight it may as well snap in half. If it wasn't such a good fucking deal, I would give in. Not only that, but it brings us right to the edge of Vancouver. Right where the Big D

Raiders are alleged to be in hiding. They think a measly border will stop us? I scoff at the thought, tugging at the strands of my hair.

My biggest concern is smuggling goods across the border. Motorcyclists aren't likely to be carrying, but we can get caught a hell of a lot easier than big rigs.

Which brings me to our plan. Heading down the stairs, I watch my sergeant at arms and my executioner eye fuck, or eye murder, each other from across the room.

Letting out an obnoxious whistle, I yell, "Tornado, round em' up!" He jumps into action, going around the house to collect everyone. I swing back up the stairs, away from everything to finish collecting files.

The house is massive, something that was built for the club when it was born. The basement used to be a dusty ass bomb shelter, but we've redesigned it to be a BDSM club. Of course, the bomb shelter was just a bonus. If there was ever a nuclear attack, we could still have fun. The main level is the basic club area where members can drink, fuck, and have a blast. The conference room and a bunch of bedrooms are down here too, probably around ten or so. The guys have no problem sharing two or three guys in a room. Most of the time, they will fuck each other or share a jacket picker.

The upper level is for offices and bedrooms for those who are higher up on the food chain. I didn't design it this way, but hierarchy in the clubs is extremely important.

"They are in church," Tornado says, propping himself on the last step. "Leather sure is something else." I scoff.

"She's a snarky one, that's for damn sure." Grabbing my folders, I pile everything together.

"I will say. She will tell you what she thinks of you." There's a tinge in his voice that puts me slightly on edge, but I brush it off.

"Leather is a bit of an acquired taste, that's for sure." He hums, tilting his head back and forth in thought. Pausing in my path, I raise a brow for him to continue.

"I don't know, I don't think she likes me," he mutters, tapping his fingers on the banister.

Rolling my eyes, I shut and lock the office door. "What makes you think that?"

"She told me." If I had water, I would probably spit it out. Like I said, she's a bold one. "She made it pretty clear what she thinks of me."

"Did you tell her why you're here?" I ask, brushing past him to go down the stairs. He freezes momentarily, face slightly pale before he exhales quickly. "Jesus, we don't have any fucking ghosts around here."

"No, no," he says quickly, following me down the steps. "She knows I'm here to take the new sergeant position."

"Is that all you're here for?" Stopping on the step, I turn to look at him. I'm not stupid. I catch body language easily, maybe not as good as my executioner teams, but I wouldn't have been voted in if my club didn't have faith.

"No, I mean yes." He huffs a laugh, scrubbing a hand down his face. "The guys weren't kidding, you can make a man shit his pants."

"I asked you a pretty simple question." Again, the guy looks like he's about to break a fucking sweat. "Look, if you fuck over me or my club, I will end your life. Do I make myself clear?"

"Crystal," he says, never breaking eye contact. I jerk a nod, going back down the stairs. I didn't have any negative emotions about him, but the dude fucking stuttered. Only those with a guilty conscious act like that.

We'll get to the bottom of this.

Chapter Thirteen

LEATHER

Don't get me wrong, he's a fucking douche bag, but he's a hot douche bag. I can't tell you what rubs me the wrong way about him, it's just this overwhelming sense of *something*. Maybe it's his vibe, or the way he holds himself. I don't fucking know, but it's giving me hives just thinking about him.

I can admit that I'm not used to change. It's something I know I don't like, that I have never liked. That's one of the main reasons why I'm still an executioner. I don't have to relearn anything or do anything new, not needing to be in charge of more than a few people at a time. I know my systems, I know my shit, and I can hunt men better than the fucking FBI. It's easy work for me, a cake walk. I get in, do my job, and get out.

Plus, the connections I have in the underworld? Fucking spicy. They know me as Leather, and they also know me as *Leather*.

Sitting down in the church room, my leather shorts immediately stick to the plastic chair. Groaning, I adjust myself a bit to get comfortable. The shriek of the leather material sticking to the metal seat makes my whole body ache.

"How have you been since the incident?" Tornado asks me, sitting down in Knuckles' normal spot. I can feel my left eye twitching, and my heart pounds heavily in its barricade of bones. Swallowing the heavy lump in my throat, I glance over at him and take in his sharp features. His energy is off, almost tentative as he kicks back next to me.

He's absolutely the tallest guy in the club, probably pushing six-five or so. His jaw could cut glass with the little five o'clock shadow he's sporting. Not only that, but his eyes are a steel electric blue, one that I have never seen before. I can appreciate a good looking man, but deep in my gut, something just isn't *right*.

"Uhm," I choke, clearing my throat a few times to keep from drooling over this man. I'm pretty sure he caught me fucking staring. I don't know what it is, but I know I could get lost in those damn eyes. I try clearing my throat again.

"Uhm?" He questions, a gentle smirk pulling at his lips. My stomach rolls. My body is screaming at me to jump his bones, but my head is demanding I run the other way.

"I have been good," I mumble, popping my knuckles. "I don't even know why it happened." Laughing in self-deprecation, I think back to a couple weeks ago. I can't believe I fucking passed out.

"Yeah, you hit your head pretty hard," he grunts, picking at a few stray strings on his jean cut. "You're feeling better? No lingering issues?"

"Not that I'm aware of." Nodding, he pats my bare knee before standing. I'm left gaping at the spot where he touched, his skin burning against mine in the most delicious way.

I have never been horny from a simple touch, but I'm ready to grab his hand and shove it down my shorts. Maybe even have him...

My face scrunches in disgust. What the fuck am I thinking? Do I want him to finger fuck me? Big yes. Will I follow through with it? Big maybe. Fucking hell, I need to get a grip. I have been horny since the incident. I haven't had the lady balls to convince Charles I'm okay for another scene. In another world, I would have taken what I wanted almost immediately. I would have swatted his ass until it was a solid shade of red for questioning me. Then I would have mounted him and given him the ride of his life.

Unfortunately, I'm a chicken shit in this world.

"Listen up," Prez calls, walking into church. "Tiny has us by the cock right now. We're waiting on the go ahead. Once we get the signal, we'll prep to ride." He plops down on his chair, slamming a couple files onto the table.

"We've been working with ops to get through the border," Tornado adds, pulling a file toward him from the stack.

"Why can't we take water ways?" I ask, perching myself at the edge of the seat.

"They tend to be heavily monitored as well. The ports have better machines to scan through shit, so we avoid them at all costs," Tornado quips back, not looking up from the papers. If anything, I feel utterly dismissed.

"Since when?" I scoff, shaking my head with frustration. "The borders are as packed as it can get."

"I don't fucking know, Leather. How about you let me do my job and you do yours," he snaps, finally leveling me. Quirking a brow, I can feel the challenge rise up.

"What's the plan? I bet I can guess it." Smirking, I kick my boots on the table.

"Be careful," Knuckles suggests quietly, his elbow meeting my ribs. Shooing his hand away, I contemplate if it's worth it. There's plenty of other battles to fight about this, but is it actually worth my time?

It is.

"You plan on having a slew of us ride ahead, get popped by the border patrol, right?" I start, my foot shaking with excitement. Prez's head snaps up, eyes narrowing on me in warning. Meeting his thunderous gaze, I continue. "Then you're gonna drive some sort of hauler rig a few cars behind us while they work on us."

"That's enough," Prez snaps, his fist slamming on the table. "You know what you're doing, so cut it out. We can figure the logistics out later." I hold the scoff back, pulling my feet off the table and sitting up.

They are telling me how to do my job. I trained for this shit. Blood, sweat, and tears were shed for me to be able to rank up. Yet, here we are. Back at square fucking one because Prez thinks Tornado can help us. I want to talk, throw some shade that they are fucking stupid. But, I don't. I decide now isn't the time, and I hold it all back. If they want to be idiots, they can.

Neither point of entry will be free of challenges. Dragging my pointer and thumb across my lips, I pretend to zip them and wave a dismissive hand while figuratively throwing away the key. Knuckles lets out an appreciative exhale as I digress, and I shoot daggers straight at him. Nonetheless, he grins right back at me.

"As I was saying, logistics will get ironed out later. Phisher, what's the catch on the CCTVs?" Prez calls, jotting shit down.

"Nothing new, unfortunately. We're working on gathering more plate info, but the ones coming out all have clean records."

"I wonder if they would've camped out, knowing we'd run records?" I ponder, tapping my nails on the table. So much for not talking. *Oopsie.*

"That's a possibility." Phiser nods in agreement, looking around the room. "Anyone from the task force find anything?"

"No, sir," a prospect denies, not bothering to rise from their seat.

"We don't have the manpower to scour hours and hours of footage, hoping for a potential bust." Knuckles grunts in agreement, but I don't feel settled. Looking at Tornado, I catch him already looking at me.

Narrowing my eyes, we stare. Chatter continues as I'm swallowed whole by his gaze. The blue in them pulls me under, the swirl of emotions being pushed to the surface just as quickly as they are pulled back under by the current.

I shake my head, closing my eyes before I get tugged into them any further. He's a dangerous creature, that's for sure. Make no mistake, I don't trust him. But my gut is also telling me not to write him off *just* yet.

Chapter Fourteen
Tornado

It's been a fucking week trying to get her to open up to me. I can tell she doesn't trust me, but thankfully I don't need her trust. I need her to just follow the orders. Go along with them, preferably blindly. It helps significantly that we've got serious sexual chemistry. Not only her, but I have noticed a little something with Knuckles. I'm not sure what, but I can't stop taking longer-than-appropriate glances at him.

A couple days ago, I walked in on him and Leather working out. He was bench pressing her like she weighed nothing. I stood off to the side, not wanting to interrupt their gaggle session. He was sweaty, probably from finishing a workout before lifting her for fun. The biceps on that man...they are drool worthy. I will admit I'm openly attracted to both men and women, but I have never been with a guy before. I was always too shy, shockingly enough.

I find them both extremely attractive. Something about the tongue on Leather just really gets me going. There's a clear picture as to why people are interested in her. She's hot as balls, quicker than a whip, and knows how to nail a guy in more ways than one. Once she follows through with this, I can go about my own shit.

What I don't understand is how she would get wrapped up with those people? They are dangerous, even for her. Unfortunately, I know from personal experience.

"Tornado!" A baritone voice calls, snapping me out of my thoughts. "You daydreaming, princess?" Prez asks, an uproar of snickers following.

"No," I scowl, pulling my feet off the table and straightening in the chair.

"Then why don't you tell me what the plan is?" His smug expression makes me want to punch him.

"Something about crossing the border and a hauler. Is it a done deal?" I question nonchalantly. The key is to act disinterested. It works sometimes.

"Good try," he muses, shaking his head. And sometimes it doesn't work.

"I exist to please." They continue to snicker, muttering to themselves as Prez and I have a mini stare down. Not wanting to challenge his position, I break eye contact.

"As I was saying," he starts, giving me a pointed look. "We'll have to split man-power around the club if we get this contract. We're working on implementing the sign on's for the club. Ramping up security will be necessary while we get shit sorted. Bookie said we're starting to flatline since we're waiting for this to pull through."

"Why haven't we taken smaller contracts in the meantime?" Leather asks, plopping a piece of gum into her mouth then leaning her elbows on the table as she glances at a file in front of her. "We can't just sit with our thumbs up our ass. They are not used to being pressured by clubs and their records indicate this is the first time they have used manpower."

"And?" I quip, turning fully to look at her.

"And," she stretches, leveling her gaze on me. "That's not suspicious? The contract was pretty fucking vague what we'd be moving. I have other leads that I can track while we're twiddling our thumbs. There's one on that side of the border that I think we can run. While we're there, we can scout. Give us some intel on the CJNC and if the contract is granted to us, we're already there to help with diversion."

He stares at her for a moment. "How long will you be gone?" We all watch as she glances through her file.

"I would say about a week. Two at the most," she responds confidently. Prez tilts his head back and forth, obviously debating.

"What would you be doing?"

"Funny you should ask," she responds, a wicked smirk on her lips. It's definitely the version that gets men to drop on their knees for her. "We're scouting for intel on another cartel that's running interference there. It should be an easy in and out. The tip came in from one of the understudies in CJNC and we're scouting possible scouts. I know it's odd, but I confirmed it with Tiny. It'll be a few days there, a few days scouting and a few days back. There can be weather delays, but the upcoming days are all supposed to be pretty clear."

"Where?"

"You sure do ask a lot of questions," she sasses, flicking a brow up. He folds his arms, waiting patiently while they have another little stare down. She gives in with a pathetic eye roll. "Ugh, fine. It'll be *in* Vancouver."

"If you're up there, we have a few other deals out there that need to be completed," Phiser calls from his spot. "It's up to Prez on whether or not you'll do them." His gaze flicks up from the computer taking a quick glance at Prez himself.

"Who would you take?" He asks, his voice still sounding on the edge.

"Knuckles would come, he's gonna be my ticket in." She flashes Knuckles a wicked look before looking back at Prez. "Probably a prospect or two who shows interest in the executioner lifestyle. Can't roll up solo, you know? Too long of a ride, might get lonely." Smacking her gum, she blows a bubble, watching Prez closely as it gets bigger.

"You know my next question?" He asks, challenging the small but feisty female. Her face pulls back in a smirk, flashes of different emotions flying through her hazel eyes.

The bubble in her gum breaks with a loud *pop.* "Depends on the cut size." She shrugs, the look on her face is one of challenge. I have no doubt that she would want to do this on her own, but I'm glad she's at least taking precautions. It's not a lot, not even close to anything I would force her to have if she were my girl. I have to remember that something is better than nothing.

Wait.

My girl? I must be fucking hallucinating. She's not my bitch, and she never will be. I have no fucking time for a woman. Period. Plus, she's elbows deep with some pretty vicious men. I don't want to get anywhere near that with a fifty-foot pole.

She doesn't even look in my direction as she challenges Prez silently, everyone's gazes volleying between the two as their eyes remain connected.

"Normal," he prompts, leaning back in the exec chair.

"Twelve-five," she snaps. Prez's brows jump to his forehead and confusion takes over from before. "Let's chat about this after?"

"We need to make a group decision," I interrupt, knowing that Prez would have absolutely fallen for her puppy eyes. That woman is nothing close to innocent, but the energy she projects is fairly clean. Shocking.

"Tornado's right," Knuckles chokes, almost as if those aren't the words he wants to be saying. "We can't have closed door discussions with everything going on. We talk about transparency, we need to preach it." Leather turns on him, her eyes blazing with rage and...lust? The hazel orbs are narrowed to slits, the pupils blown. But it's gone as quickly as it came. I question whether it was actually there or not.

"Club cut?" I ask, nodding to Prez as he sits back. It's my job to focus on them being in line.

"Twenty-five, the usual." She shrugs, blowing another bubble. "Contract is fifty-thousand. There'll be three of us, so it'll be split four ways. Twelve-thousand five-hundred per person."

"That'll put us back in the green until the contract comes through," Bookie mumbles, clacking away on his computer next to Phisher, who is also working on the laptop.

"Then add fees from *Backslide*, I think we'll be fine." The club mumbles amongst themselves, mulling over the ideas.

"Those in favor of adding Leather's added *excursion* say 'aye'." From the sounds of it, the whole damn club is in favor of her trip.

"Those against say 'nay'." Church is silent for a few moments before Prez clears his throat, nodding for Bookie to add the values.

"Anything else?" Prez asks, glancing passively around the area. "Great. Leather's taking the lead for her trip. You're all excused."

"Prez," I call, standing from my seat as everyone else does too. They all pause, waiting for my next move. He dismisses them, waiting for them to leave before I speak up. Leather grips the back of her chair, obviously waiting her turn to speak with him.

"I would like to be included in Leather's mission."

"No," Leather butts in, pushing her chair under the table roughly, black painted nails gripping the plastic. "You had time to say something earlier and didn't. Plus, I don't take strays."

"Leather," Prez snaps, narrowing his eyes at her. She doesn't look the least bit intimidated. If anything, her face heats as he looks down at her.

"What?" She scoffs, rolling her eyes. "He had time. I get that he's here to be a spy, but I can't afford this one to go wrong. Big D Raiders are active, and I need to be on my A-game. While I'm sure he would be an asset elsewhere, this isn't the best case."

Prez sighs, glancing at me over his shoulder. "He's going."
Turning to me, he gives me his famous death glare. "You won't be
getting a cut, but you'll get your stipend from the club when the
club cut shows. She's right. You should've spoken up when church
was in session, not waited until we voted it in."

"Understood. I just didn't want to pop-out and have Leather eat
me alive with everyone present." Prez rolls his eyes, grabbing his
jacket off the back of his chair.

"No offense, but I don't give a shit if you're scared of a few snickers. Rules are rules. You know them, you follow them." Slipping
his arms into the sleeves, he struts out the door quickly. Knuckles
hesitates by his own chair, obviously debating whether or not he
should go. Neither of us move or blink, so he also dips, leaving
Leather and I to compete in a stare off.

Chapter Fifteen

KNUCKLES

Leather's been super quiet since the meeting a couple hours ago. She's not a fan of the outcome, which is fairly easy to see, and I will admit that I'm not particularly happy either.

I can admit that there's obvious tension between those two. They have been practically eye-fucking since they met. On the other hand, I stare at Tornado's ass as he breezes past us, hustling to get to his bike.

That man has her wrapped around his finger metaphorically, and vice versa. They may not know it yet or may not be ready to admit it, but just watching them...it's clear they are just working themselves up.

Readjusting myself, it dawns on me that I would be more than happy to watch them together from the sidelines. Leather could absolutely top from the bottom. My throat grows thick. I'm craving *him*. Not only Tornado, but I'm salivating at the thought of Leather and Tornado together. Maybe even add Prez in there.

I'm fucked.

Being attracted to men isn't an issue, besides being surrounded by them every fucking day of my life. The downside? I have never looked at a guy and thought '*I would let him fuck me*'. No. If anything, I gag at the thought of dicks. They are ugly. After seeing them constantly between the jacket pickers and *Backslide*, I have never wanted to be associated with one.

Thinking about Tornado dominating Leather? Leather being switched between Tornado and Prez...

I readjust myself again, my throat suddenly too dry. "You sure you don't want me to talk to Prez?" I ask Leather as we walk to the bikes. "I can get him to keep Tornado back. I'm sure there's plenty of shit he can do here."

She doesn't say anything as she straps her gloves on, her heeled boots clicking heavily on the concrete of the club parking lot. From the far-off look, she's pretty deep in thought. So much so, that I doubt she actually heard me. I pull my own gloves on, strapping all my shit down onto my body.

Her hips sway back and forth as she struts to her ride, her phone peeking out of her jacket pocket before she zips it, hanging her helmet on the handle bar.

"Nah," she finally mutters, straddling her bike. She pushes the key in, firing the baby beast up. I put her small pack into her saddle bag, clasping it shut. "If he fucks up this mission, I will just kill him myself." In one fluid motion, her helmet is snug on her head, her braid secured down tightly. The visor is up, her eyes peeking through as I watch her closely.

"Dibs on the second hit," I say. She sends a wink my way before popping the screen down, covering her face fully. Kicking my leg over my own bike, I settle all my gear on and start her up. She purrs loudly, a gentle rumble between my legs almost enough to give me a hard on.

In true Leather fashion, she doesn't peel out of the parking lot. She knows better than to disrespect her bike like that. We hit the open road, taking curve after curve up the winding back road, the breeze hitting us in the tail and pushing us faster the farther we go. I take up the rear, ensuring that everyone in the club is accounted for, minus Tornado. I don't think anyone would put up a fuss if he just miraculously went missing.

The ride to Vancouver is a long one. One of the guys popped a tire on the drive, forcing us all to stop and wait for a truck to show up. We didn't want to bring a van with us, as it would probably just slow us down. Except that backfired because they would have had everything we'd need. On a positive note, the shop we called just happened to have an old, usable spare he could buy, and it put us only a few hours behind schedule.

Walking back out to the hotel lot, Leather locked eyes with Tornado. Every time they would look at each other, there'd be some sense of longing in their gaze. I wasn't the only one who noticed. A slight *zing* of jealousy shot up my gut, only for me to force it back down. The hardest part wasn't watching them, no. It was choosing which one. I wanted both. I want all of them.

After witnessing Leather and Prez, even if it was only the aftermath of it all, I came to terms with the fact that I'm not against guys. In fact, I have been caught by Prez on a few occasions checking him out...we may or may not have gotten a little bit closer than we both anticipated.

"That's my ass," Prez grumbles, a smirk twitching on his masculine face. His plump bottom lip gets tugged between his teeth, a curious look on his face. Quirking a brow, I watch as his eyes lazily draw over my body. My dick twitches at the attention, and I swear I can feel every spot his eyes graze. An involuntary groan releases from deep within my chest and he snaps back up, a devilish glint in his e yes.

"It's definitely a nice one," I quip, sending a lust-filled wink at him. A small whimper sounded from him, and I pounced. Eating up the distance between us, I gripped the back of his neck harshly, digging my fingers into his short hair and gripping tightly.

"Aren't I supposed to be in charge?" He mutters, his breath minty. A mirthless laugh follows, my nose brushing his before going down to his throat.

"Yes, but it's my turn." Gripping his skin between my teeth, I bite harshly without breaking the skin. Prez's hands fly to my jacket, gripping the material roughly.

"You want my ass, Onyx?" Prez groans, tipping his head back to give me more room. Pushing my free hand between us, I cup his cock, putting a bit of pressure on his jeans.

"If you're willing to give it, Hendrix," I retort, using his govern-ment name. Just as I'm about to claim him, a door slams in the distance. We both jump back, my teeth dragging his skin roughly and leaving a deep red mark. His hand flies to the spot, a look of pure shock on his face. I'm sure mine matches.

"We can't..." he pauses, a sharp inhale following. Shaking my head, I turn on my heel.

Shaking the bold memory out of my thoughts, I step between the two having a silent quarrel. Her eyes flick toward me, a silent thanks ebbed in them.

"What's the game plan, folks?" I ask, reaching for my key card from her outstretched hand. Before I can grab one, her hand re-tracts and a slight pained look crosses her face. "What?" I glance between her and a couple of the prospects. They look like they are trying to withhold their laughs.

"Some of us have to share rooms," she mumbles, only holding four cards. "Three to one room, two to the other. They only had two available for the next couple nights."

"We can all band together in one if you want your privacy," the prospect, Bear, says quietly.

"It's fine. Just know that I will get a bed for myself, the other two will have to share." With that, she turns on her heel and heads up the concrete stairs. The rest of us are stuck staring at one another. None of them *wants* to be with her. There's a rumor that's been going around for as long as I can remember that Leather doesn't sleep. Either way, I would gladly volunteer if it didn't cause weird looks my way.

"Rock, paper, scissors?" The other prospect, Twelve, asks. I force myself to hold my groan. A feminine laugh echoes in the night, and Leather stands over the metal railing. Waiting.

"Really?" She scoffs mockingly, tapping her nails on the rail. "You're *that* scared?"

The four of us look at one another, determining whether our manhood would be ruined after this. Almost in unison, we shrug.

"Okay, it's rock, paper, scissors, then throw your sign on *shoot*, got it?" I ask, narrowing my eyes on the two prospects. They all shuck their jackets off, getting ready for a fight to the...bed?

Is it bad that I actually want to lose so I can bunk with her?

Chapter Sixteen

LEATHER

H oly shit. They are not joking. I swear my face is bright red as I watch them duke it out in the age old game. Pulling out my phone, I hold it up to take a video of the group. Four burly men, guys who are considered deadly...are playing children's hand games.

"Fuck!" A deep roar shouts. "Best two out of three." Looking past the phone, I catch Tornado pouting like a schoolgirl.

"Nah, dude. You agreed to death first." Bear shakes his head, stepping back. My laugh finally erupts, all four turning toward me. I can't help the wicked smirk as I point to my phone.

"Hurry up, I'm tired." They roll their eyes, turning back to their little pack. I can hear Tornado pleading for them to let him try again, but they all refuse. His back muscles ripple under his shirt, the dark shadows casting over his body just accentuating the look. Knuckles is no better. His biceps ripple with irritation as they continue their game. Tornado groans and moans at the fact that he lost, definitely not happy with the results. Knuckles looks like he's determined to lose this little charade.

"Ah!" A deep voice shouts, arms pumping. The other three look at him like he grew three heads. "Dibs on the side closest to the bathroom." Knuckles grabs his gear off the seat of his bike and bounds up the stairs toward me. His arm is around my waist before I can blink, grabbing the room key from my hand and pushing our way inside the bedroom.

I can't help the little laugh that breaks free, this grown man throwing me around like I weigh nothing. Not that I'm against being thrown around but...*Heckles.*

Shaking the name from my head, I slap his ass with effort and the *smack* is loud. He yelps, nearly dropping me into the corner of the dresser thing. Setting me on my feet, he eyes me. The look is deep, full of something I'm too scared to admit.

I clear my throat, taking a cautionary step back and throwing my thumb over my shoulder. "I'm going to, uhm." Pointing, I don't wait for a reply before I slip into the bathroom. The door shuts gently before I sag against it, breathless and slightly needy. The sudden ache between my thighs isn't from riding on the bike for the past few days. No, it's from watching two grown ass men play hand games with the two prospects.

My body threatens to go straight into an orgasmic spiral if I don't take care of it, but the guy who haunts my dreams flashes before my eyes. I squeeze them shut, praying that it'll end the damn suffering I have endured for years on end. His fucking face curls into that sadistic smirk I used to love, his yellowing teeth taunting me. The way his teeth would snag on my throat, breaking the skin for him to taste my blood...

"Leather?" My eyes pop open as a banging knock pulls me abruptly out of my thoughts. Taking a deep, shaky breath, I open the door to see Tornado there, his hardened eyes assessing me before softening slightly. I grasp the metal knob tightly in my hand, putting my free hand in my pocket. My body is open. Exposed. The deep colored iris's lock onto mine, keeping me in place. It's like a tornado of emotions swirling behind his depths, waiting to pull someone under. I wouldn't mind being pulled under.

"Uhm," he croaks, grunting to clear his throat. "How long are you going to be? I smell like exhaust and want to go to bed."

"Give me ten," I say, but it sounds more like a question. He nods, not moving from his spot. His fists clench at his sides, his forearm veins popping from the tension. Biceps ripple with strain. I swallow several times trying to clear the damn egg in my throat. Once I realize he isn't going to move, I take a tentative step back. A part of my brain wants him to step inside with me, swim the depths of my mind with me. The more logical part tells me to slam the door quickly and to save myself.

His spine snaps straight, his knee bending as if he's going to follow. Instead, he swiftly shakes himself and turns, walking back to the main room as I shut the door.

I strip quickly, wanting to be done with this shit as much as the next guy. With steam billowing from over the curtains, I hop in.

Washing myself thoroughly, I do my best to keep from fading into taunting memories with *him*.

Unfortunately, it's like a black hole mixed with a vortex. It'll suck you in, and you'll never be the same again.

"Oh, Leather," he sneers, shaking his head as he rolls another set of chains over his fist. "I can't wait to see how these shred your pretty skin."

"They won't scar?" I ask softly, knowing better than to question him loudly. He will snap. He kneels in front of me, a mocking coo leaving his lips.

"I thought you liked my scars, whore?" A whimper escapes me, one that I can't help. It's not one of pleading, if anything, it's the opposite.

"I'm sorry, Master," I mutter, keeping my eyes cast to the floor just like he taught me. He jerks my chin, lifting my face to meet his.

"You'll be sorry for questioning me. In case you needed reminding, you're my blood slut." He throws my face the other way and my body tilts as I work to keep myself upright. In the shadows, I can see his arm jerk back just as the chains slam onto my body.

"Stop," I hiss to myself, looking between my breasts. A deep, pale scar sits jaggedly on my sternum, taunting me at every turn.

"Please stop, sir," I rasp. Liquid pours down my shredded back. To seal the deal, he sprays bacitracin right over it because it apparently has lidocaine in it. I can't keep the animalistic scream from ripping out of my lips when the stuff hits my skin. The alcohol burns, the jagged pieces of my skin seers for a few more moments as the pain slowly dissipates with my consciousness.

My scars taunt me. They are my formal sign of weakness.

"You're not weak," a voice says, startling me so hard I damn near piss myself.

"What the fuck!" I shout, covering my body with my hands. There's so many places I don't want others to see, scars that some would use as trophies, but this is torture that was sold to a forbidden paradise.

"Why do you hide?" He asks, yanking back the shower curtain. My mouth falls open, unable to give him an answer. Knuckles stands there in a white tee-shirt that hugs him completely and his jeans, which I'm sure will fit snugly against his pert butt. Water splashes off of me, slowly turning the material see-through.

"Get out!" I shriek, trying to stay focused. I grapple with the curtain to use as a cover up, but he immediately denies me of that luxury. He reaches out, pulling my arms away from my body. I struggle slightly, my tired body no longer willing to fight against my mind.

"What the fuck are these?" He grits, stepping into the shower with me, pinning my arms over my head while my back presses into the cold tile. No words form in my mind. I'm too damn shocked by his proximity, and the fact that he stepped into the damn shower fully dressed.

The warm water splatters around us, his body getting soaked. He wants an answer, but it's one I can't give him. Not yet, anyway. Not when I know he can run.

I avoid his eyes, looking at his wet shirt and watching his abs ripple with every struggle I give. Effortlessly, he holds my arms up and away, inspecting my naked body with intent. Heat creeps up and over my breasts, straight onto my neck.

"I can't tell you," I mutter. Gathering the courage, I meet his gaze. There's lust, but there's also concern. Fear. It's a look I'm not familiar with nor am I comfortable with. Unable to see that shit, I go back to admiring his abs. That's something I'm more than okay with.

"Blaine," he whispers, letting one arm go to grab my chin. He drags my face back up, forcing me to meet his eyes. The way his depths flicker between mine causes an involuntary shiver to race straight to my crotch.

This man may just be the death of me.

Chapter Seventeen

LEATHER

I can't breathe. My lungs are seizing as this man devours me with his eyes.

"You don't have to hide from me," he mutters, his eyes dropping to my mouth as his thumb drags over my bottom lip. "I won't let you hide from me anymore." The air can't seem to enter my body, caught in my throat as this man I have only ogled from afar claims me in his own right.

"I'm not ready," I whisper, wanting nothing more than to jerk my face from his hand and slam the door between us. Something. *Anything* to get a barrier back over my heart. His eyes glisten as he quirks an eyebrow, barely letting it move from its rightful place.

"If that's the case, then you'll never be ready." He doesn't give me a spare second to move before he's on me, lips smacking onto mine in a rush. My hands fly between us, my fingers digging into his shirt as he pulls me close, his body finally drenched as he commands my mouth. In an instant, I meld to him, eyes fluttering shut with desire. His warm heat pouring into my body as the water slaps us both. Dominance is fought between us, one that I am debating on letting him win.

It's like those stupid fairy tales that talk of sparks flying, butterflies in your stomach, the whole nine yards. Except, this is more. This is more than anything I would have imagined. It's like a ton of motorcycles revving inside my stomach, my exhaust dripping with need. I can't compare it to Prez by any means, but it's almost equally aggressive, possessive, and *hot*.

An involuntary whimper escapes me as he bites my bottom lip, pulling away from me and letting it drag between his teeth before it pops back into place. The carnal desire that sweeps low into my stomach, the wetness of the hot shower mixed with the arousal dripping out of me pushes me past any point of solid thinking.

This man is all consuming, his hard body tucking me into his as he takes me. My brain misfires as I try to fight for air, fight for any form of coherence before he moves away from my lips. Dipping his head and panting against my neck, he bites, licks and sucks on the sensitive skin. My legs shake as he goes further down, right above...

"Wait," I pant, pushing him back slightly. "Wait." He straightens to his full height, his eyes controlling his every emotion as he looks at me. Looks *through* me.

"There's no more waiting. You've had time to control your demons, Blaine. The chains around mine are breaking, and I can't hold them back much longer." His voice is deep, heavy, and thick with desire. The thread of need snaps in an instant, my doubts washing away as his strong, calloused hands grope my body with bruising pressure, kneading on my ass like he simply can't get enough. We can't get enough of one another.

"It's not that simple," I reason, tilting my head back into the stream of hot water. A literal growl leaves his throat as he ravishes the sensitive skin.

"Make it that simple." His mouth captures mine in another searing kiss, the air failing to replenish my lungs. The way he molds his lips over mine, fighting his tongue with mine, my knees threaten to give out. Muttering one word, my legs lock around his waist, back slamming into the cheap motel tile wall.

"I want to devour you until my lungs give out," he grunts, shifting my hips slightly and pushing his covered crotch against my bare one. The heavy denim pushing apart my lower lips, a rough sort of chafe edged between a sense of bliss and a pinch of irritation.

"Please," I stutter, grinding my hips into his wet jean clad erection. It's odd, the fact that I would never seen him as more than a friend, then suddenly I want nothing more than to rip his clothes off, lick his abs, and let him fuck me into oblivion.

While I'm not one into monogamy, I want him to fuck me hard and fast, cum into me so hard he sees fucking stars behind his eyelids. I want his hand around my throat, squeezing so hard my face flushes hot and I struggle to breathe. I want to fucking tease him, edge him until he's begging to cum inside of me. Fuck a baby into me...

"Fuck," I whimper roughly when he suddenly drops my legs, taking a step back. I reach for him, but he grabs my wrists and spins me around. Another deep growl reverberates off the walls. I can't help the flinch in my body as he lightly drags his fingers over my back. Thanks to the tattoos, they are hard to see, but my back is shredded from whips and chains. An abusive dominant who took advantage of my submissiveness.

"These are beautiful," he mutters, coming up closely behind me and kissing my neck. I attempt to push back on the iron-rod in his jeans, but he denied me, shoving my hips forward. One slow, long lick is met from the base of my neck to my ear.

"Finish your shower, because I'm going to get you even fucking dirtier."

Chapter Eighteen

Knuckles

Walking away from her has to be the hardest fucking thing I have done in a long time. To say I wanted nothing more than to undo my pants far enough to pop my dick out and bury myself deep enough to hit her stomach, is an understatement.

I shove myself out of the shower before I can convince myself to do just that, almost eating shit on the wet floor and my sopping clothes. It takes a fucking year to peel myself out of my pants and shirt, finally hanging them on the cheap rack.

How have I not seen her back before? Thinking about it, most of her costumes for her scenes all pretty much cover her body. Skin isn't a hot commodity with her, and I'm just starting to realize this. I could see the rippled skin under the ink almost immediately, but the piece drew me in just as quickly. Black and gray ink, it was a beautiful lady head with skulls dancing around it in different eras of decay. Some of them were fully skinless, others had shadings of where the skin peeled, then the one lady head that was perfect.

It was almost like those lapses of the moons, where they are in different stages. Remarkable.

Shrugging off the odd feeling, I open the door and leave the steamy bathroom. Much to my surprise, Tornado is there. With his pants off, cock in hand. Stroking himself.

Holy. Fucking. Shit.

"Jesus!" He jumps from where he sits, covering himself a moment later with a stray towel. Too late for him, I already copped myself a look, and hot fucking damn...he's *lengthy*. He's on the thinner side, but he would pierce a girl's cervix, if that were even possible. It's definitely made to breed, forcing her to take his cum.

"Can you cover that fucking monster?" He grunts, tightening his hold on the towel over his lower half. Looking down, I completely forgot I'm stark ass naked. Not only am I naked, I'm still harder than a rock. "Fuck, you've got your dick stabbed?" His gaze stays locked on my cock as I reach down and slowly stroke my length.

"You mean a Jacob's Ladder?" I retort, a single brow raising. His own jumps beneath the cover of the towel, fighting against the covering to get out. Licking my lips, I debate on whether to go and suck him off...

"Whatever it is, fuck dude," he grimaces. This is like nothing I have encountered before. Have I had a few fantasy's of him? Sure. Have I stroked off to the made-up image of his hand instead of my own? Yes. Did I anticipate them to come true? Not a fucking chance.

But here we are, both buck ass naked, staring at one another. His abs aren't rock hard but they are there, covering his whole torso in tattoos. While he gawks at my cock, I point to his body with my free hand.

"Do those go all the way around?" I mutter, taking another long stroke as he stands shocked. Gulping, he nods, turning slowly to show me his back.

Fuck.

His ass is just as fucking plump as I would imagined. Seeing his ass in tight fucking jeans before made me want to pin him to the bed and drill him, but seeing it like this...

Taking cautionary steps forward, I trail my fingers over his giant dragon tattoo. His shoulders shutter, breath stuttering as I caress his golden tanned skin. I'm not sure what force is pulling me, but I lean forward and inhale his musky scent, grazing my teeth over his neck.

"Knuckles," he groans, taking a small step backward right into my bare body. Reaching both hands around, I gently feel the plains of his body all the way from his pecs to the slightly defined V on his lower abdomen. I tease the area where the towel is stopping me, before gripping it and ripping it away.

"What-" he starts, turning around and rubbing himself over me unintentionally. His cock is rock hard, pre-cum leaking from the tip. Mine rubs with his as I take both of us in fist. Pumping my hips, a rasped groan falls from his lips.

Before I can think it through, I'm dropping to my knees in front of him, hands staying on his hips for support. I feel animalistic, like I can't get enough of him. While he stares at me with wide eyes,

I may as well feast on this beautiful man. I drag my rough hands down his body, reaching behind him to cup his ass. His eyes are tentative, but he doesn't stop me.

His hard cock juts in front of my face as it waits to be sucked down deeply into my throat. I peer up at him from under my lashes, coaxing him on.

I have never done anything like this before, but the sudden confidence in myself has me second guessing if I was maybe a jigolo in another life.

Licking the underside of his lengthy erection, one of his own hands slams into my hair, gripping the thin tresses tightly. A guttural groan of satisfaction peels from me. The thick head beads with pre-cum, and I just can't help myself. I suck him into my mouth and flick my tongue over his hot tip.

"Fuck," he rasps, hips jarring slightly in surprise.

"Well, well," a feminine voice teases. Tornado jerks out of my mouth, swiping the towel again. I stay on my knees, looking over my shoulder at the woman who's captivated my mind since the day we met. She's gotten scars that would scare a weaker man, but boy do I think they make her look ten times hotter...

"I would love to say I'm shocked, but," she trails off, shrugging slightly as her own towel gives us a peep show of her leg.

"Woman," I growl. Twisting on my hands and knees, I slowly crawl over to her. After seeing her perform and having a moment to clear my head, I realized that I could probably get to her better if I appealed to her dominatrix side.

Her breathing shutters as I get closer and closer. Bending on my elbows with my ass in the air, I lick from the tip of her toe to her ankle. It's slow, and I take my time placing gentle kisses in my wake. Moving further, I creep along her shin, nibbling on the side. She shakes above me as I go, and my hands trail to caress her thigh. Clamping down on the side of her knee, she yelps while I take the liberty of peeling the towel away from her. It lands somewhere behind me.

Sharp inhales reverberate off the old stricken walls. Peering over my shoulder, Tornado stands there like a man possessed. Fists tightly balled at his sides, brows dipping low on his face, his eyes blazing with lust and conviction. He burns just as brightly for her as I do, that much is evident.

"I want you," I rasp, looking back at the beauty above me. Her pussy is bare, exactly as I imagined it. Not a single hair in sight. Tattoos cover her entire left leg, up her rib cage and onto her back where the masterpiece sits. Funnily enough, I notice quotes from her favorite books from over the years etched into her delicate skin. Kissing each of them one by one, I leave behind a promise for continued support in her darkest days. She's known since I joined the club that I would protect her with my dying breath, even if she's the one stealing it away from me.

"How do you want me?" She purrs, tracing a hand through my damp hair. Pushing higher on my knees, I sink my teeth into the soft flesh right before I meet the apex of her thighs. Instead of jumping like I anticipated, her fingers lace tighter into my hair, tugging me closer to her body.

"With my tongue." Shoving my nose between her lower lips, I inhale her sweet scent deeply. Due to the shower, the smell is muted, but I will eventually have her over the mount of her bike. At that point, she will be sweaty, hot, and fucking delectable.

Her legs tremble around my head, one hand grabbing the wall to keep steady but getting no purchase. Her other hand has a death grip in my hair. With how hard she's tugging, I wouldn't be surprised if I lose a few strands.

"Right here." Shoving my tongue into her opening, I take one long, slow lick. Her pussy is the best tasting thing I have ever fucking had. With how hard her fingers are laced in my hair, she directs me to where she wants me. Using my lips, I suction her clit into my mouth, biting on the bundle of nerves as she quivers and sputters around me.

Chapter Nineteen

TORNADO

H oly. *Fucking*. Shit.

I don't even know how to react with the erotic scene in front of me. My entire being is telling me, *begging* me to join in on their action. But the more logical side is telling me that I'm here for a bigger purpose, that I can't let my cock be the head of this operation.

Knuckles crawling to her is one of the most possessive acts of submission I have seen. I had to do some research, sure, but I'm out of my fucking element here.

A loud *smack* brings me from my slight panic, and I catch where her hand finally manages to grip to the corner of the wall, knuckle gripping in an attempt to keep her upright. His dark hair is tangled in her other hand, the short strands pulled taut off his head.

Suddenly, his hands come to land on her hips and turn her harshly. Her back slams into the wall as he grabs one of her legs and swings it over his shoulder.

"Much better," he purrs, diving back into her cunt.

Fuck it.

Sinking to my own knees, I take Knuckle's lead and crawl my way over to this vixen of a woman. There's a slight burn on my knees from the rough carpet, but I ignore it when I see his tongue shoved deep inside her delicious pussy.

"Where do you want me?" I ask, rolling my eyes up her body, I take in the harsh lines covered in tattoos. *They* never mentioned anything about her being marred...I will need to follow up about this.

"Suck my clit," she demands as her other hand comes down off the wall and laces into my hair. Knuckles scoots further between her legs and hiking her one higher up on his shoulder to give me better access.

Who am I to deny her?

My cock rubs against Knuckles as I shuffle closer, and I have to stifle a groan. Fists clenching, I wrap one arm around her leg and hold her hip to keep her steady while the other wraps around my cock. I have to keep some semblance of my manhood, so I wrap my other hand around my cock in an attempt to stop from spurting all over the carpet.

Sucking her clit between my lips, I swear I feel like a teenager again with his first taste of pussy. A deep, guttural groan vibrates out of me as I suction her between my lips. Pushing my tongue forward, I alter between working my teeth over her nub, occasionally flicking my tongue.

"Shit," she hisses, and her fingers tighten. "Touch each other. Give me a show." We both sit back on our heels, contemplative looks shared. Resignation etches over his face as he reaches a tentative hand out. His fingers are coated with her juices, so I also reach up to coat my hand with her. Nodding, I shoot my hand out and grab him around the base, using the slight lubricant from her cum to tug him to the tip. His hips jump, his cock pulses.

Following my lead, he grips me tightly.

"Who is going to suck off who?" She teases, petting our heads like animals. I snap my head up to her. Her eyes are darkened in a lust-filled haze, one that makes some deep-rooted part of me slowly giving into the submission.

Knuckles hoists her leg up, motioning me forward. Shuffling on my knees, he sets her leg on my shoulder as he moves backward. He situates himself behind her, her hips pushed forward a bit, and he leans down on his forearms with his ass back in the air with his hot mouth breathing on my erection. It juts out, hard and solid, ready to do with as it's asked. My face is directly flush with her glistening cunt that's just waiting to be eaten.

Taking one last glance up my body, he takes the tip of my cock and sucks it into his mouth tentatively. A rumble vibrates on my length.

"Holy," I gasp, my brain working to figure out what the fuck I'm supposed to be doing. Thankfully, Leather knows what she wants from me. Both of her hands wind tightly in my hair, guiding me back to her slick center.

Slapping her thighs, I use my thumbs to spread her wide while my own eyes roll up her body. Her head is tipped back, but she needs to be looking at me. Us. With my sudden, cool breath lacing her heat soaked clit, her head snaps downward. Auburn hair floats around her like a halo as she admires Knuckles and I. I'm honestly not sure what she sees, but I can guarantee that my face is slack with pleasure.

Her jaw drops like she's going to say something when I dive tongue first. The bundle of nerves is hard, proof that she's extremely turned on. Taking a single finger, I dance it along her weeping entrance. She droops backward once again, and I pull back.

Jerking downward, "why'd you-", and I suck her clit back into my mouth just as I shove a single finger in. Her leg quivers in time with my whole body. If I wasn't using Leather as a fucking post to not fall, I would have Knuckles hair twisted tightly in my own fist.

He pops off, licking a long trail up my abdomen. "I think our female wants to fuck, isn't that right?" He coos, his voice dripping with sarcasm. She looks ready to clam up and step back, when he helps me tongue her deliciousness. It's like she latched onto *our*. She is ours, she just doesn't know it yet.

"I will even let Tornado have my ass while I take your pussy." At that, we all freeze. Even Knuckles seems shocked that it came out of his mouth. "Shit, fuck, nevermind," he sputters, bewilderment crossing his entire body. His own rock hard cock is straining to be touched, precum oozing from the tip. Just as he's about to start scrambling...

"Wait," she commands, halting his movements. "Is that something you want?"

"I..." Knuckles pauses, confusion warping himself. "I have never..." We all nod in understanding. This is a first for everyone, apparently.

"Have you?" She turns to me, raising a questioning brow. Shaking my head, I swallow harshly. I have not even fucked a girls ass before, shockingly enough.

"Are you positive?" She asks, taking a single step toward him. He looks about as pensive as she did a few moments ago. Hesitation coats his features before he nods slowly.

Chapter Twenty

Leather

I t's intoxicating just thinking about the things I could do to them both. They put their trust in me, both by giving total submission. Knuckles willingly sucked Tornado off, just because they knew I would like it.

Now, here they are. Both staring at me with wonder in their eyes, waiting for my next more.

"What are you waiting for?" I mock. Taking their momentary lapse in sanity, I use the heel of my foot to shove Tornado backward. "Though, I think I would much prefer if I had you both to myself."

"I don't do well with being bossed around." Tornado glares at me from his position on the floor. I just smirk. Grabbing Knuckles by the hand, I lead him toward the bed. He stands off to the side, waiting for my command.

"See," I pause, gesturing toward Knuckles. "This is what I call a good boy." Tornado scoffs, pushing to his elbows. His thick cock bobs proudly, jutting up and waiting for more.

"It would be a real shame if you only watched," I sigh tauntingly, dragging my nails over Knuckle's chest. He releases an audible shiver, goosebumps peaking through the flesh on his arms.

"I will just take matters into my own hands." Tornado's fist wraps around his cock, stroking himself tightly.

"You won't cum until I say you do," I bark. He stops dead in his tracks, his fist tightly wound around the head of his dick. "There's nothing a little deprivation won't fix."

"You wouldn't." His eyes narrow on me, my hand gliding down my companion and dragging my full hand over his cock.

"Try me," I deadpan. Opening my hand, I spit into it and put it back on Knuckles's cock. He groans, knees shaking like he's forcing himself to stay upright. "So, here's what you're going to do. Are you listening?"

"Yeah," he grumbles, removing his hand. Leveling him with a glare, he obviously isn't too happy to be in this position of submission.

If he wants to play, then this is what he will get.

"Want to try that again?"

"Yes, Mistress," he seethes, obvious anger reddening his face.

"Good boy." Stepping away from Knuckles, I pad back to where Tornado is lying on the floor. I crouch down to his level, allowing him a full view of my cunt. He stares directly where I want him to, his fingers rolling into fists almost immediately as I touch myself. Lust overtakes his features, brows pinching together with neediness.

I straddle his hips and shove his shoulders back into the musty carpet. He doesn't fight me, letting himself fall backward. The feeling of his cock brushing against my pussy has me shivering with anticipation, yet, I'm not going to be giving into his demands anytime soon.

"You think you can boss me around?" I ask, trailing a nail over his pec. No answer. "I bet you think you're a big man, don't you?"

"No, Mistress," he says, though it's as if I have to put a gun to his head for him to say it. That simply won't do.

"Now, now," I coo mockingly, grabbing his chin in my hand. He tries to fight it for a moment before giving in. "Do I need to tame a brat today?"

Tornado lies there without another word, fists still tightly balled and knuckle white. Glancing over my shoulder, Knuckles remains exactly where I left him.

Turning back, I catch the male below me eyeing between my breasts. An indescribable look crosses his features, one that I have no desire to question him about.

One hand holding his chin, I lift myself off him for a moment, only to use my free hand to line his thick cock at my entrance.

"You want my cunt?" I question, rubbing him along the slickness that was brought on by my previous orgasm.

"Yes, Mistress," he says. He tries to nod but fails due to my tight hold on his chin. Without another word, I sink the tip of his cock inside of me. The flared head feels amazing, stretching me further than before. Lifting off, he visibly restricts himself from grabbing onto me.

"On the bed lying on your back." The command comes out sharp, no room for questions. I stand and step off of him, letting him scramble to do as I asked. Knuckles remains completely still and watches the scene with wide eyes, almost as if he can't get enough. Snapping my fingers, he quickly pops out of his gaze, kneeling down at the foot of the bed.

"Where would you like me, Mistress?" Knuckles questions, keeping his head down. His position intrigues me. The crawling could have been a one-off, but the near perfect submission posture? His palms face up on his thighs, his spine straight and chest pushed out. The only thing that isn't right is the span of his legs. They are not quite wide enough for my liking, but it'll absolutely do.

"What do you think, Knuckles? Should you fuck my ass while I ride him, or would you like to fuck his ass while I ride him?"

"Wait," Tornado squeaks, shooting up.

"Is there a problem?" I ask, knowing damn well I'm out of both of their comfort zones. Knowing Knuckles, he won't make Tornado do the deed just yet, though I anticipate they will be getting dirty at some point in the near future. Especially after the little show I got.

Tornado watches me closely, his brows and eyes portraying vulnerability.

"I will take your ass, if you'll have me, Mistress," Knuckles announces to the room, answering my question. I don't acknowledge him, though. Tornado and I have a stare down instead. If anything, this will determine that I'm the one in charge, not him.

After several moments, he relents. His back bounces lightly on the bed and his cock bobs above him, leaking pre-cum.

"I think you liked the second option." He huffs a laugh but doesn't deny it. I could tell straight away that he's not against being fucked in the ass, but that's a boundary we'll push on another day.

Bending at the hips, I grip Knuckles' chin and tilt his head back. "You want my ass?" He doesn't hesitate before ripping into his pleas. Meeting my eyes, he waits for me as his whimpers die off.

"I think you've been a good boy," I admit as I drag my thumb across his lower lip. "I'm going to take his cock in my tight pussy while you watch. No touching, understood?"

I don't wait for his reply before crawling up the bed and hovering over Tornado. There's a whirlwind of emotions passing his features while his eyes flicker between mine. It's almost hypnotic, observing his contemplation about his next moves.

Well, good thing he doesn't have to worry about that since I'm the one in control.

Lining him back up to my entrance, I don't give myself a moment to adjust as I slam home. His shoulders jump off the mattress, features painted between shock and ecstasy. Gyrating my hips over him, I catch my clit on his muscled abdomen, rubbing just the right spot.

"You feel so good," I moan, tossing my head back. His hands fly to my waist and grab my hips in a white-knuckle grip. *Tsk*ing, I pry his veiny, calloused hands away from my body and shove them above his head. "No touching without permission." I should probably tell him it's a soft limit but that's not information that needs to be divulged at the moment.

"Yes, ma'am." I don't bother correcting him.

"Knuckles, get up here." The man in question wastes no time, climbing onto the bed and positioning himself behind me. His face is between my cheeks, right where Tornado and I meet. Flicking his tongue out, he takes a long, slow lick up Tornado's cock and circling at my entrance.

I want to admonish him, punish him for breaking a rule. Yet, he looks so happy just to be licking up our mess that I decide to let this one slide.

"Prep my ass, boy," I demand. Immediately, he gets to work. Pushing a finger inside my pussy, the slight stretch almost turns me into a whimpering mess. The smidge of pain amplifies everything. He swirls in another finger, bumping my sweet spot right along Tornado.

Just as I'm about to reprimand him, he takes his soaked fingers and pushes one slowly inside my tight ass.

"Yes, just like that." Leaning on my elbows over Tornado, I can't help the delighted groan that escapes me. Being filled to the brim is one of the best feelings.

Knuckles slowly pumps that finger in and out of me, swirling around before adding another. Again, he moves them in sync and stretches me by scissoring his fingers. He constantly spits, lubricating my ass for his fingers. This would be better with lube, but I didn't think I would be fucking my friend and sergeant while on this trip.

That thought alone has me freezing. Holy shit.

I'm fucking my boss and my friend.

"You're so tight, Mistress," Knuckles growls from behind me, pumping simultaneously with Tornado as he rears upward. The impact catches me off guard, almost throwing me straight into detonation.

"Can I please fill you with my cock? This naughty boy needs to be suffocated by your tight ass," Knuckles begs while kissing my ass cheeks. I don't say anything, I don't even move for a few moments.

You know what? It's too fucking late now.

"Be a dirty boy and fuck your Mistresses ass." Jostling the bed, I can feel the warmth of his chest on my back even though he isn't touching me. It's like he's a fucking radiating heater. One of his arms drops next to Tornado's head, the other not in sight as the burning stretch of his cock enters my ass.

My eyes roll, head spins, jaw tightening. He moves slowly at first, switching with Tornado to keep me full.

"Fuck me." The demand is simple, yet it's as heavy as a boulder. Wasting no time, they both slam into me at the same time.

I didn't realize how worked up I was, because as they yank themselves out and fill me up again...I detonate.

Screaming, my legs shake and quiver. Stars erupt from behind my eyes, white light guiding me straight through my orgasm. Actually, they are relentless as they fuck me. Not giving me a chance to breathe, they continue to pound mercilessly into my holes. I don't have enough air to stop them, even if I wanted to.

Chapter Twenty-One

KNUCKLES

B right light shines from the cheap motel curtains. It shines directly in my eyes. Groaning, I go to roll over, when I'm met with a muffled *oomph*. My brows dip into my nose, and I rocket out of the bed. Leather and Tornado lay snuggled together, and I can see where I was playing big spoon with her. My eyes dart around the space, trying to comprehend what's happening.

Correction.

I'm trying to comprehend that it *actually* happened. I fucking know that my dreams basically came true last night, I was there. I felt how great it was. Yet, digesting that simple fact has now turned into a big frog in my throat.

Pacing back and forth in front of the bed, my brain slowly tries to recollect the night's events.

I sucked off Tornado.

Leather sucked me off.

I ate her, and Tornado did too.

Gears turning in my head, I'm sure my face is composed of shock and awe. There's far too much happening for my brain this morning.

"Too early," Leather grumbles, throwing Tornado's arm over her eyes. "Shut off your damn brain, Knuckles." Tornado chuckles and lets her do what she wants, cuddling further into his arm. I open my mouth to address what happened last night.

It's been a long time coming, and it happened.

My stomach feels hollow, clouds looming over me for the day. I would have preferred us to be in candle light, but I know she's against that.

From what I gathered, Leather suffered some shit at the hands of someone who was supposed to protect her. I mean, who hasn't endured some trauma? Except, hers was clearly an abuse of power dynamics, and he used her soft side to do it. Unfortunately for the rest of us, that means we get the cold exterior and killer glares when anyone mentions anything about love or relationships. She doesn't say anything against it, but it's clear from her dynamic that she's not happy with sappiness.

"We should-" Pounding on the door cuts me off, the hollers of the guys on the other side.

"Let 'em in," she mutters, throwing the blanket over her partially naked body.

"Absolutely not," Tornado and I both bark in sync. One look at her and the whole damn club will know about our late night debauchery.

"Get in the shower, we'll let them know you're running late." Tornado rolls out of bed while Leather looks irritated.

"Why am I the late one?" She sasses. Sitting up, her sweet tits bounce almost perfectly in unison. Tornado isn't affected as much as I am, but who the fuck cares?

"Uhm, because you're always running behind," he says, though it's like he's throwing a question back at her.

"Not on missions, idiot," she huffs, glancing down at her phone. "Sucker, it's not even six."

"Will you guys hurry?" One of the guys calls while still pounding on the door. My brows dip to my nose, curiosity killing me. Glimpsing through the peephole, it's just the two of them, though they look antsy.

Just as Bear goes to pound on the door again, I rip it open. They hustle inside, not bothering to second glance Leather's level of nudity.

"Intel is saying that they are...expecting our arrival." A huff echoes from the bed, and Leather shakes her head.

"I figured as much. I suppose that's not a bad thing." She looks pensive for a moment. "Knuckles, your friend is running coast, yeah?"

"Yeah?" I drag, unsurety glazing over me.

"Think we could get through easier that way?" Bear asks, crossing his arms. Tilting my head from side to side, I debate on it. "Would it be better if we just trailed through the backroads? What about taking the ferry or something?"

Pondering for a moment, I say, "Probably not." He nods, slumping down into the chair. "Honestly, it's not going to matter which way we go, they know we're coming. Our best chance is to go full balls to the wall," I laugh. I grab a shirt from my backpack and pull it on quickly.

"Uhm, excuse me?" Leather pipes up, attitude already penetrating her tone. "I don't have balls, so what next?" She tries, but fails, to hold in her laugh. When none of us respond, she huffs.

"I'm going to check us out," Tornado says without acknowledging the conversation. Once he leaves, Leather and I simply glance at one another. Neither of us want to even deal with that right now, so instead, we start gathering our belongings to hit the road.

"We're going to pack our stuff, why don't you guys get ready too?" She asks, shooing them away.

"We already packed," Twelve starts before catching her gaze. It's hard, one that doesn't allow for argument. "You know what, we better do a double check." They exit quickly, leaving just Leather and I alone.

Clearing my throat, I awkwardly fiddle with the strap of my backpack. "I think we should talk about last night."

Her heavy sigh says otherwise, but she doesn't comment against it. Instead, she lets the sheet fall from her chest and onto her lap, showing her perfectly sculpted breasts. I'm captivated for a moment, enraptured by the sweet treat in front of me.

Shaking my head, I turn away with heated cheeks. "Look, we really *need* to talk about what I saw last night, and everything that went down."

"What is there to talk about?" Shuffling has me looking back at her, only to see her tight ass on display. I can't hold in my groan of delight. I send up a prayer to whoever is above for some mercy on my soul.

"Leather," I start.

"Knuckles," she interrupts me, holding up a hand. "It happened because we both wanted it to. It was mutual, can we agree on that?"

"Leather," I try again.

"We just happened to be in the moment, right? No hard feelings."

"Leather."

"It was bound to happen, especially since we-"

"Blaine!" I shout, finally catching her attention. Her rambling seizes, her eyes wide with shock. I haven't called her by her real name for a long time, only when she's freaking the fuck out and won't calm down. Like now.

She must have changed while I was looking away because she's donned her usual leather attire, her pert ass tucked tightly in her pants.

"There's no regret on my part, if that's what you're thinking." Walking over to her, I sit on the bed and position myself to face her. "I just need to know you're okay. That you're not going to do anything stupid while we're out because of what we did. Being with you...it's been a long time coming, and I hope you can see how happy it made me to be with you. I'm honored that you shared that piece of you with me, but I hope that you can trust me to talk about the horrors you endured one day."

Clasping her hands in mine, I bring them both up to my mouth and plant gentle kisses on the backs of them. There's small scars from years of hard work with the club, being an executioner isn't for the weak.

I set both her hands in my lap and brush away the hair that fell in front of her eyes. The scar she's had for as long as I can remember has faded to a light pink, but I know it bothers her. What she doesn't know is that it makes her so much more sexy.

"Knuckles," she pulls her hands out of my lap and clasps them together. "I don't know what to say." She doesn't meet my eyes.

"I don't want you to say anything. I just want you to know that I'm here for you. Not just your body. Though, that is fantastic too," I tease. She fakes shock, smacking my chest with the back of her hand. Catching it, I peck the back again, letting my lips linger on her soft skin. "I hope you know that you can always come to me, whether it's for something miniscule or something life threatening. You're my ride or die, and I will do everything I can to make sure you're okay."

"I'm supposed to be the one protecting you, remember?" She retorts, sniffling slightly. I don't comment on it knowing how hard emotions can be for her.

"Technically yes, but my ego says no." Shrugging, I cup her cheeks and lean my forehead against her. "You're mine, do you understand that?"

She nods against me, exhaling heavily.

"Yours."

Chapter Twenty-Two

TORNADO

They continue talking, something about the scout knowing we're coming. Being in the same room as Leather and Knuckles was a lot harder than I anticipate, so I announce that I'm going to check us out. They don't say anything as I leave, giving me a moment to breathe.

Stepping outside, I take a long, slow deep breath. Regret is the first thing on my mind, but it's also the furthest thing. Feeling his cock running along mine from a slim barrier, it's like nothing I have felt before. I have done threesomes, so it's not that. It has to be because it was with them.

That thought also brings more confusion to my mind. I'm not here to make friends or fuck buddies. Yet, the longer I stay around, the more I talk with her, the more I realize she's not who she was made out to be. A woman who was villainized because she was protecting herself. Either way, I'm here to do what I was hired to do.

Pulling my phone from my pocket, I head down the stairs of the hotel and make a call.

"How is it?" He grunts, not bothering with a proper greeting. It's strange, really. It hasn't been too long since I have been with the Silent Renegade's, but I will admit that it does feel like a lifetime. Leather may not trust me, which is evident in the way she treats me, but everyone else? They act as if I didn't just drop in out of nowhere. Whatever their president says, goes. Again, with the exception of Leather.

"Fine," I retort. I attempt, and fail, to keep the snappiness out of my tone. He catches on immediately.

"What? Not enough pussy for his majesty?" He barks a laugh at my expense. Usually, I would be laughing along with him, telling him that there's plenty of bait for me, but that's not true. After getting a taste and feel of the best pussy around...

"Oh, someone has a magic pussy?" He asks, though there's a menacing edge to it. It's near impossible to tell what he's thinking since I can't see him. If I had him in my line of sight, I would absolutely be able to read him like an open book. Over the phone is a totally different story.

Shaking myself out of it, I clear my throat. "First of all, that's not a thing. Second of all, it's going fine. We're talking about different missions, but nothing exceptional at the moment." *Lie.*

"No?" He questions, his voice raised just slightly, enough to put me on edge. "You guys aren't going on any trips soon?" Swallowing thickly, I debate on whether to tell him the current trip.

"Like I said, nothing crazy. Just a few small jobs here and there. Some tracking, but that's it."

"Any mentions of the Raiders?" My chest squeezes, heart hammering heavily behind my ribs. He's my boss, for fucks sake. Yet, I want nothing more than to protect the little auburn haired beauty currently cursing up a storm in the hotel room. She curses worse than a sailor, but she's also one of the most loyal people you'll ever meet.

"Minor mentions, but nothing notable. It's everything we already know." Silence. "Just how they are going to destroy them, but again, you already know that." Silence.

Pulling the phone away from my ear, the timer for the call still ticks. Neither one of us say anything. I let the silence continue on without giving him anything else. While I want to trust him, I have a sinking feeling there's so much he left out when telling me about her or this club. Even still, I'm just going to do what I'm told.

"Alright," he sighs. "You remember what you're supposed to be doing, correct?"

"Yes," I sneer, irritation burning red hot in my veins. "If I didn't, I would get a bullet, I know."

"Good, good." He goes silent once more. There's only so much fucking silence I can take.

"Alright, I'm going to get going," I mutter and stop outside the business office.

"Where are you going?" I audibly groan.

"I'm done answering these ridiculous questions." Without waiting for his response, I pull the phone away and end the call. Stuffing it back into my pocket, I pull open the door to the hotel.

Right as I walk in, there's two officers standing with the reception-ist. They are talking to her, but she doesn't look like she knows what they are asking her.

Taking a few steps back, the officers realize that someone en-tered. Turning fully away from her, they both put their hands on their belts.

"Are you Jaxon Wrath?" One of them asks and the other grabs their notepad. Furrowing my brows, I debate whether to be honest or not.

"Uhm, who's asking?" I clasp my hands behind my back, using the backs of my hands to feel for my gun.

Shit. I left it in the room.

There must be a reason if they are asking...

"Are you, or are you not, Jaxon Wrath?" There's a buff guy on the left, who would be pretty intimidating if I was a weaker man. He raises a single brow.

"Who is asking?" I retort, keeping my tone clipped. "I have shit to do today, so if you want to spit something out, that would be great."

"You got ID?" Skinny dude on the right says. Brushing my hand on my back pocket, I grab my wallet out and whip it open. Keeping eye contact with the skinny guy, I grab my license and flash it at them.

They both squint, scanning my I.D. "We're sorry to interrupt your day, Mr. Edwards."

Smiling, I give them a curt nod.

"No worries, fellas. Just got to do a job, I totally understand."

Chapter Twenty-Three

PREZ

Walking through the doors to the club, the party seems to be in full swing. Their moods are light, smiles plastered, and yet, I don't feel any of it. It's odd to think that there's two individuals that have my hackles raised, simply because they are not with me.

When they left, it was literally like a piece of me went with them. It's only been three days but those days have felt like a fucking year. I also need to keep in mind that they are basically just biding time. Tiny hasn't given us the determination on whether we're getting the weapons contract or not. Usually it's not a big deal, but Big D is just on the other side of the border. If we don't have a reason for being there, we're more likely to be rampaged.

Who the fuck am I kidding? The whole damn mission is fucked, but I will be damned if we don't get to the bottom of the bullshit going on in our area.

When my grandfather was president of the club, he once told me about how children were being sold around the area and there was little they could do to stop it. Excuses were constantly stopping us. Now? We have the technology and manpower needed to take these fuckers down.

We may not be the best people around, but we don't stand for harm against women and children. That's where we draw our line in the sand.

Slugging myself into a table, the waitress doesn't hesitate to bring my usual. Plopping down the glass, she pours me three fingers of whiskey before turning away. Calling back to her, I motion for her to just leave the damn bottle. Pointless to take off with it when I will be needing a refill before she can get back to the bar. She plops it onto the table and gets to work with the other regulars.

The cool glass meets my lips, and the slight burn from the alcohol as it coats my throat is blissful. Serene.

Ever since we implemented the registration and membership for *Backslide*, our numbers initially dropped. It was a shock for everyone, but when we explained that it was due to recent safety concerns, most of the members were on board. Now, our members are more protected from the inside out, and not just the outside in.

"You look like you could use a pick-me-up." A female plops down in the chair next to me, her shirt barely containing her tits. She's definitely someone I would go for, except...she's definitely not anymore.

"And you are?" My arm stretches out over the back of the seat, opposite to her while occupying my hand with the glass. I don't want her to think I'm interested or willing to be...persuaded.

"I'm Amber," she smiles. We sit and stare for a moment. She twirls her hair and pops her gum obnoxiously. I take several slow sips from my glass, taking in the female.

"Amber," I muse, looking down at my lap. "What can I do for you?"

"It's more like what *I* can do for *you*." Her hand lands on my thigh gently, slowly stroking my leg. As nicely as I can, I bounce my leg and get her touch to fall away. Her expression drops for a moment before returning just as brightly.

"Are you an employee, or a patron?" I ponder. Grabbing the bottle, I pour myself more whiskey. There's clear hesitation in her eyes, and I'm not entirely sure why. "Oh, were you not honest about your name?" I *tsk* condescendingly.

"It doesn't matter if you're not interested," she huffs, attempting to scoot out of the vinyl seating. The short shorts hug her slim figure, her long legs on display as she tries her best to stand graceful without sticking.

"Who said I wasn't interested?" If I want to know her angle, I need to play the long game. She freezes immediately and glances seductively over her shoulder. After watching Leather in action, seeing how she can manhandle someone without even breaking a sweat...witnessing her ability to carve humans into canvases...no one else will compare.

But for the sake of the club, and our livelihood, I digress.

"I just assumed..."

"Assumptions are what dreams die on." Waving at the waitress as she passes, I order Amber a vodka soda. I can tell she wants to reject the order, but one sharp stare has her shrinking.

We sit quietly for several moments, her breathing heavy as I take several long, slow looks over her. She's fit, seemingly in good shape, though she doesn't have a cut nor a club tattoo. Anyone who wants to be a member *has* to have one of those two things, if not both. Finally, the waitress returns with the drink, giving Amber a long look before taking off to help another person.

"So. What brings you to this club?" Using my free hand, I gesture around us. Exhibitions of all sorts are going on, some already in the process of fucking like animals, while others are still leading their submissive like a fucking dog.

It's great.

"I had a friend recommend this place, so I applied and was accepted," she shrugs. Her glass meets her lips, throat bobbing as she takes several quick swigs. There's tears forming at the corner of her eyes from the burn, most likely, and it's fascinating to watch others who aren't used to the burn. People who haven't had the chance to familiarize themselves with it.

"Really? How cool." I wrack my brain for anyone with her name and come up short. I know for a fact that no one with that specific name has come through, not even on the alias cards. "What friend?" She sputters slightly, just enough that an untrained person wouldn't catch it. Yet, I'm specifically looking for characteristics that wouldn't be seen by the normal eyes. I look for mannerisms, eye movement, speech styles.

She's trying to take me for being a fool, and I don't fucking like it.

"Oh, you probably wouldn't know them." Waving her hand through the air dismissively, I roll my eyes back down to my lap.

Initially, I was thinking that she might not know who I am and how I'm associated with the club. After that simple conversation, I have no doubt in my mind that she knows exactly who she's talking to. She's also got a goal in mind, one that I don't think I will like.

One thing I believe she underestimated? The fact that I'm the one who does all club admissions.

"I bet I would," I toss back teasingly. I need her to slowly build trust in me. She scoffs with a laugh, taking another long drink from her cup. Catching eyes with the waitress across the bar, I use my free hand and motion for her to keep the drinks coming for the female accompanying me. Flicking my finger, I signal I need something a little bit stronger for my friend. She nods without missing a beat.

"His name is Tornado, I'm not sure you'd know him. He's new to the club." Schooling my features, I give her a single nod.

"No, he's not ringing a bell. What does he do in the club?"

"You seriously have no idea?" She asks, her eyes wide with glee. *Shit.* Maybe she doesn't know who I am after all. Shaking my head, she immediately goes into who he is and how great he is. Not just how good he is, but how *great*, if the jist is gotten.

As she talks, I try to drone her out.

After a couple hours, she's easily five or six drinks in. Her inhibitions are long gone.

"...Raiders weren't always like that, but I'm so glad-"

"Wait a second," I stop her, holding a finger off the glass. "Did you just mention the Raiders?"

"Uhm, yeah?" She squints at me, obviously skeptical. "He was their vice for a long time while Armstrong was in the presidency. Once Armstrong stepped down, so did Tornado. Something about trafficking, blah blah, I don't know. He didn't want anything to do with it. But, there was a new guy who totally was an asshat, but who cares? We're out!" She cheers, clinking her glass with mine.

"How did you get out?" I ask, pretending to be genuinely surprised.

Again, she scoffs, "usually it's blood for blood." She waves the waitress back for another refill. "Except, when Daryn...oh gosh, what's his last name!"

There's no fucking way...

"Oh! Daryn Finnigan! He's hotter than a southern summer, but man...he's a douchebag. He came in with all sorts of new ideas. When he was initiated..."

Again, I space her out. Reaching into my pocket, I pull up the eFile I have on my people and search.

"...and they told everyone he was abducted! Can you believe that? How fucking crazy?" She continues cackling, and I swear I'm whiter than a ghost. Everything starts slowly clicking into place, and before long, I realize that I can make this into something better. There's no guarantee that it'll work out, but it's worth a shot.

"Oh! And get this!" Her slurring has ramped up, almost to the point where she can't even talk in a straight line. "Daryn still has Tornado by the balls somehow. It's crazy, man. We got out, but he's still hanging around them like a dumbtard. Daryn, which I don't know if he has a road name or not because he's an asshat, even implanted a stupid tracker on Tornado. I tried to warn the dude, but he wouldn't listen..."

If shit wasn't bad enough, it's definitely going to hit the fan.

Chapter Twenty-Four

LEATHER

Rolling across the border was a lot easier than we anticipated, which put our previously behind schedule now caught up. The guys were all cracking jokes, having a great time while we rode. I simply couldn't get into it. They asked me, tried to engage with me. There's only so much I can say without spilling my guts.

I slept with two of the three people I deemed off limits for myself. They were temptation in the purest form...and I did myself dirty by giving in.

Regret isn't the word I'd use to describe how I'm feeling, though. If anything, I feel crummy. Almost as if I took advantage of them. Yes, I know they are grown ass men, and yes, I know they can make their own decisions.

Knuckles has been trying to "woo" me for as long as I can remember, then after him...even just the thought of the asshole has my hackles raising. My heart feels heavy as I pull into the parking lot we were ordered to go to.

After that first night, I told the guys that they would be sharing their own room, and I'd take my own. None of them made complaints. When their door would shut, it was like a party on the other side of the wall. I couldn't fault them for having a good time, either. If I were in their position, I might have been doing the same thing. Instead, my eyes remained nearly unblinking at the boring ceilings as I zoned the night away.

Now that we're riding into day four, exhaustion has crept into my bones after sleepless nights and extremely long days, but this mission was at my insistence. I won't let them down simply because I'm feeling less-than great. It's imperative to our overall objective that this goes right.

Dropping the kickstand, my phone lights up with a call. Unfortunately, we keep playing phone tag. Prez has tried to call me several times today, but when we pulled over for gas and I tried to call him back, he wouldn't answer. If he ever needs me for something, he'll just send a quick text, but he doesn't just call over and over again. Which means it's because there's something going on. My small group doesn't have all day to stop and go. We can't just stop for me to answer his call, so we kept moving. Until now.

Yanking on the strap to my helmet, my phone goes dark before lighting back up again with Prez's name.

"What's so-"

"You need to leave!" Prez demands, his voice taut and heavy. "Get out of there, and we'll talk when you're back." There's an edge of desperation in his voice, one that has my brows pinching together and bad straightening.

"Woah, we just got here," I start, frustration and concern already taking root. There's no fucking chance I'm leaving a drop spot without a good reason.

"There's no time to explain, Leather. You all need to leave, *now*." Opening my mouth to ask questions, the distant sounds of motorcycles start up. The rumble of their engines takes over the call with Prez, hushing his voice into the background. Glancing around at the guys, they all seem to hear them too. Three of the four guys shove their helmets back over their heads and wait for my call.

The only person who doesn't look surprised...is Tornado.

"Go, Leather!" Prez shouts down the line and his voice kicks me back into gear.

"Let's go!" I shout down the mic, kicking my stand and screaming out of the lot. I hear the bikes start up behind me, their own tired squealing to race away. I take a sharp hook to move out of their way and motion for them to move ahead of me. I refuse to let members of my club suffer.

The sound of bikes gets a lot louder. Three of the four guys whiz past me while the last one stops, his bike right beside mine, and idling along with me for a moment. Swallowing thickly, a sinking pit in my stomach knows exactly who it is.

"This is a direct order. Get back to the club, let Prez know you're alright." All three immediately start blowing up my side of the line, asking what's going on, their voices carrying over each other. Reaching up, I switch off the mic and speaker, unable to hear their frantic questions.

Just as I'm about to hit the throttle, a hand stretches over, hitting the killswitch. I could easily turn it back on, but the distance of the bikes...

If this is my fate, then I'll gladly take it to ensure the others are safe.

But I'm not going down without a fight.

As the rumbles grow closer and closer, I have to fight my hands from turning the bike back on. Flipping my visor, my eyes meet Tornado's as he stares at me.

"Why?" I ask, pulling off my other glove. His throat bobs, his swallow audible.

"I'm sorry, Leather." Nodding, we continue to sit in silence.

There's so much I want to scream at him. Sorry is an excuse for people who aren't thinking through their actions, and it's far too late to go back on. Sorry isn't needed for people who are intentional in their actions. Maybe that's plenty of reason for me to forgive him, the fact that he's not able to own his actions.

Who the fuck am I kidding? I'll never forgive him.

We wait with bated breath as a group of five guys roll into the lot. My three are long gone, hopefully on their way back to the club and listening to my direct order. Since Tornado didn't take off after them, I can only assume I'm the person they want.

"Why?" I snap, this time using more force behind the question.

"Misled circumstances." He says something else but the mufflers roaring with life barrel toward us at an alarmingly fast rate. Neither Tornado nor I move out of the way.

We're both watching. Waiting.

"I promise if I had more time..." Turning to look at him, he almost looks guilty. Almost. There's absolutely more to it than he's leading on. It's just a travesty that they won't be alive to see it.

"You should have thought about that before agreeing to whatever plan this is," I scoff. Arms crossing over my chest, my breasts get shoved between each other and create a bit of a distraction for him.

Boys. Not even men.

The first guy finally stops in front of us, his chopper a deep shade of orange with flames painted on his exhaust pipes. Wracking my brain, I try to figure out where I know a design like that. It's so familiar, yet it's such a distant memory.

Four others tail behind him, shoving their kickstands to the ground and standing at their full height. Tornado shuffles off his own, his gloved hand reaching out to shake the hand of the first guy who has yet to unveil himself.

"What the fuck is going on?" I ask, pretending to be absolutely fed up. In reality, taking on five guys, not including Tornado, it's going to be near impossible. Especially when my gun is under my jacket and would be far too obvious to grab.

A deep, gravelly chuckle escapes the first man. Ice burns in my veins as my blood suddenly freezes.

There's no fucking way...

"Blaine, or should I call you Leather?" He laughs, unclipping his helmet. It doesn't take long for him to unceremoniously take it off, but it doesn't make my panic any less real. "It's been far too long, don't you think?"

Chapter Twenty-Five

KNUCKLES

I wouldn't say it was fear that I saw on Leather's face, but it was resolution and conviction. Whatever they told her on the phone, she immediately knew that something was up. It was like a light bulb had gone off in her head, and she immediately knew what to do. Once she stopped, there was no doubt in my mind that she was going to try and cut them off for the rest of us. I don't know if it was something on her face that tipped me off or if I just know her that well, but I knew she wasn't going to let us stay there with her. She's the lead executioner for a reason, one that will take a bullet and laugh it off, as long as it means she's saving those around her.

Unluckily for her, I don't always do things the way she wants me to. I refuse to leave her to the wolves, I just need a second to catch my breath.

"We need to stop down the road and form a plan," I inform the others, getting uncomfortable silence from their ends. I don't wait for them to determine if they are going to follow or not. They know their role.

"Hey man, she made a clear order to-"

"Who is in charge right now?" I bark, merging onto an exit ramp. "Where is she right now and where are you? Is she here?"

"Well, it would be you because she's *not* here, but-"

"I don't want to hear it, dude. She's not here right now. Yes, she gave a direct order, and I will deal with the consequences if there are any. What's one of the motto's for the club, Bear?"

"Uhm, all for one and one for all?"

"What does that mean to you?"

"Leave no man behind," he says sternly, with more conviction than before.

"That's right. We're not leaving her behind, and the fact that you were willing to just let her order you back into a fucking shell has got to dock some brownie points off you." Traffic is light at this hour, not the worst, but rush hour is only a few short hours away. Having ridden early this morning, we intentionally avoided the shitty traffic. Now, we're going to make a plan to figure out how to tackle said traffic.

"Not only that, but you know Leather would never do that to us..." Bear says quietly, as per his usual demeanor.

Pulling into a busy parking lot, Bear and Twelve flank me, and I almost end up tail spinning. The kickstand scratches on the concrete as I rush to grab my phone. It doesn't take long for Prez to answer.

"What the fuck is going on?" He asks, his own tone on the edge of frantic. "I told her to get out of there, but I can't reach her."

"She stayed back," I huff and flip the visor on my helmet. "She thought she was fucking saving us, but Tornado stayed with her. I didn't see much, she just ordered us to leave and not come back." I can't stop my leg from bouncing, my calf starting to burn from how rapidly I'm moving it. It's like trying to contain this horrendous rage that's just begging to be let loose.

"That's fucking stupid," he starts.

"Believe me, you're preaching to the choir." Pinching the bridge of my nose through the open area, my brain tries to grasp at straws on how to get back there. "We're going back, but I need a plan."

"What are you thinking of doing?" His agitation is beginning to grate on my nerves. Or maybe that's just me being a fucking idiot by not having something already decided.

"I don't know!" I grunt. "I have no fucking clue, and this isn't one of those times to be teaching me!"

"I think you're wrong. You *know* what you're supposed to be doing. Do it." He leaves no room for argument, pushing further. "You're Leather's right hand for a reason, Knuckles. Take fucking charge and get back there! I got locals trying to get to them, but you'll have to meet them."

Without waiting for my response, he immediately ends the call.

Staring out onto the busy roadway, cars slowly start flooding the streets. There's not a ton of time left for us to avoid rush hour, and who knows what's happening right now...

"We'll discuss the plan on the way," I state, my own decision now made.

Chapter Twenty-Six

LEATHER

"I would love to say that this reunion is unexpected, but..." he trails off, shrugging his shoulders nonchalantly. His helmet is suddenly tugged off his head then placed on the seat of his bike. Looking back at me, he smirks. "It's not."

My frozen veins instantaneously thaw with raging fire. "What do you want?" There's more ferocity in my tone than I'm currently feeling, and I can only hope that it's sending him 'don't fuck with me' vibes. It's easy to see that I'm pissing him off, which is exactly what I need.

Tornado doesn't move from beside me. I don't take my eyes off the predator in front of me, but there's a good chance that Tornado is standing like there's a metal rod shoved in his spine.

"Leather," he sighs, *tsk*ing like he's scolding a small child. Taking his time, he pulls his leather riding gloves off one finger at a time. Besides the natural sounds of the city surrounding us, the group is completely silent.

"Fuck off," Tornado grunts and moves several steps away from me. "You weren't supposed to be here." That catches my attention, though I refuse to take my eyes off Heckles.

"Maybe not, but I'm the one who showed up. Plus, did you really think the boss believed the whole spiel about nothing going on?" Furrowing my brows, I know better than to start asking questions. However, just because I know better doesn't mean I won't do it.

"What the fuck does that mean?" I demand. Crossing my arms over my chest, I do my best to put puzzle pieces together. Unfortunately, they just aren't forming.

"Oh, my," Heckles laughs, shaking his head. "I presume that our dearest Tornado hasn't caught you up to date? At least I know he's loyal to someone."

He turns to face Tornado slowly, looking at him like he's ready to bury him six feet under. A quick glance to the other men, and I realize that I'm absolutely at a disadvantage. I don't think I would be able to sneak my gun out of my waistband. There's no telling where they are looking since they all still have their helmets on and visors down.

"I'm not falling for that bullshit," Tornado spits, his own irritation finally rising to the surface. "Get the fuck out of here, Heckles." There's a sense of finality in his tone that would have me cumming...if he didn't just commit a cardinal sin and turn on a fellow member. But, that's just another issue. Is he a member of Silent Renegade? Or is he a member of a different club?

My brain hurts trying to keep up with everything.

"Can you both just cut the shit?" I shout, fire burning in my stomach. Reaching behind me, I grasp the handle of my pistol. Just as I'm about to yank it out, another hand lands on my wrist and holds me tightly against them.

"I wouldn't do that if I were you, sweetheart," he snickers, his head tilting down to breathe right into my ear. A disgusted shiver trails through my spine.

"Now, here's what's going to happen." Heckles saunters over to me and the other dude and kicks rocks along the way. "You're going to be a good whore and get into that van." He points to the vehicle I hadn't even realized was here. It must have been here this whole time and none of us clocked it.

"Absolutely not," I hiss, fighting the tight hold on my body. "I would rather die than go anywhere with you." With rushed steps, his chest is mere inches away from me. His hand lashes out, smacking me harshly across the face. Blood instantly pools in my mouth.

The guy behind me lasso's my arms and tugs me off the ground. Not realizing his disadvantage, I swing my legs up and slam my heel into Heckles' face. He staggers as the dude and I crash onto the ground. The hold on my shoulders loosen immediately, but it's pointless. The remaining men form a semi-circle around me. Jumping back to my feet, I manage to grab my gun and aim it dead at Heckles. If there's any shots I take, it'll be killing that motherfucker.

"Do it," he taunts, advancing on us. My finger hovers over the trigger, but it's like my body refuses to push it down. "You're a weak little girl who needs someone to dominate her."

His remarks continue to hit the target, my own feelings of betrayal surfacing once more. It's been years since I have felt the struggle of his hold. Yet, now that he's found me and is standing right in front of me, the submissive girl wants to fall back on her knees for him.

"I'm not weak," I snap. Taking aim at one of the other guys, I let the round fly steadfast. It lands and makes a loud *crack* as it punctures his helmet. I can only hope it hit him smack between his eyes, because he drops like a wet noodle onto the concrete. I would love to rip the helmet off his head and stare at the liquid oozing from the wound, but there are others around me that I simply can't trust.

Finally taking a glance at Tornado, his body language is tight, shoulders rolled back and hand poised over the butt of his gun. His eyes...they are the only thing that betrays him. They are dull and emotionless to those who can't read people. I can see right through him. He's not torn, he's regretting this decision with everything in his being. From his earlier astonishment, Heckles wasn't meant to be here.

"My, my, you've grown a back bone!" He claps slowly, his voice haughty and monotone. "Now quit playing games, stupid girl, and get into the van." My entire body is trembling as I fight against the command.

"You know what happens to girls who disobey?" He whispers in my ear, the tips of his fingers dragging along my naked ribs. A shiver wracks through me. The vibrator is tied between my legs, stuck on my

clit as he torments me. I'm unable to stop him. "Aren't you going to stop me, little girl? Fight against your master." The demand kicks my brain into action, squirming against the tight holds. My body is hunched over like a girl praying at church, except my arms are tied together and tucked tightly into my body. Almost to the point where breathing is difficult.

"Red!" I shout, but that doesn't stop him. It never does, even as I scream it over and over again. The jagged knife pressed firmly into my tight skin, he rips away my last barrier.

"Now, now, girl. I think you'll like what I have coming." Cool air meets the wounds, effectively also helping my overheated body. The moment of reprieve is gone. His cat-o-nines lands harshly on my flesh-

"No!" I shout and pull the trigger. I wait for the gun to discharge, for him to drop. Except...it doesn't. Clicking the weapon over and over, I realize the chamber is jammed. There's no way that I will be able to fix it.

Heckles charges me, and I bolt away from him. Taking off in a sprint, there's no way I can outrun him in my boots. He's also almost twice my height, so his leg span doubles mine.

Pushing myself faster, it's not a pace I can maintain for too long. Before I can think, I'm being tackled so hard my head clobbers on the concrete. My arms cover my face, fending off his continued punches. Shifting my hips, I try to buck him off of me and flip him like I was always taught, but he knows exactly what I'm trying to do by counteracting it.

"Quit fucking struggling!" He screams, spit flying onto my face as we grapple. I don't want to leave my face vulnerable, but I have to fight back in order to survive. Shrieking, I shoot my hands out, get a tight grip on his face, and smash my thumbs into his eye sockets. His own shout of pain echoes around us. I can't clock anyone's location, but that's not on my agenda right now.

His body weight still sits heavily on top of me. Jerking my hips upward, he topples to the ground as he cradles his face in his own hands. I struggle to stand, my head swimming and vision cloudy from the hits I took. Two men converge on me, both with looks of pity. I try to find Tornado, and I see the other guys struggling to put him into the van.

"You can tell Hendrix," Heckles spits, referring to Prez's real name, "that you'll see him in hell."

Before I can block the hit, a pistol jams right into my temple, and my vision goes dark.

Chapter Twenty-Seven

Prez

JUST BEFORE...

The phone call ends before I can rip into him. How could they let her trick them into leaving? On the other hand, I can absolutely see how she can do that. She's strategic, and I can guarantee that there was so much going on, they expected her to follow. Unfortunately, she didn't.

I wrack my brain for names, anyone in the area that would be of use. There's really only one name that's popping up, and if we use them, there's no doubt they will want something in return. That's how the world works.

You scratch my back, and I will scratch yours.

Dialing Tiny, I swear he leaves me in suspense until the very last moment. "Look, I already told you that the contract negotiations are still going on."

"I'm not calling for that." Pinching the bridge of my nose, I can't help but groan out loud. "We need your help."

"I'm listening." Explaining the situation to him, he remains quiet on the other side. I have to pull the phone away from my ear a few times to make sure we're still connected.

"What do I get in return?"

"Guess it depends on if you guys get there in time." Hopefully that will encourage him. Just as he starts talking, I hang up. He's absolutely a contract we need, but we need our members alive. That's a priority over anything else. Unfortunately, I don't think he will. I may need to rely on someone else...though, I only have one other person in mind, and it's not someone that anyone would guess it to be.

Not only that, but Leather...it's hard to imagine the club without her. While I would like to pretend that it would be a lot calmer, I know for a fact that it wouldn't be. She levels them out, keeps them on their toes and adds just the slightest hint of estrogen that the guys need.

In reality, we need to come up with a better game plan, and fast. My phone vibrates in my pocket, and it's Tiny on the other line. I do exactly what he did for me, waiting until the last possible moment to answer the phone.

"It would help if you'd tell me where the fuck I'm going," he grumbles and shouts at his men in the background. I provide details about where their drop was supposed to be, and I also inform them of who I think went to meet the team there. There's no way for sure to know, but I'm definitely not stupid. He continues to grumble and bitch.

"Just know that this doesn't make the contract shit go faster."
With that, he ends the call. With the amount of stress slowly
starting to stack up against us, I don't know whether I need to
laugh or punch something.

Whistling loudly, it startles most of the guys hanging around
the bar. "Church!" I call out, watching them scramble to make
their way to the giant conference room that we use for their choice
services. Plopping myself onto the barstool, the bartender laughs
at me and grabs my usual whiskey. He sends it down the wood, and
it lands perfectly in my opened palm. Raising it in salute, I down
the contents. Per usual, the burn is soothing and grounding.

Once everyone has filed into the room, I move quickly to follow.
Usually, this is when Leather and Knuckles would flank me, but
neither of them are here. Even my second in command isn't here
right now.

"Before the rumor mill starts, we need to make some things
clear," I start, hoping like hell that I can get this out in one piece.
"As you all know, Leather and a few men went on a mission into
the Canadian area to do some scouting. We don't know all the
details, however it is believed the Leather and Tornado were both
grabbed." I won't tell them my suspicions of Tornado, not without
solid proof.

"What can we do to help?" Phisher questions. His laptop lands
onto the plastic table loudly, jolting everyone. For some reason,
that single movement is enough to push reality back onto me.

"There's not a ton of details. From what it sounds, they were cut off by a group of bikers. Leather and Tornado rounded them off to let Knuckles and the two prospects leave. They didn't know the two didn't follow the group."

"Let me see if I can find location on her GPS." His nimble fingers fly across the keyboard. "If we can at least get their last ping..." he trails off, continuing to work.

"What happens now?" One of the guys from the back row grunts.

"We already tried to get to them before it escalated, but by the time the guys got there, the premise had been vacated." The hole in my chest seems to grow as the reality sinks into me. Once we lose members, we rarely ever get them back. If they are returned...well, let's just say that they are not usually in one piece.

Chapter Twenty-Eight

KNUCKLES

I have never been more anxious about anything as I am right now. If I could go back in time, I would have forced her to go first, forced us to all run as a group. Unless someone has a time machine, we can't turn back.

"We need to try to get there without making too much noise. We're going to pull into the other side of the lot and run to where the drop spot was," I announce down the com.

"What about our defense?" Twelve asks. We move through the streets effortlessly, cutting lanes and going as fast as possible.

"You've got your side pieces?"

"Yeah, but we have the drop stuff in the saddle bags. We can't just ditch them," Bear retorts, as if I didn't think about this shit.

"If you'd fucking shut your pie holes, you'd hear the rest of my goddamn plan," I snap, anger permeating down the mic. "Now, should I wait for commentary or are you both done?"

The light turns yellow right as I hit the crosswalk, but we just cruise through it. Past the point of no return and all that.

"Now, as I was saying," I start but get cut off by the sound of sirens. Jerking my head to the side, red and blue lights light up the early morning sky. "Fucking hell. Meet me at the drop spot in ten. Go!"

Splitting up, the officer doesn't go with them. He stays on my ass.

"You've gotta be fucking kidding me," I mutter. Still in range with the guys, they laugh at my expense.

"Your plate was down," one of them garbles before the line breaks off. Pulling onto the side of the road, I look over my shoulder and watch as he pulls right up on my ass. His door opens, and he takes several steps in my direction. I take off. Opening the throttle, I leave him behind me. My speed accelerates quickly, gaining from zero to ninety in mere seconds. Thankfully, my plate is a fake, but that means it's a use for identifying, and we just came through the border.

The cop drops back as I fly between cars in the morning traffic that's quickly building. I don't think I have ever been so grateful for other people as I am right now. Reaching a light, there's another cop waiting for me. His lights are already rolling, and I don't hesitate to push my bike to its limit.

Wind crashes against my body as I fight to keep hold of the bike. The two officers give chase, following me diligently through the traffic. Passing through lanes of traffic and intersections, they continue to ride my ass. I know there's some bullshit law about speeding with motorcycles, yet they don't let up. I'm almost certain that one of them is going to try to do the pit maneuver and throw me off the damn bike.

I don't have time to think about another plan. Leather is most likely in danger, and I'm getting chased by the police.

"Siri, dial Prez," I command, waiting for my phone to listen. It takes a few moments for it to come through. It dials for a few moments before I get sent to leave a voice message. "Fuck. Redial." Again, voice mail.

The line goes dead.

One of the officers manages to get in front of me, slamming on their brakes. Barely swerving out of the way, the other cop slowly crawls closer to me. Looking to my side, there's a deep ditch that I don't want to land in. I know if they manage to get me off the road, I'm done for.

I also realize that there's no way I will be making it back to Leather in time which pisses me off even more.

Thinking quickly, they both manage to box me in, but just as they go to converge, I slam the gas and barely skim between the two officers. Pulling into one another, the guards on the front of their vehicles smash together. The helmet does little to hide the grinding of metal. I don't wait a single moment to fly out of there.

Looking around, I have no fucking clue where I'm at.

"Siri, call Bear." The line rings once.

"Where the fuck are you?" He asks, obvious panic in his tone.

"Two cops tailed me, I finally lost them." I sigh. Noticing a gas station ahead, I pull into the lot to catch my breath. It's small and quiet, a few stops off the main road. Perfect for getting out of the way. It may sound insane, but I have never had to lose cops before.

"We didn't get here in time, but I'm pretty sure I just saw that dude Prez warned us about when we first joined." The blood in my veins runs ice cold. "I wasn't close enough to get an exact, but Knuckles...I think they got her."

The words don't seem to compute in my brain. A sense of numbness takes over, my body sensing the panic rising in me.

"Repeat that," I croak, gripping the handle bars tightly. There's no fucking way...

"I think that Heckles dude took off with her. Twelve agrees." Swooshing takes over his voice as he talks.

"Hold on." Inhaling deeply, I work to shake the foreboding feeling. Impending danger. The alerts are blaring my head for me to save her, but I have no idea how. "I will send you my location. Meet me here. We need to get back to HQ."

Neither of them say anything else, waiting for my location to ping through. Once it does, they end the call. Sitting in the parking lot of the gas station, I reach back and flip my plate over just in case those stupid officers put out a BOLO or some shit.

Slumping down, my helmet clunks on the tank of my bike, the heavy sound mimicking how I feel. There's ideas pinging around my head if Tornado had anything to do with this. It's odd that he didn't take off with the rest of us. Why would he stay behind if we were all booking it?

I try to shake the negativity from me. I'm trying to place blame on someone who wasn't involved in it. He just so-happened to be collateral damage, plus, he's the new VP. His job is to protect us, and Leather's natural instinct is to take charge. They probably had a power struggle or something fucking stupid.

"You good?" Someone shouts from the pump, throwing me thumbs up and down. I don't respond, just throw a thumbs up toward them. They must take that as a good sign because they take off without another word.

I don't know what I'm going to fucking do, but I do know that I want to curl up on Prez and beg for him to make this shit better. I have never pictured a day without Leather, and now that I have to...I don't even want to think about it right now.

Once we get back to the club, we'll make a plan. We'll get her back, that much I know.

Chapter Twenty-Nine

LEATHER

Needles burn my flesh as I struggle to open my eyes. ". ..stupid whore!" There's incessant shouting, then more pain slicing across my skin. I'm not coherent enough to figure out what's happening, but I refuse to let my pain be heard.

"Fucking pussy, this is how it's done." Ice cold liquid is suddenly drenched over my body. A prod stabs into my skin, and a slight jolt forces my muscles to twitch. It happens several times, my body beginning to cramp up with each length of electrocution.

"What the fuck are you doing?" A voice booms through the room. I'm half tempted to shrink into myself from that voice alone, but I don't. It doesn't help that my skull has its own fucking heartbeat.

I wonder if a lobotomy would feel better than this pulsating pain in my temples.

"We were just waking her up, boss," one of his cronies laughs, stabbing me again with the cattle prod. The jolt shocks me, and I barely manage to withhold a hiss of surprise.

"Did I tell you to wake her up?" He growls, his anger burning so damn hot it's practically radiating off of him. I'm glad I'm not in his line of fire. Yet.

"Well, no, but-" Heckles doesn't wait a moment before lodging a bullet into the man's arm. He shrieks like a child who scraped their knee.

While they go back and forth, I take the chance to look at my surroundings. I'm seated at the center of the large, dirty cell, my hands tied behind my back and ankles taped to the legs of the chair. How cliché. There's a metal table off to the side of me, with chains dangling from different posts on the wall and one from the ceiling. A chair is perched in the far corner with a body slumped into it, but I can't tell who it is from here. The pain in my temples doesn't bode well with my eyesight, unfortunately.

"Look," he points in my direction, false sadness coating his features. "Now she thinks we're here just to play a fun board game. What do you think, boys? I think we're here to have a lot more than just some fun." They grumble their mutual agreement to his shitty speech. Their eyes gaze hungrily over my body. Looking down, I realize I'm only wearing my white undershirt and white boxers. Both of which are now see through because of the ice bath I got.

My fear of Heckles hasn't gone away. Ever since he was banished all those years ago, I have been under the protection of the club. It's been great, knowing what true freedom looks like. I have gotten ballsy, I know that. I can agree that I was practically luring him toward me. We could say that I'm the reason he attacked me the second time, but I will never give him the gratification of taking responsibility for my abuse.

Forcing his presence to appear smaller, he walks over to me with his shoulders hunched. I know it's simply a ploy, but I can't get a read on him. There's no way for me to tell what his next move is, which means I can't brace for it either.

I want to scream, thrash, and threaten to kill him. I don't. Refusing to speak unless spoken to, I'm trying to lessen the target on my back. Sadly, the target is a giant red mark that I will never be able to get rid of as long as Heckles is alive.

"Perhaps you'd love to spread your legs for my men, hmm? Give them that thrill of playing with your blood the way I loved to?" My face burns hot, the anger inside my body slowly threatening to reach boiling levels. I need to get myself under control and not give him the satisfaction of working me up. It definitely doesn't help that my brain is screaming for reprieve and the soaking clothes on my body mixed with the cold air are starting to affect my thinking.

"I don't think she's interested," another guy laughs like I'm the most hilarious joke in the world. Which, I suppose, would be correct. I'm just the funniest mother fucker around. They will see how fucking funny I am once I get out of these goddamn restraints.

Opening my mouth to give them a piece of my mind, my chin won't open. Trying to pry my mouth open, I finally feel something sitting in my mouth. Blinking slowly, I adjust my jaw and realize there's metal on my face.

How the fuck did I not see that before. Why didn't I feel it? As a matter of fact, I still don't really feel it. I attempt to scrunch my nose. Either it doesn't move or my face is numb.

There's no amount of effort I could use to make my words make sense. Jerking against the restraints angrily, Heckles whips around with a wide, evil smile. It's the one I saw right before he almost killed me...

"Ah! She finally figured it out!" His hands smack together with a loud *clap*, sending a painful zing into my skull. Like bouncing off a wall, it reverberates around my head for a few moments. My eyes slam shut on their own accord, and I do my best to stop the slamming pain from worsening. The light of the room is so bright that I can see it from behind my eyelids, and it doesn't give me any reprieve or relief.

My head is swiftly yanked back, the force of the pull causing a painful pop in my neck that surges down my spine. A garbled cry rams its way through my mouth and escapes into the air around us.

They cheer, whooping and hollering along with the deep voiced male behind me. I can feel them getting closer, their breath coating my wet hair and over my ear.

"You think you can get away from me, little girl? You think I will just let you go? You're in for a real treat, naughty girl." Shoving my head forward, he kicks the legs of the chair from the side. I don't think anything of it, until the sounds of groaning wood echoes from under me. Freezing, I don't make any moves because I don't want to force it into breaking. There's no movement for several long moments.

Their cheers of victory continue to grow louder, more vicious. My vision is still hazy, fogged over from fatigue and pain, but I can finally make out who the figure is. His jacket is the same as earlier, and his body isn't quite as hunkered down as mine is.

His head is dropped to his chest. I can't tell if he's even breathing, until he tilts up just slightly, winking at me from the corner of his eye.

Furrowing my brows, I can't decide what to make of anything.

Tornado and Heckles knew each other. They weren't strangers, but I don't think I would classify them as friends, either. Heckles mentioned something about switching sides, something about Tornado betraying someone.

As I wrack my brain, I'm so tempted to scream at everyone to shut up so I can think. Two reasons that I can't do that. One, because of this fucking device strapped around my head. Two, because I would rather stew in silence than announce that I'm planning their murder. However, if they were smart enough, they would know that I was planning it either way. If I don't make it out alive, Prez knows all of my torture secrets.

Or at least he should, unless he wasn't paying attention when I explained different ways to kill someone.

That brings me back to the conversation at the drop spot. Tornado led me to believe that he orchestrated everything. So, was the informant real? Was this just one giant set up?

I'm usually the one who reads through everyone's bullshit, but I don't think I would have caught this one from a mile away. Though, this would explain how he knew exactly who it was that startled me all that time ago...

When I collapsed on stage after thinking I saw *him*, Tornado immediately knew who I was talking about. There's no way that he would have that information unless someone told him. Which then leads me to now try and figure out who the fuck would divulge that. If I didn't know any better, I would instantly blame Prez for outing my secrets. He's been doing that since Tornado has been involved, but I don't think Prez saw who it was.

Shaking my head, I realize there's far too much happening here. Another groan from the wood makes me realize my mistake. The sharp *crack* doesn't make its way to my brain. I can only register that I'm falling, and no one is there to catch me.

Chapter Thirty

Tornado

Having chloroform shoved in your face definitely doesn't bode well with your nervous system. The rolling in my stomach is just one of the symptoms of the shitty stuff. I can feel the heat building in my face from holding back the hacking cough I'm working hard to suppress. My body is confused as fuck right now. I'm both tired as fuck, but I feel like I could throw a bus.

When Heckles kicks her chair, I have to physically restrain myself from looking at her. The wood definitely crushed under his foot. Glancing around from under my eye lashes, they are focused on her. The group of guys are spitting at her, laughing at her expense. She's having an internal struggle that I could definitely relate with. I would like to think hers is probably on a deeper level.

I can see the moment she realizes that she fucked up, confirming my thoughts. She was trying to not move, trying to stay as still as possible, but her thoughts caught up to her. All of the idiots in the room are throwing a fucking party around us while Leather tries to stay as still as possible. Winking at her, I want to show her that I'm okay, but I will be honest, I don't think it helped anything.

Being as discreet as possible, I'm able to track only one official entrance and exit. There's no windows or vents in the room. It's made of concrete from ceiling to floor.

Her chair sways. The groan finally snaps, and she topples to the ground. I brace myself for the land. No one is concerned about me, all focused on watching Leather fall. It happens in slow-motion for me. Her brows pinch together, her matted hair flows outward before the sharp *crack* of her head on the hard floor. Blood pools around her almost immediately, the dark lighting barely making the darkening of her hair visible.

Cheers grow louder after watching her tumble down. It's a power move also, because now she's fallen from her status and is considered to be nothing. She's no better than the gum found on the bottom of a shoe.

The crackle of a can opening startles me, and I'm praying to any higher power that they didn't see me jolt.

Those prayers go unanswered.

"Oh shit! The traitor joined the party!" Jason slurs, tipping his can in my direction. Some of it sloshes out from the opening, but he doesn't seem to care. He wasn't part of the drop, and it's apparent that he's been drinking for a while.

"Fuck off," I grunt, working the knot behind my back. Whoever tied this shit doesn't know how to actually tie anything. He spits at my feet and gives me his back, obviously not worried about me in my current state. Keeping an eye on everyone around me, they don't even seem bothered that I'm here. If anything, they only have

Leather in their sights, not me. My bleary eyes struggle to focus on her, failing to zone into her chest to check if she's even alive.

"What do you think, boys? How long will it take for her to go crazy?" Heckles laughs, chugging his beer like it's water.

They talk over one another, brainstorming how they plan to torture her and how they are planning to make Silent Renegade pay for what they have done. Quite frankly, I have no idea what all happened. I was under the impression that Leather hurt Heckles, but no one disclosed how or why. Then, they brought up that Silent Renegade attacking them for their resources. Yet again, they didn't bring up clarification. Now, I'm stuck in these fucking bindings and have no idea what the fuck is going on.

The knot suddenly slackens, the ropes dangling. I quickly pull them back tightly around me to mimic being trapped. None of them even notice.

"Pick her up," he orders. "I think I have the perfect thing for our girl." I pretend to struggle against the bindings again as two of the guys haul her body upward. They cut the bindings off her, her head dangling every which way as they sling her around.

"Where are you taking her?" I shout, keeping the ruse. "Leave her alone!" My screams fall on deaf ears. There's no way we're going to survive if I don't get out of here.

Instead of acknowledging me, all laugh and ignore me, telling me how I'm a traitor and how I'm next for whatever torture they have planned. Removing her swiftly, none of them stayed behind with me. They carry her like she's a fucking trophy they obtained.

Like they are rallying around the fact that she's caught, which is fucking disgusting. At least from what I have been told about Leather, she doesn't parade around her kills. She may have a reputation of being heartless, but I don't think I have seen that side of her. Even in her own words, she terminates those who don't deserve to live.

Perfect. Now I'm fantasizing about the girl who I was supposed to be turning into Big D. That's just another dilemma. How do I know that Heckles is going to return her to Big D? Daryn made it clear to not harm her, that he just wanted to talk to her. Now, I don't know if that's the case. It's hard to gauge if Heckles went off on his own or not, but I'm going out on a limb and assuming he's not under the command of Big D. Fucking Christ.

The door slams shut behind them. I wait for their cheers to drown out with the distance. They are definitely a loud bunch. Telling time down here is practically impossible, but it has to be several minutes. Once I can't hear them anymore, I fully pick my head up. I work to have my eyes and ears focus at the same time. If I don't get them to work, there's a good fucking chance of getting caught. I definitely don't want that.

Time suspends as I hold myself to the chair for a few more moments. Once I'm sure they are gone, I check the room fully for cameras. Not seeing any, I bring my hands to my lap and bunch the rope together. There will be another purpose for it, that much I know.

Body trembling, my head swims from the chemicals I inhaled. Taking several tentative steps, my knees threaten to drop my body weight for a few moments. I clench my fists tightly. There's no fucking way I'm going to fail this.

It started as me getting Leather to Big D on Daryn's orders, then Heckles overheard and got involved. I let him cloud my judgment on her before I got the chance to connect with her. We did not have many conversations, and she was always far too skeptical of me. Not that I blame her, because I would be the exact same as her. After connecting with her on a physical level, I realize that she's not all that they made her out to be. Daryn made it clear that there were no hard feelings against her, that she wasn't his target, but he needed her. He didn't get into details, and as his enforcer, I didn't ask questions.

Now? I'm skeptical of everything around me. Heckles insinuated that Daryn knows about this. I honestly don't know what to believe at this point.

Righting myself and my mind, I pull myself together. The door is cold against my face as I press my ear on it. No noise greets me back. I sink onto my knees and look under the door for any movement or people.

Nothing.

Praying to the powers above, I stand back up and slowly open the door. The hinges squeak, but no one seems to hear it. Through the barely opened door, it sounds like they are having a party up stairs. I don't know where Leather is, and I don't know how much time I have before they come back down for me.

It's a battle between my head and my heart as I stand here, debating over whether to look for her or not. For all I know, she's at the center of their party. From what I counted earlier, there were at least ten sets of feet. That doesn't include anyone that may have been waiting up stairs for them to come back.

Finally making a decision, I take off down the hallway. Another thing to notate is that this basement does not resemble that of the Big D club. That means I can confidently say Heckles went rogue. If Daryn finds out about him taking Leather...I don't even know what would happen. There's too much shit for me to keep up at this point.

I round the corner, slamming into another person. They flail backwards and land on the ground with an *oomph*. He slowly sits up, glaring in my direction before he realizes it's me.

"Hey!" He shouts, backing up like a coward. "You're not supposed to be down here! Hey!" Advancing on him, I grab his mouth and pin him into the cemented floor. There's no way that no one heard him shouting, so I quickly remove my hand. He starts screaming as I grab the back of his head and his chin, then sharply twist his head to the side. The silence is instantaneous. Refusing to wait and see if anyone heard the commotion, I continue running in the direction I started.

Chapter Thirty-One

PREZ

P acing the entrance of the club house, my heart hammers behind the bone cage in my chest. Knuckles informed me that they were heading back this way and were going to try and form a game plan on the way. He's not clued me into what he's thinking, not given a single hint as to how we're going to find her and bring her back.

"Prez," Phisher calls, landing a hand on my shoulder. "It'll be alright man, we'll figure it out." He takes a swig of his beer, smiling as if one of our most honored members hasn't been snatched right from under our noses.

Like the asshole I am, I shrug his hand off of me. It feels wrong of me to want to celebrate three of the five coming back. I'm glad that three were able to escape, I'm pissed that Leather fucking did that, and overall, I'm confused as to why Tornado got involved. What does he have to do with anything?

Whirlwind emotions spiral through my head as I pace. I don't think I have ever been this wound up over members being taken. It's not uncommon, and yet, it feels like a complete failure on my part. Was there anything I could have changed? Anything different we could have done?

I shouldn't have let them go on that fucking mission. They shouldn't have-

"Boss!" The familiar voice shouts, catching me off guard. Knuckles stands there, his leather jacket hidden by his cut. Seeing him...it's different. My frantically beating heart suddenly happens for an entirely different reason.

I don't hesitate.

Taking several large steps toward him, I'm sure he thinks I'm probably pissed off at him. His brows pinch inward as he pulls his helmet off his head and props it under his arm. Fisting his jacket, I smash my lips onto his. I don't wait for his response before trying to deepen it. He's definitely in shock, but I refuse to take no as an answer.

The softness of his mouth against mine, molding into one...it's unreal. There's a spark that I never thought I would have without Leather, but I have been missing it all along. *He* is right here.

Wolf whistles and cheers resound around us. I couldn't give two shits if I'm kissing him in front of everyone. It's not about them, it's about us. His tongue softly massages mine, finally melting into me. He's accepting it fully.

The struggle to breathe finally takes over the fog of lust in my brain, and I pull away. He doesn't seem to mind, instead laying his forehead against mine and gasping for air. It doesn't take long for me to feel the tremble of his shoulders, wetness seeping from his eyes and onto our cheeks. Cupping his face in my hands, I try to get him to meet my gaze, but he refuses. I can only assume it's from embarrassment.

"Give us a little bit," I announce to the club. Thankfully, they don't argue with me. Leading Knuckles from the main room, we take the stairs into my office, and I shut the door. The silence is deafening. Within moments, Knuckles' knees are buckling underneath him, and he's falling.

I barely have time to catch him before his body is racking with sobs. There's never been a time where he's cried, that I can think of. In fact, he's usually the one telling everyone to suck it up.

"Woah," I mutter, sitting us on the couch side by side. He wraps his arms around my waist, head perched on my shoulder. My arms wrap his shoulders, keeping him as close as I can. I can feel the wetness seeping through my clothing. Patting the back of his head, neither of us say anything as I absorb what has happened.

"I tried," he croaks, his voice breaking off. "If those stupid fucking cops hadn't..." again, he's cut off by his own choked sob and tears. Unfortunately, I have been in a similar situation as him. It wasn't with someone nearly as close as Leather is to him, and I had to quickly accept that it wasn't viable to try and retrieve them. It's just the way club life works, but I have done a lot of work to change that mindset. Losing members is not an option. If they are taken, we do our best to get them back. Sometimes, it's not possible, then we hold funerals for those around that person to give them a sense of closure.

Shushing him softly, his head remains on my shoulder as I rub his back. There's no words I can say to make him feel better. I could attempt to convince him that it's not his fault, but this is Knuckles we're talking about. Those two have been thick as thieves for as long as I can remember.

"I didn't mean to kiss you earlier, I'm sorry," I mumble, placing a soft kiss on his head. His hair tickles my nose a little, but this position is just too good to move away from.

"I'm not," he chuckles gently, sniffling. Taking me by surprise, his hand reaches up to cup my own cheek. I don't really have any response to him, so I wait for him to continue. "I can't tell you how confused I have been about everything. The jealousy I have felt...I didn't want to admit it. I suppose I'm already at my lowest right now, so I might as well admit that you're the only one who has actually believed in me like this."

"If we're confessing our feelings..." my heart beats rapidly, my lungs squeezing with nerves. "Nobody wants to be on their own, and when we were standing there, I was just thinking...is this the moment when I find the one I want to spend forever with?" He tilts his head back, leveling me with his eyes.

"Did you just..." a watery laugh bubbles from him. "Did you just quote Nickelback?" I can't help my own chuckle.

"You caught that, huh?" It was definitely from the heart, but I knew it would get a laugh out of him. His happiness is a better feeling than seeing his sadness.

His lips land on mine as we both continue to shake with laughter. It doesn't take long for us to open up, his tongue lapping against my bottom lip, and I give in. It just feels so fucking right.

"You have no idea how long I have waited for this," I mutter, a smile breaking out on his face as he pulls back.

"I think I know." Sitting up, he turns to me fully, leg coming up and over my hips to straddle my lap. I have no choice but to grab his hips. His hardness grinds against my stomach. Repositioning myself on the couch, I nudge his ass with my own erection. Even if it's between clothing, the pressure of him against me along with the feeling like my life is finally coming together. There's a shift between us, one that neither of us were prepared for, but anticipating all the same.

"I don't know what's going to happen...but I'm prepared for wherever life takes us." The devotion brings goosebumps to the surface of my skin. He doesn't realize how deeply I needed to hear that. Some might say we're moving too fast, but I think we're just making up for lost time. A possessive feeling rears itself inside of me causing me to grip his hips tighter, pushing him down onto me harder.

"You're mine," I grunt. Our mouths collide. Capturing sparks is impossible, but the light behind my eyes from this connection...there's no way we're not connected as one. Like a wandering soul searching for its mate. It feels complete, but also hollow. Leather is out there, lord knows where.

"We're going to find her," he growls with conviction, bringing me back to our bubble. "Bear and Twelve already know they need to be giving information. Stay with me, just for a few more moments." Nodding, we both meet in the middle again, continuing the kiss. This time, it's not frantic nor rushed. We take our time, savoring the taste of each other and soaking in the body heat from one another.

Ever-so slowly, his hips rock against my own. The erection he's sporting digs into my stomach from behind his jeans, the rough material both irritating and invigorating. As he moves, my own hardened length digs into his ass. The friction doesn't help the dirty thoughts swirling in my head.

All I want to do is flip our positions, lay him out on this couch, and fuck him into the next year. I want to fill him so full of my cum that there's no doubt who he belongs to. I want Leather here with us, have her riding his cock like she owns him while I own his ass. Maybe I will even own her ass too...Tornado could fuck her mouth while Knuckles and I dominate her pussy together...

There's so many possibilities. Ones that aren't available right now, and they won't be until we get our girl back. Not only that, but I had too many thoughts racing through my head about Tornado. It's all just too much to comprehend right now.

Chapter Thirty-Two

LEATHER

What is up with people coming for my head? Two sets of heartbeats pound inside my skull, dragging me between consciousness and sleep. Struggling to open my eyes, the first thing I realize is that the room is far too bright. I give myself extra time to adjust to everything around me. Squinting through my lashes, I notice the entire room is white.

My face is planted into a plush floor, one that seems too luxurious for the concrete basement.

Am I dead? Did they kill me?

"Shit," I hiss, my shoulders threatening to give out from under me. "Yup, definitely not dead." My head feels like it weighs more than the rest of my body, there's no fucking way that I will be standing up anytime soon.

"Good morning!" Shouts a voice from somewhere in the room. Whipping around, I kink my neck and a radiating pain shoots down my back. "Don't hurt yourself, I have plenty of plans for you," he cackles, one that surges deep within my bones. There's something about the way he says it...

Sucking on my teeth, classical music suddenly starts playing. My brows pinch in confusion. What the fuck? Again, I remain silent. Tapping against the floor, it's soft and squishy, like a mat of some kind. Just as I'm about to push up onto my knees, the volume of the music cranks up. Collapsing onto the mat, I rush to cover my ears. Tucking myself into a ball, I press tightly to try and stop the music from overwhelming me.

The song ends after a while, leaving silence in its wake. I count to thirty and slowly unfurl myself. Taking a moment to assess what the fuck just happened, I prop myself on my hands and knees. In a sudden rush, it's like the lights got even brighter, and I have to squint just to see. Even that seems to be far too bright. There's heat hitting my skin. I can't open my eyes enough to figure out where it's coming from.

White light slams through the back of my eyelids, and I'm forced to ball back into myself to fend off the abrasive lights. However, being tightly wound into myself is hot and stuffy. I can hardly breathe. Just as a sweat starts to break on my skin, the air suddenly blasts cold, classical music playing softly. The breeze slowly freezes the perspiration. As the temperature drops, my body begins to ache and creek with movement.

It switches back and forth, switching between hot and cold air, then blasting music and having it in complete silence. It's hard to concentrate on getting out of here, instead I'm trying to figure out if there's a pattern going on with this fucking torture.

The speaker crackles, and I slam my hands over my ears to stop the screaming sounds. No noise follows the crackling, only having the speaker sit with static playing. I don't test the noise, just waiting for it to stop.

Time can't be told in here, no sense of sun up or sun down. The crackling happens again, but a voice follows immediately.

"We're so happy to have you here with us!" The voice cheers brightly. Heckles wastes no time. "In case you weren't aware, we decided it's time for you to go through everything I endured."

"Let me go!" I scream, slamming my hands on the cushion. That immediately gets me punished by blasting music. Heavy metal screams through the speakers, and I shriek in surprise. After a few seconds later it cuts off with his obnoxious laugh to follow.

"Welcome to your own personal hell, Leather. Why don't you get comfortable, it's going to be a while."

Chapter Thirty-Three

KNUCKLES

"Any hits?" Prez asks, shifting in his chair. I'm perched right on top of his lap, his hand splayed on my thigh possessively. After the moment between Prez and I a few days ago, it's been a complete one-eighty. Ever since then, we've been touching more and overall just inseparable.

"Nothing yet. Her tracker is still down." There's irritation radiating around the room. We're all trying to figure out how to get Leather back, but it's been a lot harder than we imagined. The installed microchip that we all have to get isn't working. While trying to connect with hers, we ensured that the others are all working also.

"You don't think it was removed, do you?" Twelve voices what we all are thinking. No one speaks, knowing there is a potential truth to his words. If it's removed, no one will know her actual whereabouts. Prez's hand squeezes my thigh, and it's the only indication from him that the pressure is sinking in.

Swallowing thickly, I realize I will need to be the one to break the ice. "We have to consider the possibility-" the door slams open, the bang on the wall echoing through the church hall. Prez and I are facing forward, but everyone else swings around, guns drawn. A male stumbles into the room, falling flat on their front as they heave for air.

"Medic!" Prez shouts, lifting me off his lap and approaching the guy. Whoever it is doesn't move, staying face down. One of the other guys runs out of the room, going to get medical while we all wait in stunned silence.

Prez slowly rolls over the individual, who groans in disapproval, but goes over. We all gasp, catching sight of Tornado. He doesn't look beaten up, but he's definitely dirty and doesn't look too good.

"What happened, man?" Prez asks him, tapping his cheek lightly. Tornado's eyes slide shut, and Prez smacks him again, this time a little harder.

"Not...Big D..." he croaks. Someone pops up with a bottle of water next to them. Shaking my head, I book it over the entrance and help him sit up. He greedily drinks the water, his throat bobbing with each gulp. If it wasn't under these circumstances, I would say he's fucking hot.

I mean he is either way, especially with his throat bobbing...clearing my throat, I have to look away from him to get the thoughts to go away. He's a freaking cum-boat that I would ride...

"Shit," I mutter, shutting my eyes in another attempt to fend off the wicked thoughts.

"You good?" Prez asks, brows furrowed as he feeds water to Tornado. I nod, refusing to use my voice. Swallowing thickly, I try to clear the frog from my throat.

Once the bottle is half gone and several minutes have passed in near silence, Tornado's body weight gets heavier as his eyes close. Just then, the medic comes through with a back board thing. A few of the guys heave Tornado onto it, and haul it out.

"What did he mean, it's not Big D?" I ask, watching brows furrow on multiple different faces. "Why would he come in and just drop that? I don't fucking get it." Sitting back on my heels, I run my fingers through my hair a few times. It happened so fucking quickly.

A hand lands on my shoulder, Twelve coming up behind me and consoling me quietly. The room remains silent, waiting for words from our president about what just happened.

Honestly, it's like someone died. Which very well may have happened. That's the problem, we don't know. Our minds are filled full of the unknown, and that's the hardest piece. Seeing Tornado brings hope and terror. If he's here, where is Leather?

Where could she possibly be? There's only one person who actually knows now, and he's currently being treated for God knows what. Then, there's another branch that's weighing on me about him. Seeing him running in, barely hanging on and then collapsing down when he knows he's safe...I can admit the horror I felt when both of them were reported missing.

He and I had gotten together on a whole new level, one that probably wouldn't have happened without Leather there to coax us along. It was a bond that we quickly built, and there's no doubt in my mind that he belongs with us. Now, after Prez and I confessed how we felt, I'm beyond confused.

A shaking pulls me from my thoughts, and I look around to see everyone is gone.

"You zoned out for a while," Prez mutters, brushing hair away from my face with the back of his hand. "Do you want to talk about it?" I shake my head. Pulling away from him, I lose my balance and land straight on my ass. I can't think straight when I'm being touched, but when I look up and see his face, it makes me want to smack myself.

"I'm fine. I'm just struggling to process everything," I admit. Bringing my knees to my chest, I rest my head on my legs. He comes to sit next to me, but doesn't touch me. There must be some shit radiating from me, because he respects the distance I need while keeping me company.

"Do you want to talk about it?" I ponder for a moment. Honesty has always been the route that I take, as I know what it's like for someone to lie straight to my face. Having grown up in my own form of abuse, I get it.

Taking a deep breath, I decide to just take the plunge.

"You promise not to get mad?"

"Why would I be mad?" Reaching over, I grasp his hand with mine and let them lay in the open space between us.

"I have been having...thoughts," I start, hesitant to continue. Taking another deep breath, I continue. "While on the way to

Vancouver, Leather and I had a moment in the shower. I don't want to betray her trust, but she was hurt so badly, Prez..."

"It's okay, you don't have to talk about it if you don't want to." His thumb runs over the back of my hand, soothing me more than he realizes.

"I saw things that weren't meant to be seen, or at least she didn't want them to be out in the open. She opened up to me just slightly...and I fear that I might have taken advantage of her vulnerability. She was struggling, and I was struggling to understand everything that was going on. But Prez, we had a moment. Then one thing led to another and Tornado got involved." I stop there, and I don't know if I want to continue.

The one memory of Leather and I together is supposed to be good, not me reliving it because she's missing and Tornado is lying in a hospital bed right now.

"Keep going," he orders softly, obviously just as on edge as I am. Though, his feelings will be for a very different reason.

"We...uhm." Why do I feel like I'm about to admit to cheating on him?

Maybe it's because I have.

"Knuckles, whatever it is, we can work through it. Feelings arise, and we all do things we don't realize the consequences for." That breaks my heart even more, because I honestly didn't think about the inevitable repercussions of what Tornado, Leather, and I did. I just followed my heart, and now I may be tearing another finalized piece of it away.

"Tornado, Leather, and I had a fling." The words fly from my mouth, and I avoid looking at Prez all together. I don't want to see the potential looks he would be wearing. Worst of all, I don't think I could stand to see any disappointment.

He's quiet for a while, his thumb still slowly pacing over the back of my hand. I have no idea what would be going through his head right now, and I'm not even sure I want to.

If I were him, I would feel like someone betrayed me.

Chapter Thirty-Four

PREZ

He's worried about that?

Covering my mouth with my hand, I do my best not to laugh at him. I don't want him to feel like I'm making fun of him, but I could see their sexual tension from a mile away. He knows damn well that I'm not into monogamy, he also knows that I don't care what he does with himself. Though, I suppose since the shift in our relationship that lines should be drawn. I can understand his fears and frustrations though, because those thoughts had crossed my mind at one point in time.

Thankfully for him, I have no issues with his sexcapades. I debate for several moments on how long I want to draw this out and make him stew for just a little longer. Though, now that I'm thinking about it, I probably *should* be a little more upset than I am. It makes me slightly question myself and my feelings. Deep down, I know we're just fine.

"Knuckles," I sigh, pulling his hand to my lap. He doesn't look up at me, and he remains unmoving from his current position of legs tucked under his chin while staring off into space. "Onyx," I press again, fully turning my body to face him. His whole body tenses, not used to us being called by our given names. It's usually a sign of disrespect unless it's from someone you know and trust. I will say that he's one of the few people who can call me by my own name, so I hope the feeling is mutual.

"It's just too fucking much." Knuckles turns his head, gazing at me from over his knees. "A line was crossed, and I can't go back. Plus, there's the whole thing with Tornado..." His sigh is heavy, one that I rarely ever hear come out of him.

"What thing with Tornado?" My brows furrow. I want to say that it's the fling he already mentioned, but at the same time, he doesn't seem too sure. A shallow hole in my stomach starts to form, one that I have not felt in a long time.

"When we heard the bikes going off, Tornado and Leather stayed behind. At first, I thought it was weird when she shut her mic off with him right there, but his mic was still on. He just said that he was sorry. We heard her shout from the background, then he said something about circumstances and that it's nothing personal. He then said something about working both sides. None of us heard him clearly, then the line filled with static."

Breath catches in my throat, my head swimming with possibilities. I warned them that someone was coming. I knew that something was happening, but why would Tornado stay behind with her? Flipping between my head are two possibilities. One is that he thought he could protect her. Two is that he was part of orchestrating the pick-up. Which, I suppose could be something...I mean, there is that agreement between Daryn and I.

"Anything else?" I attempt to keep my tone mellow and nonchalant, yet I doubt it's coming off as chill as I would like.

"It was just so strange. There was a palpable fear that all of us could hear...I don't think I have ever heard her so scared about anything as she was then." His face turns red, tears welling in his eyes. He says that he's never heard her that scared, I have never seen him this upset.

Something definitely isn't right.

"Did you guys hear any names or see anything else?" He looks away from me for a few moments, his eyes squinting in an effort to concentrate. Then, he shakes his head.

"I think I heard Tornado say something about Heckles, but I could be wrong. Like I said, the radio was full of static," Knuckles sniffles. My spine snaps straight.

"Why didn't any of you mention Heckles before?" He sniffles again before, confusion written on his features. The once small hole in my gut is now doubling in size.

"We did? We talked about it during one of the meetings about finding her chip." Trying to wrack my brain, I continue to come up empty.

"Was I there?"

"Yeah?" He questions, fully sitting up. "Are you okay?"

"I swear no one brought him up before besides Leather..." A throat clears, jerking us both from the awkward conversation. Twelve stands with his hands shoved in his pockets, tense still swirling around all of us even as he takes tentative steps in the room.

"Can we help you?" I finally ask, my voice sounding much more gruff than intended. I don't know why he looks so fucking nervous.

"Tornado is awake and is asking for you," he rushes out before turning around and heading quickly toward the door. Without turning back, he says, "he also dropped a big ass surprise that I think you're not going to like."

"What do you mean?" Knuckles and I question at the same time, yelling at Twelve's retreating figure. So many questions, so little answers.

Standing quickly, I dust myself off and reach down the Knuckles. He seems hesitant.

"Does that mean you're not mad at me?" Exhaling heavily, I shake my head.

"I'm not mad at you for how you feel. I do think it would be smart for you and I to actually have a talk about everything we're feeling. It would be wise to just clear the air. I also think we should speak with Tornado. If you're feeling a certain type of way, then it's important for us to be able to hash it out."

I leave out anything else with Tornado. There's enough shit I need to speak with him privately about, and I would rather not have others hearing it until the details are squared away.

Hopefully that chance comes sooner rather than later.

Chapter Thirty-Five

TORNADO

My head is spinning, vomit threatening to come back up my throat, and it feels like there's sand paper on my eyes. Trying to open them is like trying to unstick skin from super glue. It burns.

"Shit, I think he's coming around." I don't recognize the voice, though it's soft. I know it's not Leather, but I can't stop the thrumming of my heart in hopes that she managed to escape. I try and fail to open my eyes several times.

The voices are fuzzy, like they are mixed with white static and something else...though I can't put my finger on it. "Prez woul..."

Actually, I can't fucking move anything at all.

Opening my mouth is also impossible. Someone grabs my hand and talks to me, obviously trying to get me to wake up. I want to scream at them that I'm fucking awake but trapped inside my own body. I think I'm wiggling my hand, when in reality, it's just the image of me doing it that builds the sensation in my body.

It's strange, really. Being so close to telling them what happened, yet so far away from being able to actually come to.

"You...while...no wait..." glimpses of conversations catch my attention, but I'm more focused on trying to get my damn eyes to cooperate with me.

Finally, my lips unstick themselves and my jaw drops open. The sounds of the room go silent. Taking a deep breath, my fingers slowly go from static feeling to moving. Someone grabs my hand, encouraging me by forcing my fingers to wiggle around. It's an odd feeling having someone manipulate how you move.

After a few moments of silence, all hell breaks loose. People are talking over one another, my body is being prodded with things that I can't tell if they are dull or sharp.

"Enough," I croak, trying to shoo them with my hand. It ends up failing and plops back on the bed. Either they ignore me or didn't even hear me because they keep going. Groaning, I fling my arm at whoever is next to me. They let out an *oomph* sound as I connect with them.

"Stop." The tone comes out more firm, but again, I may as well have sandpaper stuck in my throat. More movement before the light behind my eyelids dims and something pokes my lips. It's pushed between my lips, and I graciously take several pulls. Water. Refreshing the harsh condition of my throat, the coolness soothes the burn.

"Heckles needs to go, he fucking took our girl." I try to say it with conviction, but it comes out more like a cough. "The switch didn't fucking work!"

"Someone get Prez," a guy says frantically.

"What do you mean?" A female asks me. I can sense her coming closer and grasping my hands. Slowly opening my eyes, the bright light takes over my vision. It takes a few tries before I can finally open them and keep them open.

Looking around, I realize Prez isn't here, none of the higher ups are here. I suppose I am one of them and so is Leather. There's two out of the five people in charge. I guess I'm really not surprised that they aren't here.

The door slams open, Prez looking at the woman at my side who is holding my hand. I don't recognize her, but Prez must, because he looks like he's furious.

"Get the fuck out of here, Janet." Her eyes roll, and she stands.

"How about a fucking 'thank you' for saving his ass," she huffs, swinging her jacket over her shoulders.

"All you did was come in here and be moral support. You didn't do a fucking thing."

"Whatever," she scoffs and turns on her heels, prancing out the door all too happily. Furrowing my brows, I look after her for a moment confused before Prez clears his throat. He glances at the few other guys lingering in the room and tips his head to the side, silently excusing them.

"I was told you dropped a bomb?" Grabbing a chair, he pulls up to the side of my bed and plops down. He steeples his fingers, resting his chin on the tips of them.

"I went to the drop like you had asked. Daryn was supposed to be there, but Heckles showed up. Him and a bunch of his cronies came for Leather when they heard that a meeting was arranged. I don't know where Daryn is, but we both tried fighting them off." He doesn't say a word as I take a breath. His face doesn't give anything away, just a blank stare. "When Leather and I got to wherever they took us, she was tied pretty tightly. Whoever tied me did a shit job, but I didn't want to jeopardize one of us escaping..."

"Where was she when you left?"

"That's the thing, I have no clue. They took her out almost immediately after taunting her. I tried to show her that she was okay..."

"I doubt she would trust you after that," he sighs, sitting up and pinching the bridge of his nose.

"No shit, Sherlock," I scoff and roll my eyes. "She definitely wasn't too happy with me, but I will be honest, I don't think she even cared. I know that we weren't at the Big D clubhouse."

"Where were you?" He pulls his phone out, ready to look it up.

"We were somewhere in the literal middle of nowhere. I was more concerned with getting out alive."

"Wrong priorities," he says flatly, but a smug smirk on his face indicates that he's being sarcastic. I go to tell him more when the door bursts open, an angry looking Knuckles standing in the doorway.

"I think you both have some explaining to do."

Prez goes pale but doesn't look back. We lock eyes. Even his tattoos can't save the look of complete horror on his face for a split second. He straightens, adjusting his vest and sitting back casually again.

"What did you hear?" He continues looking down at his phone, appearing nonchalant, but I can see right through it. He's scared shitless. Glancing between the two guys, I realize there's something that I'm missing. Knuckles and Prez...holy shit.

Did they take the step that Knuckles and I did? Maybe they didn't get that intimate. Their body language isn't enough to indicate more than some soft play of some sort.

Shaking my head, I reach a heavy hand toward the water. Prez assists me, bringing it closer to me while I try to adjust.

"You both are just going to pretend that I didn't just fucking hear that?" He growls, stomping his way over to us. "Absolutely not. You're both going to start fucking talking before-" Prez snaps up out of the chair, grabs Knuckles by his vest and slams him into the wall. My brows shoot into my hairline when Prez slams his lips on Knuckles.

Holy fucking shit.

Once Prez pulls back, he presses into Knuckles once more before roughly letting him go.

"You're right, we have a fuck ton to talk about."

Chapter Thirty-Six

LEATHER

The music finally stopped after God knows how long. Switching between several different types, my brain can't keep up. A headache quickly started forming after I attempted to figure out a pattern in the music. I thought that I may be able to determine if someone else was playing DJ with music, but it's no use. They aren't following any patterns, and if they are, I'm way too exhausted and cold to care.

Right after I was brought into this room, they blasted the heat and made it unbearable to leave my jacket on. I must have fallen asleep at some point, because when I woke up, it was gone. My boots were also taken off, leaving me barefooted. I pounded on the door for a while, screaming for it back. Of course, I don't have it. Now, they have dropped the temperature in the room and there's no avoiding the cold air.

A bright shade of white cascades around the room, and it's so blinding that I have to squint constantly. I can't tell when it's morning, noon or night. They fed me dinner food a few times in a row and then did the same for breakfast. I tried to follow it. Again, pointless. Now, they have gone a while without playing anything at all. I can't hear anything in the room besides my own heart beating, and I can only smell the fixated bucket toilet they gave me for using as the restroom. They have cameras stationed on all four corners, giving me zero privacy in this marshmallow box.

Once I would get comfortable, that's when they would crank the music up. Not knowing how long they kept me here means not having the slightest idea how long I have gone without sleep. It's also hard to get cranky when there's no one to lash out at. Well, that's not particularly true. Some of the pristine white walls are covered in my blood and my fists are cracked with wounds. The walls don't really fight back, but they also make for unsatisfactory brawling partners.

I have also been guising my tantrums into looking for escape routes. If I'm screaming, they are not playing music. Probably because they want to fully enjoy my misery. I'm not going to complain. Screaming is easy and doesn't require a thought process other than to breathe every now and then. Unfortunately, there's not been much to see as far as exits go. I'm not brave enough to see if the bucket is part of a septic system, and the door doesn't have any handles that I can see. There's a piece of white puff that drops in for meals. From what my body clock is telling me, they are pushing each meal further apart.

A loud slamming on the door jolts me from my silent thoughts.

"You've got company!" Someone shouts before the door creaks open. My body is weak and sore from lack of normal upkeep, so storming that person would be idiotic.

"Just the whore I was looking for," he smiles wickedly.

"Fuck off." Spitting at his shoes, I scoot myself further into a corner. Heckles laughs at my predicament, coming closer even as I try to shrink myself into the corner. He doesn't move quickly, almost as if he has all the time in the world.

The nearer he gets, the more my brain takes me back to the time when Heckles stopped being a loving Dom. How fast he turned from this sweet, caring Dominant to a man who would make the Devil pray at his feet. The torture he put me through and erased the sense of ease from me...

Squatting in front of me, he squints as if looking at a specimen at the zoo. "Hmm," he hums, tilting his head back and forth slowly. If I were in better shape, I would lash out, striking him at this level. However, I know I'm not up to par. So, I wait. There will be a moment when he won't see it coming. Finally, he decides to grace us with his nasally voice.

"It seems your friends aren't coming for you," he sighs, pretending to be all too sad about that. Just as I open my mouth to retort, he presses a single finger firmly to my lips. Since I shoved myself into the corner, I can't tilt my head backward and away from his grimy finger.

Reaching behind himself, he reveals a folded up paper that looks like it's from Prez's stationary. It has the P on it and the parchment seems the same...with a master manipulator holding it, I can't avoid the fact that it can be a completely fake letter.

"Do you want me to read it to you, or do you think you're smart enough to do it on your own?" He holds the letter between two fingers. Moving as quickly as I can in my drowsy state, I yank the letter from him. Instead of leaving like I figured he would, he stays exactly where he is, only moving his hands away from me to give me room to read the letter.

"Leather, if you are reading this, that means we unfortunately lost to Big D. I know it was your mission in life to avenge your family when you joined the club, but some dreams are unattainable. I am sorry it ended up this way. May we meet in another lifetime.

- *Prez"*

"You expect me to believe this shit?" I croak, my throat froggy from lack of water. His smirk only deepens when he reaches back and grabs another paper. This time, it's a torn-open envelope. It's addressed to Heckles from Prez. There's postage marks on it that show when it shipped.

One week.

It was sent one week after I was taken.

That doesn't include however long I have been here. I mean, I have no fucking clue when a week passed, but it has to have come and gone at this point.

What the actual fuck? It's been a fucking week and the club still hasn't tried to find me? What's the point of having this stupid fucking transmitter if they are not even going to use it?

Anger bubbles inside of me. You can't rely on anyone anymore, not even the members of your own fucking club. The motto of leaving no one behind must only be for special events or for someone of a higher status. There's no rescue. No one is coming for me. They surrendered to the fucking Big Douchebag crew.

What's the point of being in a club if they are just going to leave you to fend for yourself? It's fucking pointless, that's what it is. It's stupid and irritating, and I could have saved myself so many fucking tears. If I had known they weren't going to try and come get me, I would have executed my plan to bust out of here already. But, no. I gave faith in my club, only to be devastated and disappointed.

I suppose that teaches me to never rely on others.

"Believe me now?" He asks, metaphorically rubbing salt in the wound. Tossing the paper away from me, I bring my knees to my chest and cradle my head in them.

There's no fucking way that's real. Prez wouldn't fucking do that. He wouldn't leave me here, not when the club motto is to leave no man behind.

They are not leaving you behind if you're kidnapped.

I would smack my own head if I didn't want to seem more like a fucking looney. So, instead of doing that, I focus on the way Heckles taps his dirty boots on the white floors. The aglet of his lace is crunched up, almost like someone chewed on it. I focus on the way his jeans appear to be dirty like they haven't been washed in a few days.

"Is the whore getting horny?" I snap my eyes up to meet his, only to realize my mistake.

You never look your master in the eyes without permission.

Diverting my gaze back to his boots, I fervently shake my head. He reacts exactly like I thought he would.

Stomping his boot right in front of me, I fight the instinct I pushed away for years. As a slave, you learn certain cues from your Master. If they did something all the time, they usually didn't want to ask for it, so they would create an action. When he wanted me to worship at his feet, he would stomp his foot in front of me. Usually, it meant me licking his shoes clean. Before he turned into a Master asshole, he kept them clean for me. After he decided to turn into a megacunt, they were always dirty. Unfortunately, my brain wouldn't shut off long enough for me to deny him.

I'm afraid that if he stands here for too long, I won't be able to tell him no.

"You know what to do, slut," he growls, kicking at my legs and stomping again. Instead of cowering like he wants me to, I make an instantaneous decision.

I have nothing to lose.

"You're going to have to fucking make me," I retort. It sounds slightly petulant, but that's the least of my worries. His smile drops when he realizes that his mental hold on me is not as strong as it used to be. There's still an incessant nagging in the back of my head telling me that I'm going to get lashed for this. I'm simply going to ignore it.

I have wasted so much time in my life listening to the little voice in my head telling me to be careful. It kept me away from connecting with others, stopped me from being able to actually enjoy my life. I'm choosing to take my life back from his clutches. I refuse to give anyone the satisfaction of having anything over me, even my own inner monologue.

"You'll do right to fucking listen when I tell you to do something," he spits. His hand darts into my hair, and yanks me to my feet. I wait for the perfect moment as he starts dragging me out of the room. I grab his wrist, turn around, and drop onto his elbow. Immediately, there's a sharp *snap* followed by his high pitched scream. His hold on my hair gets released, and I bolt. He's shouting things that I can't understand, but I don't care.

I'm depleted, and I have no doubt that they have probably been putting sedatives in my food. Good thing is the spacing between meals. While I'm getting less food, I'm also not getting whatever they are putting in the food to make me drowsy.

Adrenaline pumps through my veins as I try to navigate the basement. You'd think it's all one big space. It's not. There's multiple stairways, and I have no idea where they go. I don't want to just take one and hope for the best, but with the pounding of boots that are coming this way, I don't have time to think about it.

Saying a quick prayer to whoever is listening, I bolt up a set of stairs. It loops around a corner, and I immediately run into someone. They lock their arms around me and cover my mouth.

Screaming, I thrash against their hold and try to break it. They don't budge.

"Shhh. It's me," they whisper. My body freezes, and I go completely still.

Chapter Thirty-Seven

KNUCKLES

ONE WEEK PRIOR

"**Y**ou're right, we have a fuck ton to talk about," I snap, unable to believe what I just heard. Are they fucking kidding me right now? "I don't want to play your games anymore. I want the truth, and I want it now."

"It's not information we just give to anyone," Prez informs nonchalantly. I swear the blood that was boiling in my veins turns to magma.

"I understand that our...whatever," I say exasperatedly, "might not be a deciding factor for you, but you don't think this was a decision that the club should have made as a whole?" Tornado clasps his hands on his lap, not wanting to look at me nor Prez. Not that I blame him, but at the same time, he was in on this. He fucking *agreed* to do this shit. Do I know the whole story? No. Do I know that they put not only Leather's life at risk, but also three other members of the club?

"Look," Tornado sighs, picking at his nails.

"I don't even want to hear from you," I snap, pointing at him. "I have no remorse for you being in that bed right now." He simply nods.

"Knuckles, it's not personal," Prez admonishes, and I'm honestly appalled.

"You think this is just about me? Are you fucking serious?" I shout, shoving my hands in my hair to try and ground myself. I need to get a fucking grip. "You..." I laugh, unable to form the right words. I'm so pissed, I have to look away from him and stare at a blank spot on the wall.

No one says anything for several minutes while I try to gather myself.

"I understand you're upset that we didn't tell you," Prez says softly. Taking a deep breath, I finally look at them both.

"This has *nothing* to do with me, and everything to do with the safety of the club. You believe that we wouldn't have agreed? Probably. There were so many risk factors and shit that could go wrong." Scoffing, I shove my hands in my pocket to keep myself from punching them. "Would you look at that, it went wrong. This dumbass had to fucking hike his way back here, and Leather is still M.I.A. So, tell me, was it worth it?"

"Yes," Prez answers without hesitation. I stay silent, staring at him incredulously until he can explain himself. "I think it would be a good idea to speak to everyone about this."

An involuntary laugh huffs out of me. "Too little too late. I will round up the troops though. I'm excited to see how this goes."

Turning on my heel, I take a few steps before I'm quickly spun and slammed into the wall. Instead of complying, I shove against him, fighting for dominance. There's no fucking way that I will give that shit up without giving him a run for his money.

"I am still your fucking President. You'll do right to fucking listen to what I have to say."

"Do I, though?" We grapple for a moment as I work to get his hands to release my shirt. Unfortunately, his grip is white-knuckled and he's not letting go.

"You do, and I'm going to tell you why," he pulls me close then shoves me back into the wall, my head clambering backward.

"I mean, I thought you were all about involving everyone? Keeping everyone informed? Isn't that what you do during church and shit? You made it clear that discussions needed to be open, or is that only for everyone else?" I taunt, spitting at his face as he snarls. Honestly, this is probably going to end in a brawl.

"Break it up, gentleman," the nurse huffs, shoving herself between us. "You're grown men, take it outside or something." He finally lets go of me, still red faced and angry.

"Until you learn to be less of an ass, don't talk to me. Obviously Leather isn't a priority for you, but she is for me," I spit, turning around and walking out of the room. I can tell he wants to say something else, but the nurse takes his attention away from me and back onto Tornado.

Stewing silently, I decide not to round everyone up just yet and just to go to the gym to cool off. They are all working diligently to find Leather, and I don't want to take them away from that just because their president is being a dick.

I can understand that he wanted to keep this under wraps, but does he seriously not see the dangerousness of the situation? Under the guise of a mission, allowed her to go off into the fucking sunset with her abuser.

How the fuck did she stumble upon that fucking mission, anyway? She supposedly got a tip from one of Tiny's men, but who knows if that's even real. Honestly, I wouldn't be surprised if Tornado or Prez called that shit in while impersonating an informant. What the fuck was the point of sending her off anyway? She gets to see her long lost brother who is supposedly trafficking children? I hate to burst their bubble, but Leather is a major advocate *against* that stuff.

None of it makes sense, and it's doing my head in. Blinking, I realize that I finally made it to the gym, though I'm not sure how long it took. Spacing out is trippy.

Looking around, it's completely empty.

Good. I don't have the patience to deal with anyone else that's being fucking stupid. Shedding my vest and my shirt, I set them on the bench then tape my hands up. Clenching my fists a few times to work out the stiffness, I circle the bag. Who do I pretend this is? Heckles? Prez? Tornado? Maybe I can take turns pummeling them all.

I don't think, I just start throwing jabs and punches, inflicting as much pain as I can onto this bag. Let's hope I'm not as angry when I face Prez and Tornado again, because their faces may just be the next thing my fists meet.

Chapter Thirty-Eight

LEATHER

PRESENT DAY

Shoving away from the person, my eyes feel as though they are going to bulge from my head.

"What..." I pause, glancing at him. "Are you fucking with me? Is this some kind of sick joke?"

"Look, I wish I could explain everything right now, but we have to get out of here." It's silent for a moment as the men chasing us seem to stop to recollect themselves.

"You're alive?" I whisper-shout, tears threatening to spill. Grunting, he grabs my shoulders and gives them a good shake. "What the actual fuck is going on? Why do you look like...*you* without looking like you?"

"We don't have time, let's go," he whispers harshly, tugging on my arm. I finally kick myself into action, releasing my brain from the stupor it's in and we take off.

That's a lie. There's thoughts clouding my brain right now, but they aren't going to stop me from getting to safety. Not only that, but who would expect the brother they lost to trafficking to come back. Though, the person standing before me isn't the brother I had lost.

No. He's nothing like the scrawny little boy I had to let go all of those years ago. Actually, my brain very well could be tricking me at this point. He doesn't look nor sound the same, but something in me just *knows*.

"Over here." I almost run past him, but he quickly grabs the strap of my tank-top and yanks me around the corner. There's boots pounding on the concrete behind us, shouts of distress and metal clinking.

Running for so long is starting to make my head go light, the oxygen barely making it into my lungs. Now that I'm really thinking about it, I don't think I have ever run this hard for anything in my life. Life or death seems to be the determining factor at this point.

A bullet whizzes past my head, and I feel the breeze whisp through my hair. Daryn curses loudly, running in a zig-zag style pattern as more and more follow. Shots start firing quickly, ricocheting off the walls as we run for our lives. Though, I feel like I'm more endangered by myself with the way my heart is pounding chaotically in my chest from all this extra activity and my life of nourishment.

Grabbing my hip to start firing back at them, I quickly realize I don't have my side piece. It's weird to not have my guns on me, and I'm not used to not having protection of my leather jacket and boots. Those are my safe guards, my protection. Honestly, I feel kind of naked without any one of them.

This entire fucking situation is fucked up.

Realizing I'm starting to lag behind, Daryn clasps my hand tightly in his, and we run until there's nowhere else to go. All that's left is a dead-end made up of stones.

"Fuck!" I shriek, yanking away from him. Grappling the stone, I growl in frustration as Daryn frantically searches for something alongside me. I'm not sure what exactly he's looking for, but I know I'm just trying to find a freaking way out.

"Aha!" He shouts as the bricks tumble to the ground and masks the pounding of boots coming toward us. Again, we take off running. I'm burning in places I didn't realize needed exercise.

"I can't," I wheeze, slowing nearly to a stop. Without warning, he jerks me around and slings me across his shoulders while barely stopping. I don't have any energy left in my body to fight him. I would usually advocate for my own independence, but I am absolutely done for. I'm not sure how long I was in lock-up nor what shit they fed me.

Flying through twists and turns, the tunnels seem never ending. I'm half convinced that we're just running in a giant fucking circle, but that would be stupid. They could have caged us off by now. From the sounds leaking in from the walls, it's almost like we're under a highway or something, which means that we're close to others.

"Grab the gun from my waist!" He shouts over his shoulder, and I gawk for a moment. I'm startled back into reality when more shots pop off.

"You had a gun this whole time and didn't fucking use it!" Yanking out the handgun, I also gawk at it. I realize it's a fucking Desert Eagle 50. They are not out of the price range, but we usually don't have anyone besides myself and a couple others that would pass a background check well enough to claim one of these.

Daryn stumbles slightly on a rock, and that's enough to knock some sense back into me. I aim backward and nail two of the several men charging us. They are getting closer and closer, and I'm not sure if we're going to make it.

"My bad, princess. I just had to save your ass!"

"Fuck off," I retort. More rounds pop off, and a searing pain wretches my shoulder. Nearly dropping the gun, I squeeze the trigger several times. One of the bullets whizzes through one guy, slamming into the friend behind him. They tumble to the ground while a few other shots ricochet off the walls and slam into the others. The empty clip clicks as they start gaining on us.

There's no fucking way we're making it out of this alive.

Chapter Thirty-Nine

Prez

THREE DAYS PRIOR

"How exactly are we going to pull all of this off?" Knuckles asks coldly, staring blankly at the room. I have tried to talk to him several times, but he just wasn't having it. Not that I blame him.

After Knuckles left Tornado's hospital room, there was no question about the sexual tension. There was also no question that Knuckles was raging and pissed at me. At first, I had no fucking clue why he would be so angry with us. I mean, yeah, we did something that is most likely frowned upon, but we did it for the benefit of the club.

We don't blame one another for our mistakes, but Tornado made it clear that I fucked up.

"You put the blame on one of the few people who takes the club lifestyle into full effect," Tornado sighs, leaning his head back and shutting his eyes.

"Fuck off," I scoff and dust my vest off. "He's just pissed off that I didn't tell him."

"Are you seriously that shallow, or are you just stupid?" He asks incredulously.

"Watch it," I warn, though it falls on deaf ears.

"I don't think I will." Sitting up, he grunts with effort. I don't hesitate to jump up and help him to readjust. He swats my hands away, doing it himself. "You put the blame of our mistake onto him. He asked about the club, not himself. Actually, I think he clarified that point several times. Unfortunately for him, that's not what you wanted to hear. I don't know what went down between you two while I was down and out, but that's not how you treat someone you care about."

"I don't remember asking you for presidential advice nor relationship advice," I sneer flatly.

"Which is sad because now I can't invoice you for it." He reaches for his water, but I manage to beat his slow moving reactions. "You and I put Leather on the spot when she wanted to talk about shit alone with you. Then, you do things privately and without moving to vote."

"If I remember correctly, the bylaws allow me to do that," I retort, though I can feel the fire leaving me. Now that I'm actually sitting and thinking, I realize just how fucking stupid that was.

"Actually, they don't. Only emergent situations or ones that need to be classified due to privacy or other discretionary circumstances."

"You wouldn't say that's a discretionary circumstance?" I ask rhetorically, knowing damn well what the answer is.

"Nope, I sure wouldn't," he answers all too smugly. "Then, you proceed to tell him that he's being selfish and wanting in on the secrets while undermining whatever relationship you two had built."

Opening my mouth to deny any relationships, I realize that he's fucking right. Not that I will tell him.

"So, what are you going to do to make it up to him?"

"Apologize?" I ask, which causes an immediate laugh from Tornado. "He's not one for grand gestures," I defend. Just as I say it, I know that's not true. He loves big things planned just for him.

"Now you just have to figure out what you're going to do," he sighs, his eyes finally closing. Once his breathing evens out, I'm left with my own thoughts.

What the fuck is happening to me?

"We can't do this alone," I say softly, looking down at the books around us. We've been trying to figure out a strategy to get Leather back, but none of them fare any differently than the last. We don't have eyes on the inside, and we don't have concept layouts for the compound. Unless we can get someone who knows the place inside and out, there's no telling what we'll be walking into.

"What about just calling Daryn?" Knuckles pipes up, his arms crossed over his chest tightly. His fists are balled tightly, and his jaw is tightly clenched shut. I can't tell if he meant to say that or not, but everyone's brows shoot to their hairlines.

"Who?" Phisher asks, pausing his incessant typing.

"Oh, has Prez not told anyone?" He asks. If I didn't know him better, I would think he was being sarcastic. Knuckles likes to give people the benefit of the doubt, always the optimistic one in the bunch. Now, he's genuinely confused, and I'm fucking irritated.

I have put the talk off for long enough, but I wish I could postpone it just a smidge longer.

"Daryn is the new leader of Big D, and is the biological brother of Leather," I start, deciding to just rip the band-aid off. There's an immediate uproar of shouting and pissed off men. It looks seconds away from breaking out in a riot. We simply don't have time to sit here to suck one another off in a pissing contest.

Grabbing the whistle off the table, I blow it loud enough that several guys cover their ears and it falls silent almost instantly.

"If you would let me finish," I start, giving them time to sit back down. "He was allegedly sold when he was a teen for trafficking. At least, that's the impression Leather has been under the past several years. Fast forward to a few months ago when we caught wind of trafficking through the area. Turns out, Daryn has been working on getting rid of the men who are trafficking. He's been cleaning the house for quite some time, and we have been keeping them in check. It's a project that has not been announced due to complexity, and I hope you all can understand."

"Who the fuck have we been hunting then?" Knuckles growls causing several people to shout in agreement.

"Daryn has been taking people out left and right which has caused some irritation in other clubs who were affiliated with them, which caused the increase in trafficking. I don't know why they have been working under the Big D name, that's still a piece of the puzzle I can't quite put together, but I'm working on it. Turns out Heckles was one of the men that was imprisoned recently. There was a massive jailbreak and they escaped."

"So?" Phisher asks, and everyone shares the same look of utter confusion.

"The mission that Leather and her crew went out on was fake and meant to be a set up for Leather to meet Daryn," I start. Again, they are furious. I knew this would come eventually, but I wish it didn't. I don't want them to lose faith in me because of this shit. To be honest, I'm losing faith in myself.

I decide not to blow the whistle this time. Instead, I let them hash out how they are feeling and sit back to watch it. They are talking over one another, not giving each other a chance to speak.

Once they have all calmed themselves down, I simply raise my hand. Faster than before, they silence themselves.

"Are we done interrupting, or should I continue to wait?" I ask, unconvinced in their ability to shut the fuck up.

To my surprise, they actually don't say anything else.

"As I was saying, Leather thought Daryn was probably as good as dead at this point. Due to other circumstances and wanting to protect Leather and Daryn's identity, we worked to keep them apart until now. It seemed like a good opportunity for them to meet then get working on weeding out the shit eaters. Now, as we all know, Heckles has Leather and we can't figure out where they went."

"What have we all looked at thus far?"

"We've looked for property in his name, looked at those who chose to follow him instead of staying loyal to the club. None of anything we found has been where Leather is at nor recognized by Tornado."

Looking at Knuckles, he's acting nonchalant, as if it's just another day on the job. The second his eyes meet mine, I can tell that's not the case. "So, I'm going to take that as a no?" He asks heavily, the weight of everything barely seeping through his tone of voice.

Leather was his whole world, whether he wanted to admit it or not. She kept him on his toes and gave him a reason to keep going. We all saw how they kept one another upright and breathing. Shit, half the time they were attached at the hip. We've all lost someone close to us and woven our way back together, but Leather and Knuckles? They sewed one another up then put pieces of themselves in there as well.

Looking over at Phisher, he shakes his head. Of course we haven't. I have kept this shit so far under wraps that no one would have even thought to call him.

Looking over at Tornado, his face is pure pity. Snarling at him, he must realize his mistake because he fixes his face almost immediately. Being in charge fucking sucks, that's for damn sure.

"Alright, I will give him a shout, yeah?" Standing from the table, Tornado exits the room swiftly. The tension in the room was too fucking high, and with his hasty departure, it doesn't make anything better. Actually, if anything, they are all even more skeptical.

Sighing heavily, I pinch the bridge of my nose. I have a lot more explaining to do.

Chapter Forty

Tornado

TWO DAYS PRIOR

"I just don't understand why this wasn't told to us earlier," Phisher says, voicing the opinion that everyone else seems to have too.

Coming into this club, I knew shit was going to be weird once they found out where I was originally from. Big D's reputation precedes them, and is making it pretty difficult to have a voice.

"If that's the case, does that mean he was involved in the trafficking?" Knuckles asks, devastation on his features.

"Absolutely not," I bark, unable to hold it in. "I didn't condone it by any means, but we were threatened. There was no choice for us to leave. It was either stay or die."

"No one makes anyone do anything. You have the ability to leave at any point. You're here, which means that you ran."

"I didn't run. I got out when there was a shift in leadership-"

"So you waited until it was safe to leave? What about the kids that you all rounded up? They can't just leave when it's safe because their lives are never safe!" His voice went from loud to shout-ing, and everyone is left speechless. "You think you can come here, play superhero, then what?"

"You have no clue what you're talking about," I hiss. He stands abruptly, stomping toward the table we're at.

"I don't care if you're president or vice president, the hypocrisy is unreal. We have an entire mission to save these children, yet we're now just throwing that all away because you needed safety!" He claps loudly, turning around toward the others. "All those in favor of kicking Tornado out, say Aye!"

It's silent for a moment, before several voices call out, though it's timid. Whipping toward Prez, his face is beet red, probably from anger. It's odd because I feel like he's also seen a ghost.

"You have no room to open the floor for vote!" Prez shouts as his hands slam on the table. The entire room jumps in surprise. "This was made as an executive decision and will not be challenged. Do you hear me?"

"Did you not hear that we're in fucking outrage?" He counters, arms swung wide. "You put our fellow member in harm's way, and we're the bad guys!"

"Alright, I think we all need to settle down," I call out, stand-ing from my seat. "Yes, we get that you're upset. We understand that we should have said something sooner, but we need to think logically now. It's too damn late to throw a fit over it, and we're running out of time. Tempers are high, we all feel the pressure with the knowledge of what not getting Leather back means. Can we seriously afford to hash this out right now?" Again, silence. Prez is fuming next to me, but I don't think anyone is willing to refute anything at this rate.

"Why doesn't Daryn know about her being gone?" Phisher asks, his hands clasped over his laptop and tucked under his chin.

"He does. He's been working with his guys to scout locations since they are a hell of a lot closer than we are."

"What are we doing here then?" Knuckles' voice stays loud, and a single look from me has him plopping down into his chair. "I stand by my question," he grumbles. After everything that's happened in the past hour, I can't help but smile at his petulance.

"Well, we were trying to get you all to shut up so we can figure out the team that would be flying with us. They are giving us room and board while we stay, but there's limited space." Like a tsunami wave, names are called out and slammed into Prez and I as we try to figure out who is saying what.

Raising my hand, it takes a mere second to have them silent again.

"If you would like to be part of the rescue, raise your hand," I call, and just like that, the entire room has their hand raised. All except Knuckles. His head down, his fingers twiddling and picking at his nails.

"Phisher, you'll stay here and run coms. Twelve and Bear will also stay and help keep everything running," Prez announces, and the two men grunt as their hands drop down. "Tornado, Kalico, Moose, Sear, Steele, Knuckles and I will go to Vancouver for the recon." When hearing his name, Knuckles' head snaps up. He shakes it, obviously uncomfortable with the choice.

"Go pack a bag with a few nights worth of shit. I'm not planning to stay more than a few days, but we'll see what happens when we get there. We hit the road to the 'port in thirty," I shout loudly, dismissing them all with a wave of my hand. Four out of the six names Prez called get themselves up and haul ass out of the room. The others linger while Knuckles and I simply stare at one another. I honestly can't tell what he's feeling at this moment, his face devoid of any emotion.

Finally, after breaking our staring competition, he stands and makes his way over. Leaning low, he says, "I can't go." My brows drop into my head, furrowed in confusion.

"What do you mean you can't go? You on your period, princess?" I scoff, irritated that he would just fucking dip after his whole speech.

"I *can't* go," he repeats, this time with more fire in his voice.

"And why not?" Prez asks, drawing closer to him. "We were all here when you made your big speech, what changed?"

"Nothing changed. I can be more useful here." Standing straight, he brushes nonexistent dust off his jacket and starts to walk away.

"You're going, and if I have to drag you to the airport with us, I will," Prez announces, and Knuckles halts mid-step. He doesn't turn around, just standing stalk still.

"Then you'll have to drag me out," he calls over his shoulder before continuing on his path. Prez looks shocked, and that's about how I'm feeling at this moment.

"You guys should really close your mouths, you'll catch flies." Squinting at Phisher, he just laughs it off as he walks closer to the table. "You both are such idiots."

"Want to try that again?" Prez sneers, glaring at his tech guru. Plopping in the chair next to mine, Phisher tilts his head back and forth, debating on his next words. I could see his answer from a mile away.

"Nah," he shrugs. Prez's eyes roll so hard into his head I'm afraid they will get stuck for a moment. "But, the fact that neither of you have caught onto it yet is really dumb."

"Caught onto what?" We both ask in unison, this time with real confusion.

"You seriously don't know?" He has the audacity to act as if we're the one's fucking around with him.

"If you could spit it out, that'd be great," I snap, my fists clenching and unclenching. He studies Prez and I for a few more moments, obviously trying to determine if we're actually idiots. Turns out, we definitely are.

"He's upset with himself," he sighs. "Did you ever think that Knuckles might take the metaphorical fall for her 'napping? Yeah, we finally realized that it was basically a set up-"

"It wasn't a set up to have her kidnapped!" Prez interjects, irritation blooming.

"Did I say that?" Phisher barks incredulously. "God, you're both so damn big headed you just can't see it. I honestly thought you were both fucking with me and just decided to ignore Knuckles. As I was saying, he left her without any warning. Yeah, she stayed behind and ordered him to keep going. Yes, if she gives an order, they have to follow it. Fine, acceptable. But for him, that's his best friend and from what I have heard it may be more than that. So, even though we *now* know it was a set up, it wasn't public knowledge then. We didn't know that, and he left her only for her to be grabbed by the man who put her through hell. Do you see where I'm going with this?"

It clicks. Slumping back in my chair, I can finally understand what Knuckles is going through. There's no way for me to know it too personally, but I think I understand why Knuckles feels like he can't go. I can't sit here and pretend that I don't know any of this.

I stand and make my way out of the church hall, following the crowd until it's time to break off. Taking the stairs two at a time, I make my way to Knuckle's room. The door is closed, so I knock. After not hearing anything for a few minutes, I try knocking a few more times. Again, silence.

"What the fuck are you doing?" His voice calls from behind me. Startled, I swear I jump a foot in the air. Bumping past me, he unlocks the door and tries to slam it shut. I slide my boot between the door and the frame, stopping it from closing. If looks could kill, I would be six feet under with the way he's glaring at me.

"I just want to talk," I start, only to be cut off by a snorted laugh.

"You can talk in the comfort of this hallway," he snaps, trying to kick my boot out of the way. I put more pressure on the floor and it doesn't move. Once he realizes I'm not going to relent, he huffs and pulls it the rest of the way open. He sits himself on the edge of the bed and clasps his hands on his lap. "Start talking."

Walking into the room, I gently shut the door and perch myself on his dresser. Neither of us say anything for long moments as I try to figure out what all I need to say.

"If you're not going to say anything-"

"I'm sorry, Knuckles," I start, cutting him off. "I know it wasn't ideal and it was a shitty way to find out. For that, I'm sorry. If I could go back and change it, I would."

He gawks at me, as if he's never been apologized to in his life. Now that I have started, I don't want to stop. Once I stop, I don't know what's going to happen. So, I just need to get it all out.

"The intention was never to hurt anyone. I didn't leave Big D because they had things over me. Blackmailing me to stay or they would turn me into the authorities. It's shitty, but I didn't know they were trafficking children. They didn't pitch it like trafficking, and it was all set up to be drug runs in containers. I didn't think anything of it until I opened one of the containers and saw..." trailing off, I realize something within myself. I'm disgusted. I may not have condoned the behavior, but I didn't do everything in my power to stop it.

Swallowing thickly, I shove both my hands in my pockets and play with the small piece of lint. I don't register that Knuckles moved until he's right next to me, his head leaning on my shoulder. He's a lot shorter than me, and the *rightness* of him curled into my side has me wanting to air out all of my dirty laundry to him.

"You don't have to tell me," he whispers, one hand curling around my bicep. Closing my eyes, I can't keep the smile off my face.

"I need to get this off my chest, and you have a right to know...especially if I can look forward to your forgiveness..." Looking down at him, I watch his lips curl upward.

"Maybe," he shrugs, pinching the material of my shirt.

"I swear I didn't know," I whisper, unable to speak any louder with the outrage within myself.

"I know," he nods.

"There was no way out. Surveillance didn't look good in my favor. Then, Daryn showed up. I wanted to move out of the ranks there and wanted to dissociate myself with them because of the trauma. Daryn heard that his sister was running with the gangs and wanted insight. Turns out, she's a fucking executioner," I laugh, unable to stop the glee in my heart. "She made something of herself and tried to be the ender of all things bad."

"Where did Heckles come into it all?"

"He wanted to continue moving kids because it makes quick money, and it's a heavy payday. We didn't want to anymore for obvious reasons. He tried to kill Daryn, Daryn put him in lock up, Heckles broke out."

"Did he know about Leather's relationship with Heckles?"

"I don't think it clicked for any of us until Heckles told me himself when he was trying to recruit us to join him. He wanted revenge on a girl that was threatening to ruin his livelihood. I didn't think anything of it with the way he described her. I was under the guise of looking for Blaine, Daryn's sister, and locating the female that tried to ruin Heckles so that he didn't ruin me, and then also get out of that fucking club. Turns out the two assignments became one. Then that one assignment turned into a hell of a lot more. I wasn't expecting the smart mouthed woman that strutted her stuff on that stage."

He laughs loudly, enjoying the shitty jokes.

"So, what now?" The question that's been burning in my brain since the beginning. I knew that this would eventually come to an end, and yet I still haven't figured out what I am going to do. I don't want to be Vice, that's for fucking sure, but the connections I made with the club has me wanting to stay even more.

I didn't want to leave, but it was always an option that I had to consider.

"Are you going to stay?"

"Are you asking me to stay?"

"Only if you promise to keep an open line of communication from here on out," he counters, leaning back and looking up at me. We lock eyes, and I'm immediately drawn in. His hazel eyes grip me tightly and threaten to suffocate me if I'm not careful. The way his eyes slide to my lips and back up has me second guessing my good intentions.

"Can I kiss you?" I mutter, glancing down at his soft, plush lips. He nods, though with a quirk of my brow, he rolls his eyes.

"Please."

Chapter Forty-One

Knuckles

ONE DAY PRIOR

The plane was delayed more than six hours. They wouldn't tell us why, and I honestly think they don't even know either. Either way, we finally made it to Vancouver, and I'm about ready to fucking explode.

"Where the fuck are they?" I groan, waiting for the damn cars to show up. "What's the point of a schedule if people can't stick to it?"

"Relax," Tornado sighs, pulling my body into his. He doesn't wait for me to give in, instead forcing me to relax against him. If I were in a better mood I might, but this situation isn't exactly the one I want to be twiddling my thumbs in.

Inhaling and exhaling a few times, I finally start to give myself a break. Just as I'm about to fall asleep on his shoulder, headlights flash right in my eyes. That forces me to wake up again.

"Welcome!" Daryn shouts from the passenger side of the vehicle while the driver's window is rolled down. No one reciprocates his joyous tone, instead grumbling and dragging themselves to the cars. I latch onto Tornado and yank him along with me to one of the cars. In club life, it's uncommon for there to be same-sex partners and generally frowned upon. Do I care? Nope, I sure don't. Does Tornado care? Honestly, I don't care if he does or doesn't. He initiated contact, that's enough for me.

"Wow, tough crowd," he grumbles as Prez takes the furthest seat in the back. Tornado and I climb into the middle seats of the van, his body leaning against the window while I lay against him.

"Any news?" Prez asks from the back, sounding far more awake than Tornado and I. The other four guys got in the other van to go to the clubhouse while we take this one to Daryn's private house.

"I got information that they are keeping her in a private sector in an offgrid home. No other information about who owns it, but I was able to pull a blueprint for it. From what the informant said, they are keeping her in one of their isolation chambers. They said Heckles keeps her occupied most of the time, not giving her time to rest and giving her melatonin supplements in her food. It's not enough to make her sick, but enough to deplete her energy if he wants to get her where he wants her."

"Where in the house is she?"

"So, the isolation chamber is in the basement. Once we get back to the house, we can look at the prints. I was thinking that I go in through one of the tunnels-"

"Woah," I call, sitting up off Tornado. Both men pause and raise their brow in speculation. "Why can't one of us go? Why does it have to be you?"

"Because I have a lot less to lose."

"And what exactly is that supposed to mean?" Tornado asks with caution. Even I caught the odd tone in his voice.

"It's not hard to see that you two are all loved up, and this idiot," he scolds, thumbing to Prez, "hasn't realized that my sister means more to him than he realizes."

"This isn't like a suicide mission for you, right?" Prez asks sarcastically, and everyone laughs out at the implication. I mean, it may be exactly that.

"Leather would definitely think you have more to live for," I pipe up and reiterate to him. His smile falters and fades just a bit before he picks it back up. I don't think I have ever seen a president act so...happy? Maybe it's the mission we're on, but even still, Prez is so nonchalant. I guess it could just be the personality type.

The rest of the drive is silent besides Daryn taking call after call about intel and movement trackers. I send a quick text to Phisher to make sure everything is rolling smoothly on their end.

Rolling into the clubhouse, there's a heaviness in my chest that refuses to leave. It nestled itself in there earlier, and now that we've finally gotten here, it's crushing itself within me. Tornado's large hands run over my shoulders, helping me further relax. It doesn't take long for us to unload our stuff and make our way inside.

"Tornado and Knuckles are through there, Prez is right there," Daryn points at two doors right next to one another, "they have a connecting door also. The other four are split between these two rooms here." He points to two doors right across the hallway.

"I will follow you to the office so we can get a lay of the land," Prez offers, but Daryn shakes his head.

"There's nothing we can do until tomorrow night. The informant said they are doing some sort of celebration, so they will be lacking security around her."

"What if the celebration is about her murder or some shit?" Prez crosses his arms, his chest puffing out like the dominant male he is.

"They aren't, it's something for one of the guys. I want to say they said it was an initiation for their own club, but fuck all if I know. I will send you the blueprints, and we'll go over them in the morning." We all nod, lingering awkwardly in the hallway and waiting for our next move. With a loud, startling clap from Daryn, he turns on his heel and walks away.

"You all get some rest," Prez orders, going to his own room and shutting the door. The four don't hesitate to leave, exhaustion evident within all of us. Tornado grabs my hand and yanks me along with him to the room.

"It's been a fucking day," he groans and flops backward on the bed. I crawl next to him, curling into his side and just following the steady beat of his heart. It starts with a soft rhythm, then slowly speeds up.

"Your heart is racing," I mutter, my ear laying directly over it.

"If there was a hot guy laying on you, your heart would be racing, too," he chuckles. He sits up quickly, bringing me with him abruptly. Neither one of us says anything for long moments, simply enjoying the silence and company of one another.

Unfortunately for me, the silence isn't usually my friend.

There are so many possibilities for tomorrow. What if she's not even at the location they are talking about? She isn't easy to trick, but it was easy for one to be pulled over on her in the past. Why does it feel like rescuing her is sacrificing someone else? After everything that we've gone through, how can we be sure that she's actually here? Why are we trusting a club that we previously were at war with?

So many questions with so little answers.

"I can hear the cogs turning up there," Tornado mumbles, kissing the top of my head. "You want to tell me what's going on?"

"I'm just nervous," I brush off nonchalantly. If he knew I was basically having an internal miniature panic attack...actually, I don't know what he would do.

"About?" He presses, obviously not going to let it go.

"There's too much happening in my brain right now, and the fact that we can't get answers until tomorrow has made everything worse. I honestly don't think I will be able to sleep tonight if I don't have some type of peace of mind."

"Is there anything I can do to help?" Nodding against his shoulder, I'm too damn shy to say it out loud. I don't know why, because

I have literally had his dick in my mouth. The idea of having to voice my thoughts makes me want to scream.

His large hand cups the side of my face and leans away from me. We stare at one another for a few moments before the heat in my cheeks takes over, and I have to look away. Holding eye contact is far too intimate, definitely embarrassing. I couldn't tell you why, it just *is*.

"Look at me." The command is gentle yet assertive. He's not giving me a choice, but he's giving me the time to follow through.

Taking my sweet time, I drag my eyes to his plush lips, watching as he bites the bottom one and lets it flop out. It's seductive, and he knows exactly what he's doing.

"Is it going to sound dumb if I ask you to help me just get lost in the moment?" I whisper, finally rolling my eyes up to meet his. His steele blue eyes draw me in, not giving me a centimeter of leeway.

"Why would it sound dumb?" He leans down, those soft cushions he calls lips barely grazing mine. I try to push forward, but the single hand still cupping my cheek doesn't let me move. "You need to answer my question."

"Because it sounds dumb, I don't know." Deciding that I'm done with this conversation, I push away from his hand and slam my mouth on his. With the amount of force I required to break his hold, my chest crashes into his. We tumble onto the bed, and I immediately straddle him to keep him from going anywhere. He rumbles a deep laugh as he relents to my dominance and grabs my hips roughly. The jean material we wear is unforgiving, though I know if I stand up, he will try to overpower me.

No can do.

"You'll stay exactly where you are, do you understand me?" I growl, nibbling on his bottom lip roughly. His hips jut up, obviously in search of the same relief I am. Shoving myself onto his crotch harder, it forces him to remain still. "I said, you will stay where you are."

"Fine," he grumbles, wiggling around. Clicking my tongue, I shake my head and don't let up.

"That simply won't do." Pushing myself to sit up on him, I yank his hands from my hips and attempt to move them over his head. He fights briefly until I manage to overpower him, slamming them down above him. I speculate for a moment that he probably let me win, but I don't really care. All that matters is that I got them over his head, and that means it's show time.

"You won't move," I command, ensuring that my eyes portray my seriousness. From the smirk on his own face, I know he's just biding his time. Pulling away from him slowly, my eyes remain narrowed on his face and body as I unbutton my jeans. His own gaze tracks my movements, his tongue jutting out and wetting his bottom lip. His arms move from the sides of his head to behind it, propping himself up to watch me and my lame attempt at seduction.

Kicking off my jeans, my shirt follows. Again, his gaze trails along my stomach and down to my already erect cock. The seams of my briefs strain against it. Hooking my thumbs into the waistband, I go to pull them off when Tornado bolts from the bed and stops my hands. Sinking to his knees, I narrow my eyes at him, he just smiles. Then, sticking his tongue out, he licks me through the tight material. It doesn't feel like much, but it's enough to have me fisting his hair and jerking my hips forward. He groans in approval.

"Take my cock out and suck it." He appears slightly hesitant, but still shimmy's down my briefs and wraps his hand around it.

"I have never done this before," he mutters, his warm breath making the small movements feel even better. Unfurling my hands gently from his lush hair, I reach lower and tilt his head up.

"You have nothing to worry about," I assure. "Unless you try to chop my dick off with your teeth, I don't think there's anything you'll do that I won't like." He laughs lightly, but he still looks unsure. Instead of letting him sit there and stew, I fist myself and rub the tip against his closed lips. Letting his jaw fall open slightly, I push forward a bit more. Once he takes the hint, he suddenly sucks me into his mouth. It surprises us both, and my hands wind right back into his hair.

"Shit," I curse, my knees threatening to buckle. Pulling away from me, he lazily licks along me from base to tip. Again and again he repeats this simple action and each time has me wanting to shove myself all the way down his throat. I barely manage to restrain my body from acting on it.

Popping off, a trail of saliva follows. Like a switch is flicking, I yank him to his feet and bring him down to kiss me. I always forget that he's several inches taller than me, but he doesn't let that show as I take the lead.

"I want to try something," I mutter against his lips. He nods, not even questioning me about what I want.

I will admit that I have always been curious about being fucked by him or Prez. Talking with guys around the club, they revealed that it's completely normal to wonder about being nailed by the same gender. It's when the lines get crossed that it tends to matter more. To be honest, I hadn't really thought about it too much besides just the odd curiousness that would pop up in my head. Now, there's two men in my life that I care more about than my will to live.

"Anything," he murmurs back, leaning his forehead against mine.

"It's something I have never done before," I whisper, eyes closing on their own accord.

"Tonight is the night for firsts." In a way, that's his form of reassurance, just like I did for him. We mirror the overall hesitation in one another, but we also reflect passion for one another.

Odd as it may seem, I actually do think I could be falling for him. Since the fall out of everything, he's been nothing but supportive. Yes, there was the whole spiel of him being a double agent, but on the other side of the coin, he really wasn't. I was angry. Leather had been missing for just over three days when he came back, and we didn't have anything to figure out where she could be. Once Tornado explained it all...it just made sense. I wish I could say it was hard for me to forgive him, but it really wasn't. My heart was already making room for him when it happened, and I'm just not one to hold grudges. The way he looks at me, holds me, assures me that everything is going to be alright...

If I'm being honest with myself, I think I have already started to fall.

"Did I lose you?" He mutters, bending down to catch my gaze again. Shaking my head, I stare at his brightly lit eyes. There's a glint in them that I feel within myself. Maybe I'm hallucinating, but I will stay on this side of reality.

"I'm right here." Standing straight, our lips graze one another, and we kiss like the world is on fire. Sparks fly between us and electricity burns brightly as we succumb to one another. "I want you to make love to me." He freezes momentarily, his hands grasping my hips tightly as he pulls me impossibly closer. While he doesn't acknowledge what I said with his words, he slowly turns us then gently pushes me onto the bed. Falling backward, he leaves me there to strip himself down.

One of these times I will have to make sure to do that for him. His own cock springs outward as he drags his jeans down his toned body. Mouth watering, it takes everything in me not to do exactly as he did and spring for a taste.

"I want to make love to you, worship your body, but I want to make it special. You'll need to prepare, and I doubt you've ever had anything up there." My cheeks go bright red, but he's right. Good thing is that it sets up the mood for the following times we'll have together. "Have you ever had your ass eaten?" Choking on saliva, I swear I get even redder. I can't speak, so I nod gingerly. It was a long time ago, but I definitely enjoyed it when she rimmed my ass with her finger. "Words, Knuckles," he demands, his eyes boring into mine.

"Onyx," I breathe out, my throat constricting as he fists me once again. "When it's just us, call me Onyx." For a few moments, he looks shocked. Given names are practically sacred in the club world.

"Onyx," he purrs, my name rolling off his tongue like the finest wine. A shiver wracks my body as his hot mouth is back on my cock. Sucking me deeper into his mouth, he scoops wetness on his finger and gently probs my tight hole. I grapple to grab onto something, anything. Finally landing with one hand in his hair and the other in the sheets, I fist them tightly. He groans against me, and the impending orgasm that's been slowly working its way through my body threatens to take over.

"I'm going to cum," I announce, my muscles tightening harshly. He grunts, his finger shoving into my ass quickly. Exploding, the backs of my eyes are pure white and stars flicker around me. My whole damn body is tingling with mind-numbing pleasure. It's unlike anything I have felt before.

It's equivalent to what I felt when it was Leather, Tornado, and I, but this is a different type of ecstasy. One that I definitely don't want to let go of anytime soon.

Not knowing how much time has passed, I open my eyes to find Tornado already has me situated on his side. We're both naked, his breathing already evened out.

Sighing happily, the hollowness that was in my chest isn't nearly as big or as deep as it was this morning.

I'm just praying that everything tomorrow will go smoothly.

Chapter Forty-Two

PREZ

MORNING OF...

Pacing the doorway to my room, I can't stop thinking about last night. At first, it was easy to ignore the slight chatter from next door. Then as the night progressed, the noises got more...explicit. I wanted to bang on the wall and yell at them to shut up. I also wanted to barge into their room and join in on the fun. It's a catch twenty-two, that's for damn sure.

Instead of doing either of those, I laid in bed and stared at the ceiling until I couldn't anymore. Now, it's morning and we're meeting in the dining hall at ten-thirty. It's only ten o'clock, but there's an itch that started in my body that can only be scratched by at least one of three people.

A knock on my door startles me from my pacing. Opening it, Daryn is on the other side with a cup of coffee.

"If you keep pacing any longer, you'll burn a hole in my carpets," he scolds sarcastically. I gawk at him. "Dude, I'm not an idiot. Your mind was pacing last night after I told you to go to bed.

The woman of your dreams is being rescued today, you're nervous. It's inevitable." Huffing, I cross my arms over my chest.

"What do you want?"

"I was going to invite you to have breakfast in the office with me so we can go over the game plan for the presentation, but that attitude isn't doing you any favors."

With an eye roll, I wave my hand outward and follow him out of the door. He unlocks the door, motioning me in front of him. There's plans scattered across the table tops, a few different types of desks are shoved against the walls. One of them is a light table that's already plugged in, a giant blueprint lit up and casting the walls around it a blue shade.

"What's that?" Walking over to it, I realize it's the print of the estate that Heckles allegedly has her in.

"That," he points to a small room on the lower half of the paper, "is where they are keeping Blaine."

"Leather," I murmur, looking around the print.

"She's my sister, I can call her by her name," he scoffs, arms crossing his chest.

"Barely," I retort. "She may be your sister, but you abandoned her when she needed you. I don't know how brotherly that is of you."

"I didn't fucking abandon her! I did it to save her." I snort in amusement at his feeble attempt at explaining himself.

"You did a great job at that," I sneer. "She thought you were dead. Sold into trafficking to never be seen again."

"I didn't want her wrapped up in the bullshit that I was, but I see that plan didn't work out the greatest."

"If anything, your scheme worked out wonderfully. She's been on the hunt for you all for years to locate you. Silly ol' you decided that you just wanted to run away and make it all better," I fume, spit flying through my teeth at the sarcastic remarks.

"Even if it didn't fucking work, she's my sister, and I can call her by her fucking name," he demands angrily.

"Wait until you call her Blaine, dumb fuck. She hates it because of you. So, good luck with that." The blood in my veins threatens to boil through my skin. Deciding that I have had enough, we move on. "What's the escape plan?" I snap, irritated that he's even questioning that shit. He shoots me a glare, telling me that it's not over before looking back toward the blueprinted map.

"I will come in through there," he points to a short hallway on one side of the house and motions across the way to another room. "This room should have a tunnel that I can access to get to the access point of her room. Then, we'll come through this hallway and come back through here." He walks me through it a few times, pointing to potential exit plans if it doesn't work out the way they need to. "This wall was put up a few years ago in the plan but it's not structurally sound and should crumble easily."

"And if it doesn't?" I ask, a pit in my stomach already knowing the answer.

"Then we're fucked." Nodding, I remain silent as we stare at the plan together.

"So, you have other exit plans until this point," I muse, trying to figure out if there might be anything we're missing. Sadly, Leather was the one who did all this. It was her wheelhouse, and I graciously let her do it. Mainly because I had zero desire to do it, and also because it didn't take her any brain power. "Planning must be in your genes," I mutter and shake my head. I can't stare at it any longer.

"Why's that?" He sips from his coffee, narrowing his eyes at the prints laid out.

"Because Leather is one of the best coordinator's we've got. She manages to have escape routes for literally everything. It could be so damn unconventional that we'd never have thought of it without her." The hole in my chest doesn't get any smaller as I bring her up. She would be so damn disappointed in me if she knew the shit I pulled. It may not have been a solo effort, but I was the one who approved it.

Not wanting to dwell on it anymore, I turn away from the plans and make myself a cup of black coffee. Thinking about the gallon of creamer Leather usually puts in her coffee makes me crack a smile. It's the simple things in life that we notice about people that aren't with us anymore.

Again, the pit in my stomach gets just a smidge bigger.

"You look deep in thought," Daryn notes, propping himself on his desk. "We need to tell the troops the plan."

"What are we going to do, exactly?" The whole plan that he laid out was only what he would be doing.

"Well, once we exit through that crumbling wall, the tunnel is likely to crumble with it."

"That still doesn't answer the question," I insist, bringing the cup to my lips and savoring the bitter taste. He rolls his eyes, motioning me back to the table with the prints.

"Here," he points to the end of the tunnel. "We'll need men stationed here. If things don't work out and we're tailed, reinforcements will be needed."

"How will we see where you are in this place?"

"I'm chipped," he shrugs like it's the easiest thing in the world.

"Leather was chipped too, and it was disconnected," I point out. Finally, a stupid thought comes to my head. "I bet they have a signal jammer. I will have Phisher look into it."

> Will you check the base out for jams?

> Got it.

Putting my phone away, neither one of us says anything else. All I want to do is run out of here and get her. Tell Daryn to fuck right off and get it over with.

"Oh, just so you know," he says after chugging the rest of his coffee. "The club doesn't call me Daryn, only my closest friends. They usually just call me Nemo."

"Nemo?" I ask incredulously. "Why would they call you Nemo? Did you get lost at sea?" I tease, finally cracking a smile.

"Fuck off," he grumbles, pushing his way out of the room. Meeting down at the dining hall, everyone waits patiently for us to arrive.

"Let's go over the plan," he announces, taking the seat at the head of the table.

Chapter Forty-Three

LEATHER

PRESENT DAY

"What the fuck are we going to do?" I scream, searching his pockets for another clip. Unfortunately, I come up empty. "Argh! Did you seriously not bring any more?"

"I wasn't prepared to carry you back," he retorts, finally turning another corner of the tunnel. "None of this was here in the plans," he grunts, setting me down and pushing me further into the wall. More boots come pounding down the hall, and even more gunfire than before. It's so loud it sounds like it's coming from both sides.

Peeking from around the corner, I realize there *are* men coming from both sides. It's hard to see anything past the haze, dust, and debris falling from the ceiling mixed with the powder of the guns firing off. Feeling around for Daryn, I realize quickly that he's not with me. I want to scream and curse, but that wouldn't do us any good. I will admit that I have never been one to run from a fight, but I'm extremely under prepared.

Just as I'm about to make a run for it, someone suddenly stands in front of me and swings. Swiftly dodging it, I manage to slam my head into the wall next to me and get an instant headache. My reaction time is sluggish as he grabs my hair and drags me out of my hiding spot. I struggle and try to break his hold, but the number I did on my own head doesn't help anything. The circle of gun fire ceases almost immediately as I scream and thrash to break free.

"Look what I have here," he shouts as his arm wraps around my throat tightly. Squeezing tightly, I struggle to get air into my lungs. "She was hiding away like a coward, nothing new," he *tsks*, holding his gun outward toward everyone else. Tucking my chin downward is pointless as I grapple and break the skin on his arm just to breathe.

"What do you want, huh? Your gang of misfits have pretty much all fallen or have surrendered," Daryn shouts from his position next to Prez. I try to look, but that only prompts Heckles to tighten his hold even more.

"You think I care about them?" He spits, pointing the gun at my head instead. "They were simply extra hands to attain what I want. What I *need*! They knew what they were signing up for, and that's on them!"

"What do you even want her for?" Prez shouts, his gun still aimed directly for me. Well, probably Heckles, but I'm the target currently as he uses me for a shield.

"She's mine!" He roars, cocking back the hammer of the gun. I want to swallow, but it just pools in my mouth as his hold finally cuts off any flow. "If I can't have her, none of you can!" Pleading with my eyes to my team, I try to tell them to leave me. If we can convince him that I'm not interested in leaving, I may be able to save myself.

"I don't want to leave you," I croak, rubbing his bloody arm soothingly. The team looks at me like I'm crazy, but I have to hope they can see that I'm just trying to live. His arm loosens a bit, so I keep going. "They didn't know that we were in love."

"They didn't, did they?" He asks, and I swear I can hear the smugness on his face.

"Don't listen to her, boss-" one of Heckles' men tries to shout, but Prez quickly silences him with a bullet to the head. Unfortunately for me, Heckles doesn't like that, and his arm tightens around my neck again. This time, I'm able to tuck my chin into the crook of his elbow, and I wait. Keeping one arm clasped tightly around his forearm, the other tries to soothe him.

My heart feels as though it's going to beat right out of my chest as I stare directly at Knuckles. He looks like he's seen a ghost, which may be for many different reasons. I will guess it's probably because my life is latched into the hands of a psychopath. I don't want to startle Heckles and give him a reason to shoot me, and my eyes are failing to portray that I need them to stop stirring shit up.

"Don't let them fool you, baby," I coo, keeping my voice soft and gentle in an attempt to coax him into letting me go. Heckles still has a ton of men on his side even though Daryn and Silent

Renegade have almost triple the manpower. All it takes is a single bullet before shit goes down hill.

"What the fuck is happening?" Daryn shouts, his voice carrying across the filled tunnel effortlessly. A few rocks come down off the ceiling, and it doesn't take a genius to realize this place isn't structurally sound. To be honest, I'm surprised it didn't crumble during the raid. More voices start shouting, Heckles following suit. More pebbles fall, adding the noise of their clattering as they drop.

Subtly, I realize the ground is also starting to quake. Meeting Knuckles eyes, I flick my gaze between him and Prez, hoping he will get the hint. Thankfully, he nudges Prez who looks at me, and I look up at the ceiling. At that moment, it seems that he's realizing what's going on. None of us want to give way to what's happening, yet if we don't, we're all royally screwed.

"Heckles, baby," I say with a sultry tone and spin around as best I can in his arm. His grip loosens even more to accommodate me, and I realize just how easy it would be to kill him. Looking into his eyes, his pupils are dilated. Like a light bulb, I realize that he must be experiencing a sense of psychosis, and the fear he's feeling of losing me has him reacting this harshly. Now that I have figured it out, it doesn't help me much. He is still refusing to let go, and unless I can get him to willingly release me, there's no hope. I would be better off sending the crew away from here and saving them instead.

I wonder...

"I think I should kill them for the pain they have put us through," I mutter, crawling my hand up his shirt. It's sweaty and sticking to his skin. Usually I would find that attractive, but the trauma really does riddle a person's way of thinking. "Don't you think that's a great idea?"

"I'm not falling for that!" He shouts, his arm wrapping tightly around me like an anaconda. I pretend not to notice, instead looking over my shoulder at the stunned group.

God, they really are idiots. But they are all *my* idiots.

"Falling for what?" I huff, rolling my eyes overdramatically. "Can't you see that I was kidnapped? I just wanted you to give chase to me, make me feel wanted again," I sigh sadly, hoping my acting skills aren't lacking me.

"This is a game to you?" Daryn asks, obviously not catching on.

"It wasn't a game to me!" I shout, praying that they understand it's all a ploy. With the real looks of shock on their faces, I'm guessing the chances are slim to none. Hopefully they are all just really good actors too.

"You want to prove yourself to me, baby?" He questions as he rubs his thumb over the revolver of his gun. Pondering for a few moments, he gives me the weapon and shoves me away from him. "Kill him." He points to Prez who goes pale.

"Easy," I scoff, walking toward him.

"From here," he calls, grabbing my wrist and stopping me. More and more pebbles litter the ground as he shouts, and I'm just hoping to whatever higher power that I can get us out of here in time.

"I think getting them in the center of the eyes is more personal, don't you think?" I quiz, pointing the gun at my head. His own face whitens as he takes a single step forward. "Nuh-uh-uh. You'll stay where you are. If you had to right a wrong, would you simply kill them from afar? No! That's too impersonal, even for you. When someone takes something away from you for so long, you have to take revenge by the horns. He *kept* me from you, don't you see?" I plead and throw my arms outward. Circling, I showcase everything around us.

"I'm sorry, my love." Like a child pouting, he takes a few steps back and rests against a wall. Him brushing against it shows how little time we have as the ground starts to audibly quake below us. "Darling," he calls with a panic.

"Don't be a drama queen, I will make this quick!" I call over my shoulder loudly, praying they start falling quicker and heavier. "Plus, I want these men to make a fuss over him. Pretend that he matters, and all that. No matter how loud it gets, stay there. If I die, you have my permission to massacre them."

"I wouldn't need your permission to do anything," he retorts. Then the uproar starts. Smiling to myself, men start shouting from everywhere. They are shouting at Heckles from behind me and the two clubs united in front of me start shouting at me.

"Louder!" I laugh and cup my hand around my ear. Finally, after what seems like hours, they start to understand what I mean. Relief plasters over the guy's face, but it's quickly masked as light shines through the cracks. That's not good.

A large boulder slams itself mere inches away from me, and that's the cue I needed to make a run for it.

Taking off into the crowd, we all book it back to where we came from. I can't tell if Heckles or his minions are behind us, not that I care. They have discharged most of their weapons. Slowing down, I halt and let them all pass us.

I refuse to let this continue on for any longer. Turning slowly, Heckles gets closer and closer. Once he realizes that I'm training his revolver on him, he stops. We both shake with the moving ground, but neither one of us makes a move toward one another.

"I love you," he shouts, arms wide. "All I do is love you, and this is how you repay me?"

"Leather, let's go!" One of the guys shouts from behind me, the pounding of footsteps getting further and further away.

"You didn't love me! You abused me, made me into something I'm not!" I scream, keeping the gun as level as I can.

"You're the delusional one. I had nothing but love for you, but you made me so angry! I had to do what I thought would make you love me! I tried to get your brother to follow, yet he was too fucking pathetic! You said you never wanted kids, but would change your mind for the right man. I tried to give you kids, all ages of them, to help us raise money for our own family!" The more he shouts, the more I realize that he's too far gone to make any sense. Trafficking children only benefits the ringmaster, and that's not who I want to be.

He was great at the beginning, that much I can admit. I honestly thought I loved him and thought the feelings were reciprocated. Until I met Prez, Knuckles, and Tornado. That's the feeling of love. Someone who brings you joy because they think your vibe is off. Someone who is willing to make themselves look like an idiot just to see you smile. There's no amount of happiness for me to describe how those three idiots make me feel, yet I have been the idiot for holding out for so long. Poor Knuckles has been trying for as long as I can remember. Now that I'm faced with the decision, it's suddenly that much easier to make.

"Goodbye, Heckles," I call out. Pulling the trigger, I watch the realization sink into him as the bullet hits him between the eyes. I thought I would revel in the feeling of having my greatest enemy struck down, but it's not a victory. It's an underlying numbness that placates me.

Turning on my heel, I sprint out of the tunnel and away from the man I once feared.

"Shit!" I scream, nearly stopping in my tracks. A hand grabs my shirt, yanking me along. "The kids! I can't leave them behind!" Trying to pull against them, Knuckles doesn't let me go.

"There's another team working on it, we have to go! *Now!*" A boulder slams behind us, then another one right next to us. Running for our lives, I watch as the rock covering the exit starts moving out of place. Exhaustion has settled in my bones and joints already, but if I don't get out of here, I'm as good as dead.

Knuckles doesn't give me the chance to jump, instead practically ripping my shoulder out of its socket to get me through the entrance in time. The rock grazes the bottom of my foot as we land heavily on the ground. I gasp for air, and struggle to push it into my lungs. A figure kneels beside me, checking me over frantically. Swatting away their hands, my vision feels like it's going to cross. That, or I'm going to throw up from overexertion.

"You're safe," Prez mutters, pushing a knot of hair away from my face. His face is blurred behind the involuntary tears in my eyes.

I finally did it.

I'm free.

Chapter Forty-Four

LEATHER

The car ride back to Daryn's is long. No one says anything, and I don't want to be touched. It is honestly hard for me to bear because I don't want silence, but I can't have the music too loud. Not knowing what to do with myself, I tucked back into a corner of the van and haven't moved. They have talked about what went down, tried to talk to me about what I experienced, yet all I can think about is the bullet I put in his mouth.

"Earth to Leather." A hand waves in front of my eyes, breaking me from my trance. Well, more like the never ending loop of me making Heckle's head explode.

"Yeah?" I ask, smiling widely. Knuckles sits back slightly, a perturbed look on his face.

"Uhm, we're back at the clubhouse," he mutters, looking over his shoulder. Tornado, Prez and Knuckles are left in the car with me. The rest of the guys have all gotten out and are already almost to the front door.

"Oh! What are we waiting for?"

"It's going to be pretty hectic inside..." Prez trails off, glancing toward Tornado. "We were thinking of maybe getting a hotel instead of staying here." Scoffing, I wave him off.

"I will be fine. We'll just go right inside and to the room." A brave face always solved my problems in the past. Unfortunately, this is the present, and I don't know the severity of what music will do to me. Between sitting in silence and music being blasted, I have no idea what my body will react to, if anything else.

"Leather," Tornado starts, reaching toward me and grasping my hand in his. "You freaked out when they started playing music too loudly on the drive here. I can guarantee they are pumping rock music through the speakers in there right now."

Shaking off his hand, I huff in annoyance and fling myself from the van. I don't want them babying me because of this shit. Yeah it was traumatic as fuck, but I will be fine. I always am.

The wind is cool against the thin material of the jacket Daryn let me use. My feet are also cold on the grass, but it's definitely refreshing. Grounding in a way.

Upon hearing the deep base of the music, I swallow harshly. They were right about me panicking with music, but I have to remind myself that I'm not alone and not stuck in that room. I have free range of this house and am able to do whatever I please. Living a life in fear isn't living at all.

With slow, sure steps, I inch myself toward the door more and more. A hand landing on my lower back startles me, and I nearly put a fist in Prez's face. He doesn't flinch, simply grabbing my flying hand and bringing it to his lips for a gentle kiss.

"I got you," he whispers and leans his forehead against mine. We stand there for several moments, soaking in one another before he finally pulls back. Tornado and Knuckles linger behind him with their hands shoved in their pockets. No one says anything, just waiting for me to make my move. Deciding that enough is enough, I square my shoulders, tangle my fingers with his, and step inside the house.

I immediately want to cower into myself, but Prez drags me behind him toward the staircase and away from the music. We don't linger around even when Tornado and Knuckles stop to speak with Daryn.

Once we get to the room, he unlocks the door and pushes it open. I hesitate. There's a perfect amount of noise from the hallway right here, but I know the second I walk into that room, the silence may be too loud for me.

"I will turn on the TV for some background noise," Prez says as though he read my mind. Walking ahead of me, I wait until there's something playing before entering hesitantly. The anxiety inside of me is overwhelming, and I never imagined I would be scared of silence. Especially since silence used to be my best friend, I can't get far enough away from it right now.

The lump in my throat threatens to stay right where it's at, not giving me any sense of reprieve as I familiarize myself with my surroundings.

"Do you want anything to drink?" He asks, pouring himself a dark liquor, I'm going to assume it's whiskey.

"Uhm, sure." I swallow again, hoping to get rid of the giant thing stuck in my throat. It doesn't budge. He extends a glass that has about a finger worth of liquid inside and shoot it back. The burn feels amazing against the dryness, the soreness of my muscles being erased already.

"It's good to have you back," he mutters awkwardly, staring into his glass and avoiding eye contact. All I can do is nod, unsure of what to say.

That's not exactly true. I know what I *want* to say. It's a matter of getting it out of my voice box and into the open air that is the problem.

I want to scream from the rooftops that I finally understand what they meant about loving someone. It's an odd feeling, the sudden realization of what being in love with someone means. The previous experience didn't work out too great for me, so I shut myself out. Made myself ice cold to the world and refused to give anything to anyone besides simple friendship.

Somehow Knuckles managed to wiggle his way into my heart further and further before I realized he got out of the friendzone. My hesitation of Tornado was immediate, but I saw what he was trying to do when he realized that Heckles wasn't who was supposed to be there. I will have to talk to him about what he was fucking thinking, but even still...my heart doesn't know if it can move on without him.

Then, there's Prez. He caught me off guard more than any of them. Being around him has always been easy, never worried about a power struggle or who does what. We simply co-exist and make it work. We balance our strengths with each other's weaknesses. Since the day he walked in on me doing the deed on myself, I haven't been able to make the mental images of him go away. Feelings followed quickly after that, and I realized that we were more alike than I realized. He brings out the best in me, forces me to think outside the box...

"It's good to be back," I smile, tucking a strand of hair behind my ear. Doing that reminds me of the lack of a shower I have had and how awful I must smell. "Do you mind if I..." I thumb toward the shower.

He nods, clearing his throat. "Yeah, of course. Uhm, the faucet in the shower is backwards, so hot is cold and cold is hot." It's awkward for a few moments longer before I bite the bullet and walk away.

The door shuts softly behind me, and I hesitate on whether to lock the door or not. After debating for a few seconds, I decide to leave it unlocked. Some small part of me hopes that he will join me. A larger, more logical part of me knows that he won't.

Turning on the water the way he said to, I strip out of my dirty leather pants and top. The material is practically glued on my body after sitting in them for so long with little reprieve. Deliberating with myself, we collectively agree to ask for help. I can't stoop much lower than I already have, so having him peel off my soiled leather pants can't be that bad.

Scratch that, I would rather cut them off and buy a whole new pair.

A knock on the door startles me from my internal debacle.

"You alright?" He calls through the door, testing the handle. The internal alarms start blaring, but I can't get myself to call out to him to get him to stop. So, with one final twist, he slowly opens the door and sees me standing there partially nude. He gawks for a moment, heat blazing in his eyes before he realizes that I'm staring right back at him. Spinning around, neither one of us says anything. His breathing is suddenly labored, while I can't voice the fact that I'm freaking stuck in my pants.

"I, uhm." The blush on my cheeks get even deeper. "I could use a hand." He nods, slowly turning back around. I can't look at him in fear of the expression, so I keep my gaze on the floor. His boots come into view, and his thumb and finger pinch my chin. Tilting my head up, his eyes bore into mine. There's heat, passion, and...guilt?

He lets his hand fall away as he assists me in unpeeling myself from my pants. Not saying a word, making a face, or anything, he simply helps. He doesn't question me, doesn't ask me how things were while I was away. No pressure on what I'm feeling or how I'm taking being back. It's exactly how we were before this all happened. We just exist together. Except now we have the story of him getting me out of clothing in a non-romantic way.

"We have so much to talk about, but I just want to hold you. Can I?" He asks, standing fully and keeping me locked in his gaze. I can't form words, so I nod.

He strips down to his boxers, guiding me into the shower stall and curling me in his arms. There is a sense of warmth and protection I didn't expect. I mean, I knew he was capable, but I just didn't see this coming. The feeling as if I have been lost until this moment. Having been guided away from my destination, only to find the north star and it bringing me home.

With that feeling comes protection. I have never been one to ask for protection or beg for someone to save me. I didn't think I needed it. Not until the moment of realization that I wouldn't be able to escape on my own. Even then, I didn't beg. Being with the guys has made me realize that I don't even need to ask. All I have to do is look at them, and they would willingly jump in front of a bullet for me.

Leaning my head on his shoulder, the warmth of the water cascades around us. My eyes close on their own accord, and I stand there in the white-noised silence. Serenity.

Everything slams into me all at once, and there's no stopping the emotions that follow. My eyes burn with unshed tears. Before long, they are streaking down my cheeks and onto his shoulders. The water washes them away, but he's not stupid. With the shaking of my shoulders and the silent sobs wracking my body, he knows.

His fingers comb the ends of my hair, but he doesn't say anything. He just holds me, knowing that I need someone to keep my pieces together for once.

Chapter Forty-Five
Prez

Holding her against me is soothing for both my soul and hers. It's strange, knowing that I may be the single thing keeping her glued together at this moment. There's a piece of me that wants her to completely break down, let go of everything that's been keeping her hostage for the past several years. After the shit she's gone through, it would be selfish of me to expect her to remain perfectly put together all of the time.

No sooner than I think that, her shoulders start to shake lightly and a sniffle bounces off the walls around us. Wrapping her tighter in my hold, I stroke my fingers through the ends of her hair to soothe her. Her silence turns audible as she sobs against me. There's nothing I wouldn't do for her, and if I have to hold her while she showers then so be it.

"I got you, beautiful," I mutter against her hair as I kiss her head. "You're going to be alright, I got you. You're safe now." She shakes her head, her nails digging harshly into my back as she clings to me.

"I can't stop seeing his face," she wails angrily, nestling her face further into my neck. Just as I go to ask what she means, she continues. "It's like a never ending reel in my brain. Moving from happiness, craziness, then the moment the bullet blasted between his eyes." Resting my head on hers, I don't verbally acknowledge it. I just nod as she unfurls into fits of crying. I think at one point she starts laughing, then it quickly goes back to crying.

I'm not usually the one to console others, and I will be honest in saying that I'm feeling extremely awkward right now. But I know that she needs me more than my being uncomfortable, so I digress.

"Let's get you washed up so we can go to bed," I murmur, kissing her hair one more time. Releasing her deathly grip on me, she sits on the ledge. Her shampoo is sweetly scented, lavender and sandalwood. Usually I would just squirt the liquid straight onto my head, but hers has the pump type. A small dollop gets squished between my hands as I lather the soap. Either she doesn't seem to notice or just doesn't care, because she stares blankly behind me. Tipping her head back just slightly, I start massaging the soap into her scalp. Her eyes shut, and a gentle exhale releases from her as she begins to relax again.

"Don't fall asleep on me," I say teasingly. Her lips tip upward, but she doesn't acknowledge it. Even if she did zonk out, I would happily do my best to keep her upright and not drowning. I don't want to sound judgemental, but this is the quietest I have ever seen her. There's never a dull moment with her, she will usually bring a sense of liveliness wherever she goes.

Now, it's like that light has been dulled. The flame has been snubbed, and I'm honestly not sure how to get it back. I do know that one of her biggest passions is BDSM, yet the amount of knowledge I have on the subject is very limited. She was the one who would teach me things, show me the ropes in all the literal and metaphorical ways.

Grabbing the stem of the shower head, I rinse her hair out with gentle quickness. I follow suit with the conditioner and lather her body in soap. I give her the rag to do her pussy, but she seems less than interested. With a stern look from her, her eyes roll into her head, and she complies with the simple demand. Leaning her head against my stomach as I finish rinsing out the last of the condition, her hands slowly crawl over my thighs. Not thinking anything of it, I wring out her hair and step away.

With a stealthiness I didn't realize she had with her level of exhaustion, she grabs the hem of my boxers and tries to pull them down. Grasping her wrists softly, I pull them away from me and bring them up for a kiss. Her pout reigns heavily on my lack of self-control; however, I am in no way, shape, or form going to give in to her until she can stand up on her own.

Finally having a solid plan in my head, I manage to keep her hands from wandering too far again. She does complain, but I don't give in. I refuse to take advantage of her in this state.

"Please don't leave," she mutters as she plops down on the bed. I smirk, combing through her hair. "I don't want to be alone right now."

"As long as you promise not to get handsy," I scold playfully. An echoing laugh rings from her, and it's almost as good as the old times.

Almost.

Chapter Forty-Six

TORNADO

Watching them go up the stairs alone leaves a weird cave in my chest. Knuckles, Prez, and I decided that it would be best to tell Leather what has been going on without hesitation. Though, after we saw her and the condition she was in...I'm not sure that's a bright idea.

Just closing my eyes I can see the blood smeared across her chest and arms, her hair stuck up in ways I didn't think was possible until that moment. Her eyes were dark, the bags severe as ever from lack of sleep. It didn't take a rocket scientist to tell that it's from their torture. While she wouldn't tell us what was going on...I could easily put two and two together.

Shaking away the negativity, the glass in my hand is suddenly refilled again. The others that accompanied us on this rescue are partying it up. For them, it was a success. Retrieving a member from something like that usually means getting them back in multiple pieces. Again, victory for them. Yet, I feel nothing but dread since we got her back. I don't know what is exactly weighing on me, but it's there and waiting for me to notice it.

"You alright?" Knuckles asks as he bumps shoulders with me. Not looking away from my glass, I nod and swig the burning liquid. "That's a bullshit answer if I have ever heard one," he scoffs, shaking his head.

"Your bullshit detector must be broken." The table laughs obviously not hearing the underlying irritation in my voice. "Seriously, I'm just worried about Leather." Looking toward the staircase, I'm more concerned with how she's holding up versus the party going on down here. Which reminds me of Silent Renegade. I need to inform them of a change in pace. We don't want Leather to feel as though it's her fault, but we also need to implement new rules to ensure she feels safe in her own home.

"You have nothing to worry about," Moose brushes off. "She is upstairs in *good* hands." He winks with the implication, and I nearly can't see past the red haze. Standing abruptly from the seat, I reach over and yank him from his chair to meet me at eye level.

"Want to say that again?" I growl. He audibly gulps over the music, his head shaking frantically. Shoving him backward, he topples into his chair. Chancing a glance down at Knuckles, he looks shocked but also approving. No doubt he probably felt the same way I did about that comment. I'm just one to act before thinking.

"Who would have thought we'd be sitting here having drinks with our enemies?" Sear asks, obviously trying to lighten the mood. It doesn't work the greatest, but he's not wrong. I used to be part of the enemy group. Silent Renegade hated us, and for good reason. If there wasn't misconstrued material hanging over my head, I would have left years ago. In retrospect, I suppose it could be seen as a good thing that I stayed so long.

If I hadn't, Heckles may have recruited someone else who would be more likely to finish out the job. He failed to notice that I don't lack social skills. I can tell when someone is being genuine or if they are simply full of shit to save their own ass.

Thinking back to when I first met Leather, I can't help but feel like a total idiot. So many conflicting emotions were swirling around my head at that time. She wasn't anything like Heckles had described, and I tried to look for that person. I really did do my best, and I tried to coax that evil villain from the depths of her that he vividly described. She never came out. In the pit of my stomach, I knew that the portrayed image of her never existed, and yet, I still tried. And failed.

I hate how much animosity there was between us, which is from my own doing. She had every right to be wary of me, and if Prez wasn't already in on the partial reason I was there, it would have made sense for him to not trust me. Being a double agent isn't as easy as it seems and having the enemy breathing down your neck doesn't make for a field trip. The enemy being Heckles.

Fun fact if it wasn't apparent, I didn't *want* to go undercover for him. But the blessing in disguise is that Daryn most likely wouldn't have taken over Big D, and I never would have been sent here to scout for Leather. So, while it's a shitty reason, I can conclude that there are happier reasons in the end.

"Is Romeo thinking about his wedding again?" Sear chuckles, sipping his bear. Slamming my beer on the table, I turn toward the stairs with one person in mind.

Leather.

I wanted to see her and ensure that she's okay. Give her anything she might need during this transition. Not only that, but she's been running on information overload and fumes.

Taking the stairs two at a time, I race to the bedroom. I stop just outside the door, not wanting to appear brash and slowly ease it open. The hinges shriek in protest, but that doesn't seem to startle the two figures lying in bed. Prez has himself propped upward with a few pillows behind him while she uses him as her own. He turns slightly to look at me, nudging his head for me to enter. Shutting the door is more silent than opening it, and I tiptoe over to the duo.

"She's out," I muse quietly, admiring the peacefulness of her face.

"Yeah, barely. Not without touching me." Even in the low lighting, his face lights up brightly as if he's proud of being anything she needs.

"Hurry up and lay down," the queen grumbles from her sleep, rolling onto her side. She kicks the covers back then doesn't move.

"That's your cue," Prez chuckles, turning himself in the bed to spoon her.

Not having to be told twice, I strip out of my clothing, leave on my briefs, and climb into bed. Tucking her into my chest, we snuggle together tightly. Knuckles better hurry up if he wants in on this action.

Scratch that, he can fuck right off for now. I just want time with her.

Chapter Forty-Seven

Knuckles

Looking around the bar, I didn't realize how late it really is. Pulling out my phone, it's just after three in the morning, A yawn escapes me right when it registers the time. Waving the guys good night, they barely notice as I leave. My feet carry me heavily up the stairs and down the hall. I don't hesitate to go into Prez's room, ready to snuggle up next to him. Just as I step through the door, I realize there are already figures in the bed. Even with squinting, I can't see very well. Lighting the flashlight on my phone, I shine the people and realize it's Leather, Prez, and Tornado are in one small snuggle pile.

A groan leaves one of them from the pile, and Leather's head shoots up for a brief moment. Her breathing becomes labored until Prez soothes her back down, informing her that it's just me. She nods, instantly relaxing back into his embrace.

"Turn that off and get over here," Tornado grumbles from the other side of the bed. I can't help the soft chuckle that escapes me as I unbuckle my jeans and kick them off.

Prez glances over his shoulder, then does a double take as my cock bounces in my boxers. I'm hard from the view of them snuggling. Rolling my eyes, it's just an obvious piece of my affection for them. It doesn't help that I saw two out of three of them naked, so...

Walking over to the bed, I look over the bed and find an open spot. After a minute of standing there awkwardly, Leather roughly jolts Tornado, and he rolls with a grumble. She pats the bed behind her and that's exactly where I crawl in. Curling into my side, she gets as close as humanly possible before going still. A second later, she's trying to squish herself even closer. Laughing silently, I push one arm under her pillow to prop her head on, and the other wraps around her waist tightly. Only after I pull her close and lock her in does she finally seem to relax.

Taking my own deep breath, I relish in the feeling of her warmth against me. I don't know how she is going to react to them telling her everything. I can't be sure they haven't already, but I also don't believe she would have jumped into bed with them right after. Maybe if they let her play Domme she might. She's too hard headed for that, so I nix that option. They didn't exactly say when they were going to tell her everything, just that they wanted to break the news to her and get it out of the way.

Taking into account how frightened she got after hearing the music in the car before we left had all of us concerned for her. I just hope telling her won't be some kind of breaking point for her. My brain runs a mile a minute, and Leather must catch on because she starts scratching my scalp. My eyes close on their own accord, my brain finally slowing down, shutting up long enough for me to drift off to sleep.

A hand slams over my face, and I startle awake, irritation bubbling inside me. Before I have a chance to snap, it moves away from me and is replaced with a set of lips. I can't tell if I'm dreaming because they slowly travel down my face, over my throat, and onto my torso. Warmth trails in the wake of them, leaving the wet spot to cool with the air around us. An arm is wrapped around my torso loosely, unaware that someone is invading the space.

Pinching my eyes open, Leather has Prez's cock wrapped in her hand as her mouth makes its way toward mine. Prez has his eyes closed, brows pinched, and I can't tell if he's sleeping or not. Tornado hasn't stirred from the other side of me, so I guess he's not affected by this display of affection.

"You want me?" She asks softly, the hot breath of her voice casting goosebumps over my skin from the cool aired contrast. All I can do is nod. The wicked grin I know and love breaks out over her face as she glides lower and lower...

"Wait," I gasp, grabbing her hand as it starts to reach into my boxers. "Wait." She sits up, letting go of Prez who looks both equally relieved and frustrated.

"Do you not want me anymore?" She whispers, her eyes pooling with wetness. Alarm bells start going off in my brain. This level of...self-consciousness has never been seen from her before. She's the secure one, telling us that she's the baddest bitch around, or whatever she actually says. Seeing her sitting here with tears in her eyes because she thinks I had rejected her...maybe she's as deep into this as I am.

"That's not it, and you know it," I rasp, my throat still partially dry from sleep. Blinking rapidly to get my groggy eyes to focus, I notice Prez is also rubbing his eyes with confusion.

She sniffles softly, her eyes glancing over my shoulder. I follow her gaze to see Tornado with a soft look in his eyes. Almost like...understanding? His hand stretches over my exposed body and grasps hers. She flickers her saddened gaze to him before looking back at her lap. From what I can see in the dimly lit room, there seems to be a pink tint on her cheeks. Thankfully, she doesn't push away from us. She holds on tightly to his hand as though it's a lifeline.

Prez lays a hand on the back of her neck, rubbing into the muscles there. She sways lightly with the pressure, her eyes drooping the longer he does it. None of us say anything, just letting her slowly put herself to sleep. Prez and Tornado make eye contact before myself and Prez lock gazes. There's a level of concern written over his face, and I can read it pretty openly.

I don't want her to feel rejected at all, but I also don't want to use her when she's not at a point to consent appropriately. If she can tell us why she wants to make love to the three of us, then we may concede. However, she's gone through almost two weeks worth of torture before we were able to locate and extract her. That's plenty of time for anyone's balance to be tilted off kilter, both mentally and physically.

Tornado keeps her hand in his while I gently lower her and I to lay back down. Prez continues to massage the back of her neck, and we all watch as she slowly lets go of the tension. I swear we hardly breathe as she goes back down. Once her soft snores are heard, we all exhale harshly.

"What was that?" Tornado mutters, reaching behind himself to check the time. It's just after seven, which is what time I would start getting up for the gym if I didn't stay out so damn late.

"No clue, man," Prez mumbles and lets out an *oomph* as he slumps back down onto the pillow. Rubbing his eyes roughly, he also looks like he's going back out. Glancing over my shoulder, Tornado and I nod at one another. We crawl out of the bed and let those two get some more rest. Yawning, we both stumble to the bathroom. I start the shower with my back turned to Tornado as he uses the restroom. We move around when he's done, swapping places so I can finish my business.

"Mind if I join?" He asks sleepily. "I don't think I can make it through the day without taking one."

"Sure." Nodding my head, I flush and step under the warm spray with him. Not thinking anything of it, I walk right into his arms and rest my head against his chest. As if we've done this a million times, he wraps his arms around my body. My eyes shut on their own accord as he rests his head on my hair. We stand under the warm water pouring from the showerhead.

We step away from one another to wash, but I didn't expect him to want to wash me. Squinting my eyes suspiciously, he just grins tiredly.

"I like taking care of you," he assures, circling his finger for me to move. I eye him suspiciously for another moment before turning around. He tilts my head up and begins scrubbing my scalp. The noise I make would not be classified as innocent even though the action is very much not sexual. It wouldn't matter, because my already hard cock that was starting to deflate juts back up to attention. I have to ball my fists to keep from grabbing it and relieving myself.

Tornado takes another step closer to me, and I feel the head of his cock pressing into my back. I'm already struggling, and I never would have thought the feeling of him or another male would get me remotely turned on. Yet, here I am. Turned on and leaking for a taste of him. Again, I remind myself that it's not appropriate right now. Leather deserves an explanation before any of us start hopping back into bed with one another. We owe it to ourselves and her to be completely transparent. Though, on the other side of the coin, it's not my story to tell. If they don't get on it, someone is going to beat them to the punch. They better hope it's not Daryn, because I can almost guarantee there's nothing worse than hearing the news of a potential betrayal from your dead brother.

"Rinse," he commands softly. I turn around with my head still turned up and rinse the soap from my hair. He brings his hands up to assist, but I smack them away playfully.

"If your intent is to get me hot and bothered, you accomplished that with the head scrub. Hands off," I tease. He chuckles and starts lathering himself up. "Do I not get a turn to wash your hair?"

"Nope," he smiles, rolling his shoulders back. "One, I'm taller and don't want to hurt my back. Two, I already told you that I enjoy taking care of you. That goes for Leather too. Prez is a different breed, and I truly think he and I will share that responsibility."

"You guys are weird, that's for sure," I chuckle before lathering myself completely with body wash. The scent reminds me of Leather and how she used to compliment me when I first got this cheap shit. I used colognes and other expensive soaps, but the second I got the stuff that wasn't more than a few dollars, she noticed. Ever since then, I have bought the damn thing. She did complain about the effects of it on my skin and the benefits of using a different one, but they don't make her as happy as this one. When she would hug me, her face lit up just a smidge. I would hear her little inhale with her nose in my neck. It would have been stupid to point it out, but I noticed.

When it comes to Leather...I notice.

Tornado and I swap places, and I get out. I dry quickly before realizing I didn't bring any clothes in here with me. Cracking the door open, I tiptoe through the room to mine and Tornado's backpacks before bringing them back to the bathroom.

"Something smells yummy," Leather mumbles to Prez, and I have to hold in my laugh. Finishing the walk to the bathroom, I get dressed quickly. I want to go downstairs to get breakfast for Leather and Prez, then to have a group conversation that could either make us stronger or end things all together.

Chapter Forty-Eight

LEATHER

The morning flies by. Prez and I didn't end up waking up until around eleven when Knuckles and Tornado surprised us with breakfast. Knuckles pulled me in tightly for a hug, one that I didn't realize I needed. I inhaled deeply while in his neck, and I immediately felt at home.

Even with the comfort of breakfast and having the three men who mean the most to me near, something still feels off. I can't explain the feeling, but it's as if they are all waiting for the perfect time. What are they waiting for? I have no idea. It's like they are biding their time. Now that it's just after one in the afternoon and the time for us to leave is coming up, I realize that I can't keep going without knowing everything.

We all sit on the bed in silence. The guys don't touch me, but they don't need to. I know they are here and waiting for me to make the first move.

Maybe I should bring up their lack of being able to find me? What about the letter? There's so much shit they need to explain that I'm just overwhelmed. I'm so damn overwhelmed that I don't know how to bring it up. Admitting honesty to myself is harder than it is to others, but I can finally digest that I wanted to use them to stave my anger. If they were willing to fuck me, then I knew they weren't serious about me. Though, now that I have a second to think about it, that makes me even angrier.

"How long?" I ask, staring at the floor. The guys brought my running shoes from the house, yet it feels weird to have my feet so close to the ground instead of my boots.

"How long for what?" Knuckles returns, his brows furrow in confusion. My gaze flickers to Prez with incredulity, and he has the nerve to look guilty.

"Almost two weeks," he says softly, meeting my gaze straight on. "We tried to come sooner." He doesn't explain anymore even after I give him a look that would kill him if it could.

"Your transmitter was working, that's why," Tornado fills in the blank. "It took us a while to find the men to figure out how to find you, then we were able to get ahold of Daryn."

"There's a lot that you don't know. We want to try and clear stuff up for you but have no idea where to start," Knuckles finishes for them in perfect sync. If the situation were any different, I would probably laugh at them. Since my irritation outweighs the happiness in this moment, I can't bring myself to even point out their synchronization.

"How about you start from the fucking top?" I spit, regressing in guilt almost immediately. Taking a few deep breaths, I look up toward the ceiling for a higher power to grant me patience.

"Tornado is from Big D Raiders," Prez announces. I immediately fly off the bed, unable to stop the natural instinct to get away. They follow quickly, standing with their hands out to stop me. Cautiously, I take several steps away from them. "He was blackmailed into staying, he didn't have a choice."

"Everyone has a choice!" I shout. Maybe it's for the best that I don't have my gun. Irrational? Yes. Do I care? No. "The stupid club is one of the largest profiting clubs in the area of trafficking, and you want me to throw caution to the wind? I saw the shit they did to those kids, the torture that they went through! I can't even rehash it because of how awful it was. If you saw that shit, you'd understand."

"Take a breath," Knuckles says, bringing his hands out toward me. I swivel toward him ready to rip into him too, but there's a look in his eye that stops me. I can't explain the look, but it's enough for me to roll my shoulders back and wait.

"I was blackmailed, as we said. The evidence was daming, but it was misconstrued and not what was actually happening. Once I figured out what they were doing, I wanted to dip. I was reaching out to sister branches to try and get out. Armstrong was willing to sign because he was stepping down, but Heckles wasn't ready to let me go. I did the dirty work without realizing what it was for. I beat myself up everyday for the part I played, but I can't change the past," Tornado explains with conviction. The lump in my throat slowly starts diminishing, but I can't take his word as gospel yet.

"Heckles forced me to stick around and see it out. He wanted insight on another club, which just so happened to be the club I was accepted into. Silent Renegade," he pauses, glancing at Knuckles and Prez. "We came for a face to face meeting. I left my phones in the saddle bags while they disconnected the wiretap Heckles put on me. We made it seem like there was a signal jam. We agreed that I would pretend to be on their side, but really trying to get things rolling here. Heckles main mission was for me to find the girl who hurt him and tried to ruin him. I came here right after Armstrong stepped down, and Daryn took over."

"Daryn..." I mutter, my knees feeling weak. I wobble slightly, and Knuckles rushes me. Putting my instincts on high alert, I fight back without questioning. They know better than to rush someone on high alert as it is. Taking a single swing, he grabs both my wrists and clamps them together before shoving me into a chair. His eyes level me and tell me not to go anywhere. I challenge him silently, but quickly give in. It's not a battle I would win, and I don't feel like fighting it.

"Your brother, yeah," Prez mumbles, sitting heavily on the edge of the bed. Knuckles stands behind me, his hands landing heavily on my shoulders. Reaching up, I grasp one of his wrists in my hand tightly. He squeezes my shoulder gently, letting me know that he's not going anywhere.

"How did he..." I trail off, unsure what to even say to that.

"Daryn wasn't kidnapped, Leather. He had a bad run in with the gang when you guys were kids. When he realized it was going to come back to you, he left under the guise of being kidnapped. When he explained it to me, it was that he knew you were safe if he wasn't around," Tornado explains softly, taking a few more solid steps toward me. I don't move, I hardly even breathe.

My jaw is definitely on the floor at this moment. The fight that was just in me has suddenly vanished as everything I have known is a lie. The training I went through, the ranks I pulled just to find him...I was lied to. He didn't keep me safe from anything. I thought he knew me. If he did, he would have known that I would search the ends of the earth for him.

"It made sense to me, but to be frank, I didn't care at the time. I wanted to get out and if going on a mission for Heckles meant leaving, I was going to hit the road."

"How do I play into that?" I ask, though after it comes out of my mouth, I realize it's slightly conceited.

"Funnily enough, Daryn asked me to keep an eye out for a girl named Blaine. He didn't know how far you'd come, not even re-alizing that you surrounded yourself around a club. He just knew that you were interested and that was it. Little did I know coming into this, I would be looking at the same girl for both guys. Of course, the reasoning isn't the same, but that didn't matter."

"How did you know I was Blaine? They never call me by my name." I hate when people say my name. That innocent girl died when her brother was kidnapped, or so she thought, and she had to reinvent herself.

"I overheard a conversation between you and Prez. It wasn't hard to figure it out and put two and two together," he explains with a shrug, finally reaching me and squatting at my knees. He cautiously places his hands on my knees, and I don't remove them. The weight of his body is somehow grounding.

I don't think I was quick to jump to conclusions. They took their sweet time explaining things to me, and I have the right to be angry. Fucking boys.

Though, this still doesn't explain one thing.

"Why did it take you guys so long to find me? Why the letter?" I question, looking between the guys. Prez stands from the bed, making his way toward the chair also. They surround me, my own circle of protection. It's refreshing.

"Your receiver isn't working. We tried to troubleshoot it from here, but we think they had the towers jammed. I tried to recruit the gang in Vancouver, who is a giant fucking dumpster fire and we will never do business with. Then we reached out to Daryn," Prez says, glancing between the guys. Looking around cautiously, I realize they are not fully giving me all of the information.

"Why didn't you reach out to him first?"

"The night you were taken?" Tornado starts, guilt evident in his face. "It was technically planned." Taking a few deep breaths, I keep myself grounded and stable. I need to hear them out. We've come this far, and I refuse to put any bullets into any more heads without a proper explanation.

"Talk," I demand, tired of the long and dramatic pausing.

"Daryn was actually supposed to meet us there. Prez and I talked it over, thinking it would be good for you two to reunite. I didn't anticipate Heckles to intervene. Yet, he did, and I wasn't prepared. He somehow managed to convince Daryn that it was a different day further in the week. Daryn hadn't been alerted that some of the others had gone rogue," Tornado continues. He sniffles, and that's the moment I realize this whole thing is eating him up inside. Despite my own anger and resentment toward the situation, I place my free hand over one of his.

"Rogue from what?" I question softly, urging him for more.

"Daryn cut off the supply for trafficking. He released the ones we already had, but Heckles didn't like that. There was a heavy cash flow in the business, and he just wasn't ready to give that up. He kept it from Daryn until the night of the drop. Once he found out they went rogue, his own club started executing left and right," Knuckles explains from above me. "He didn't realize that Heckles took off with a few of his own and a ton of the crew until we called."

"So, he's not..." I trail off, relief flooding my system. I'm absolutely pissed off that they kept that shit from me, but I'm more grateful that he's not engaging in that bullshit.

"No, he's not," Prez reassures, his hand resting on top of mine that's over Tornados. "Like the rest of us, we had to get up the food chain somehow. That's Daryn's story to tell, though."

"How can we be sure that they won't go for them in the future? Like you said, the money is great. How are they going to supplement their income?" Curiosity overwhelms me, and I can't hold back from the 'what-if's'.

"We have them on a tight leash right now," Prez answers simply.

"Can't be that tight of a leash if they didn't know I was missing for a whole week," I retort, rolling my eyes.

"They are on the leash, not us," Prez sasses back, smirking just enough for me to realize he's joking.

"Maybe you should all be on a leash. It would keep you from making dumb decisions," I snort. "Actually, that's not a bad idea. I would be able to whip you all into shape pretty quickly."

"That's the Leather we know and love," Prez smiles. It takes him a minute to realize what he said. Tornado's face doesn't necessarily fall, but it also seems shocked. I can't see Knuckles, but the squeeze on my shoulder is reassuring, as if he reciprocates the feeling.

"You love me?" I ask softly, my heart stuttering in my chest as I stare right at Prez. A blush creeps over my face, and I honestly don't know how to react. I don't think anyone has ever told me they love me. Not even when I was a kid.

He doesn't back down from my gaze, reinforcing it with a reassuring smile. "I do. You're the biggest pain in my ass, but I fell in love with you a while ago. I haven't been able to get you out of my head, and being able to say it...I feel pretty free, actually."

A grin plasters on my face on its own accord, and Prez immediately captures my mouth with his. My eyes flutter shut, and one of my hands reaches out to grab his face. He dominates me with the kiss, pouring his emotions onto it as he tries to tell me how much

I really mean to him. Tongues dancing, he shows me just where I stand in his life. It gives me a reason to envision our future together.

Pulling away from him, our foreheads touch as we lean against one another to catch our breath. No one speaks nor moves, admiring the moment that we just shared.

"I love you too," I whisper. He plants his lips to mine once more before pulling away and taking a step back.

Knuckles moves from behind me as Tornado moves away from us. I watch him for a moment, unable to take my eyes off of him until I'm forced to with Knuckles standing between us.

"I think we both know how much I care about you, and how long I have gone trying to get you to return the sentiment," Knuckles says, kneeling in front of me. "You have been the Queen in my world longer than you realized. It started off as friends, and I was perfectly okay with that until one day, I realized that you meant more to me than any friend ever had. Then we shared our emotional connection at the hotel...that was when it officially clicked for me. I have been in love with you since the day you bared your heart to me. You gave me your heart and soul, and I have been holding onto it tightly ever since. I am madly in love with you, Leather."

A water bubble forms in my throat. I feel like I'm being proposed to, having them all at my feet. Nodding, he brings his lips to mine and kisses me as if tomorrow will never come. He brings me the joy I needed in my life, brought me out of my shell and put me back together when I cracked. He gave me the ability to truly see who I am, and I'll forever cherish his friendship. Now, I have his love.

"I love you," I mutter against his lips. He growls hungrily and tries pulling me off the chair. Shaking my head, I keep my ass right where it is. There's one more person I haven't heard from and to be completely honest, I don't know how I'm going to react.

"I don't want to ruin your moment, but I would like to say that my feelings for you...I hope you can forgive me for the stupid stunt we pulled," Tornado says quietly, drawing my attention to him. "I didn't think you'd ever be able to trust me after that, but there's a miniscule part of me that prays you'll be willing to revisit the idea of us. The chemistry we have...it's not something you throw away. If there's anything I can do to make it up to you," he stops himself, staring into my soul. His eyes are captivating when you're not in a conversation with him, but when he's serious and focusing? It's like lightning in his eyes. Yet, even while being captivated...is love strong enough to overcome the pain I've endured?

Chapter Forty-Nine

TORNADO

She doesn't give anything away. Her face remains neutral after I simply giving her my heart. I didn't say it outright, but I don't think I have to. Expressing myself isn't easy and it never will be, but just looking at her is enough for me to know that she is all I will ever need.

"I will do anything," I plead quietly, not so sure of myself anymore. There was a part of me that hoped she would understand what I had to do to keep myself alive. Everyone endures things they don't want to, but we come out on top and better than ever. I just hope she can see that.

More silence hangs between us as Knuckles slowly backs away, and I take my spot back at her knees. She doesn't move away from me, but she also doesn't appear phased. The blank stare on her face doesn't settle well inside of me.

"Two conditions," she answers, finally breaking the silence.

"Anything," I plead, holding my breath in anticipation.

"You will *never* get involved with trafficking again. I don't give a fuck if someone is holding shit over you or not. You come to us and we will figure it out together, got it?"

"I wasn't even considering that, but yes, I would absolutely come to you all if there's anything going on." This is the first time I have ever had to grovel, and I have to say that it's not as bad as I thought it would be. "What's the second one?"

"You will let me dominate you," she smirks, her eyes twinkling with mischief. I can't tell if she's joking or not, but I don't care.

"Whatever you want, I will do it," I agree without hesitation. She scoots forward in the chair, sinking to her knees with me on the floor. My hands cup her face, and I wait. We stare at one another for several moments, my breath catching in my throat at the reciprocation of feelings in her eyes. Not wanting to drag this out any longer, I lean forward, eyes fluttering shut, and connect her lips with mine. The stupid sparks they tell you about in novels start flying between us. There's nothing fake about the connection.

One hand moves from the curve of her cheek to her waist, bringing her closer. I swear I hear a throat clear, yet neither one of us pulls away. A single hand lands on my shoulder, and instead of shoving it off, I grab the wrist and yank them into us. Knuckles lands heavily on his knees, and I bring his mouth to mine. Wrapping my fist around his throat, his own groan of need vibrates through my hand. Leather moans next to my ear, nibbling the flesh while breathing harshly.

"You're both so fucking hot," she mutters before her teeth clamp down on my ear. Grunting, I pull Knuckles even closer to me. The three of us are smashed together and I can barely feel the outline of Knuckles hard cock against my hip. He grinds into me in an attempt to seek his own release, but I refuse it. No one will be coming before Leather does, that's for damn sure.

"Bed," I growl against Knuckles before shoving him back. He scrambles to stand and follow the command. Bringing Leather back to me, we collide in a tangle of hair, lips, and teeth. Twisting her thick auburn hair in my hand, I tilt her head back enough to kiss down her neck. Shaking her head, she roughly pushes against me and stands.

"You will do as I say," she commands, standing up straight and shimmying down the sleep shorts she's wearing. Once they are down to her feet, she sits back down on the chair. She raises her leg and sets her foot on my shoulder while the other leg raises to rest on the arm of the chair. "You know what to do." She looks up past me, but I don't waste any time. I dive in and steal a surprised gasp from her. Taking a long, single stroke up from her hole to clit is enough for her to be grabbing my hair tightly. Her nails scrape my scalp as she opens and closes her hand, waiting for me to make my next move.

"Shit, that's hot," Knuckles calls from behind me, his words coming out in pants. I try to sit up to look at him, but Leather doesn't give me that option. Instead, she keeps my mouth planted directly into her cunt.

Darting my tongue onto her clit, I spell her name with it over and over again, worshiping her sweetness and honoring the gifts she's giving me. Her forgiveness and her sweet cunt.

"Suck his cock," she commands someone behind me. I can't see who it is, but I can take a guess that it's one of the two guys behind me. No one comes near me, so again, I'm assuming that one of them is going down on the other. It's a view I wish I had at this moment, but I will get my turn soon, I know it.

Her breath gets more erratic the longer I lick her, and I work my way further down to fuck her tight pussy with my tongue.

"Can I fuck you with my fingers?" I growl against her clit. Her hips grind against my face, and I smirk to myself knowing I'm the reason she's having this much pleasure.

"Yes!" She shrieks. Shoving two into her, she immediately starts pulsating around me. "Fuck, fuck!" Her voice echoes around me as her head tilts backward, eyes slamming shut as she rides the waves of pleasure. Releasing the tight hold on my hair, she uses her foot to push me backward. I fall on my ass, but with the wicked smirk on her face, I know we're not close to being done.

Chapter Fifty

LEATHER

"Stand up," I demand, crossing my legs to hide myself. Tornado looks as though he wants to argue, but thankfully, he doesn't. Instead, he stands without a word. His cock pushes against the zipper of his jeans, making my mouth water. I'm tempted to have him come over here so I can put it in my mouth, but I hold myself back.

Waving my hand, Tornado steps aside for me to see Prez and Knuckles. They are both sitting on the bed with their cocks in their hands. Once they realize I'm watching them, they immediately let themselves go. Their cocks bob as their hands drop, and I can see them pulsating from here.

"Suck his cock," I order. It comes out clipped and gravelly, but it gets the job done because they both jump into action. Prez leans back on his elbows while Knuckles happily brings Prez's cock to his mouth. Both of their eyes roll to the back of their heads when he shoves Prez to the back of his throat.

Tornado keeps his eyes on me but his muscles tense with obvious need. He has to physically hold himself back, and I'm here for it. While he won't look me directly in the eyes, I know that he's wishing for more leeway. I suppose I can be forgiving.

"What can I do to please you?" Prez asks distantly, his voice harsh yet submissive.

"Firstly, you will all call me Mistress, is that clear?"

"Yes, Mistress," they say in unison. Like a rope snapping, the Domme in me is ready to play.

And she's not going to be easy on them.

"Strip." The order is clear, and none of them seem to hesitate while their clothes practically fly off their bodies. "Very good, you all know how to follow simple instructions," I taunt, finally standing from the chair. Since I didn't remove my shirt, it falls just below my hips and hides my pussy from their gaze. Knuckles is happily sucking away on Prez while his own eyes feast on my legs. Shimmying over to Tornado, I grab his shirt and pull him along with me to the bed. He doesn't say a word, following along easily.

"Secondly, I want you to suck Tornado's cock for me, make him nice and wet, will you?" I goad. He knows what I'm trying to do, and yet, he doesn't give in to me.

He wants me to earn my power back.

I can fucking do that.

"I don't think I will, Mistress," he retorts back as Knuckles tenses above him.

"Release his cock, boy," I demand. Like the good boy he is, he pops off quickly and moves away. "Prez, stand." He does as asked. Moving away from Tornado, I fist Prez's shirt in my hand and yank him upward. I know if he didn't want to move, he wouldn't. But he comes along easily, getting upright and standing. I shove him into the bedpost and hold him still.

"What are you going to do, Mistress? Tie me up?" He presses, looking down at me with his own evil smirk.

I snap.

"Tornado, Knuckles, hold him," I sneer, turning on my heel and walking away. Digging through his bag, I find two belts. I tuck one under my armpit while I double the other and make it *crack*. The sound echoes across the room as all three men jump. "Not so high and mighty now, are you?"

"You think a little leather will hurt me?" He asks, though I can hear the double meaning in his words. Clicking my tongue, I take my sweet time in getting back to him. Both guys don't let Prez go, keeping him in their firm hold for me.

"You see," I start, finally reaching him. I drag the metal buckle along his torso, and a shiver rakes through his body. "This little piece of leather won't hurt you, but me? I will make sure you're marked and ready for the world to see that you're mine. How does that sound?" He gulps, the realization of taunting me has hit its mark, and there's no stopping what I'm about to do.

I hand a belt to Tornado and Knuckles, where they tie a smirking Prez up for me. Watching, I wait for them to finish. Once we confirm that he's tied up nicely, I take a step back to admire their work.

"Tornado, I want you to bring Knuckles to the edge three times, is that clear?" His face lights up while Knuckles goes sheet white. "It will be good for you in the long run. These sessions won't only be three minutes, you know." I know that they don't last three minutes in bed, but it's fun to poke fun at their male stereotype.

"Yes, Mistress. How would you like me to do that?"

"Come here and get on your knees." He comes toward me confidently, his knees hitting the soft carpet next to mine. Tilting my head back and forth, I crook my finger for Knuckles to come closer. He obeys without hesitation. Tornado doesn't wait for me to command him again, instead starts sucking Knuckles into his mouth and working him over. I grab Tornado's large hand and place it on my pussy. "You know what to do." He groans around Knuckles, who slams a hand into Tornado's hair to steady himself. His index finger starts to strum my clit lightly, and I rock gently. I don't necessarily seek friction, but I definitely want more.

"Now, who's being a naughty boy?" I ask, my hands grazing over Prez's impressive thighs. He huffs a laugh as he struggles against the tight binds of the leather belt.

"You'll have to make me be good," he retorts, his shoulders shaking with effort. *Tsk*ing at him, he doesn't stop until I bring his rosy tip between my lips. I let him balance on my bottom lip, my tongue brushing his slit. Watching as his knees stutter, I keep my gaze locked onto his.

Jerking back, his engorged length bobs in front of my face. "Too bad, only good boys get a treat."

He releases a string of curses as I trail my nail over him. The black polish is overgrown and chipped, but it makes for the perfect persona.

I'm on my knees for a man, but he's not the one in control. I am. Not only in control of him, but two others who willingly let me be in charge. I know they would give me more if I asked. Yet, this is the perfect balance for me.

Prez on the other hand...

"Do you not like watching Tornado suck Knuckles off? What about him playing with my pussy, hmm?" I jeer, rocking my hips a bit more for effect. He tries to look by bending over but the binds stop him from seeing anything with my shirt in the way. "Oh, dear me! I must have forgotten to take this darn thing off. Good thing only good boys get to have a taste," I hum, shrugging with nonchalance.

"Please suck me, Mistress," Prez begs through gritted teeth. I shake my head in mock disappointment.

"No." I give a simple answer, but the effect is there. He struggles with the belts again, and I watch his fingers try to grasp the loops. Fisting his large cock in my hand, I squeeze tightly. Not enough to hurt but enough for him to understand that *I'm* in charge.

"Faster, Tornado," I command, and he simultaneously starts pumping his head faster while pushing two fingers into my pussy. "Use your mouth on him. Start prepping his ass." Dropping my hips just a bit, I ride his fingers as Prez glares down at me. I can only keep a satisfied smirk on my features. Knuckles groans are enough to see that Tornado's hand disappeared behind Knuckles, and his dropping elbow shows us that he's putting those thick fingers to use.

"I'm going to cum," Knuckles announces. I grab Tornado's hair and yank him off. With a few quick jerks of Prez's cock, he starts getting bigger and bigger. I know what's coming.

"You will not cum, hold it," I snap loudly. All three men jump, and Knuckles has to squeeze the base of himself to keep from releasing. Prez doesn't have the same luxury as he fights himself. "Keep fucking his ass, Tornado. If he cums, he will be punished." Both men whimper on my account.

Taking a deep breath, my body is already more relaxed than it has been in months. Doing a scene with Charles was great, but being able to have three men that mean the world to me ready to fall at my feet? Actually, it's only two. One is being a brat and needing tamed. That's okay, I'm willing to put him back in his box. Either way, it's a feeling that I didn't realize I needed. I never needed someone to make me feel better or give me a boost. Now, I don't think I can do that without them.

"Please let me have a taste of you, Mistress," Tornado begs from next to me, his fingers pumping faster inside of me as I bounce on them.

"Edge him two more times, and I might give you a taste." Tornado gets to work back on Knuckles once he realizes his companion isn't going to explode. Dragging Tornado's fingers away from my cunt, I bring them to Prez's mouth. They are just a few inches too far from his mouth. He stretches to try and get a taste, but it's useless. The binds keep him from reaching.

Knuckles snaps that he's on the brink before long, and Tornado quickly moves back before he does. Taking a sneak peak of Tornado's cock, he's rock hard from getting Knuckles and I off, yet he hasn't touched it. I think he deserves a reward.

"Are you ready to be a good listener?" I ask petulantly. He nods but doesn't say anything. Clicking my tongue, I scoot away from him to show him that I'm serious.

"Yes, Mistress," he groans. It's apparent that he's not really willing to listen and just wants to get his way. Unfortunately for him, I don't play that game.

"Awe man, I guess you're really not wanting to be a good boy like these two." I wave a hand at Knuckles and Tornado. Knuckles brows are pinched in bliss while Tornado looks about ready to snap and fuck someone. My stupid joke causes Tornado to laugh, which in turn causes Knuckles to pull away from Tornado's mouth to keep from coming.

"That's three, Mistress!" Knuckles announces proudly, but like he's also ready to snap.

"Such a good boy for me," I cheer brightly. My praise seems to do wonders for him as his face lights up brightly. Tornado doesn't stop fingering me, instead staying right where he is and adding another finger to the mix.

"Get on the bed, both of you," I order. Tornado removes his hand with a pout. "Tornado, I want you to fuck Knuckles while I fuck him."

"What about Prez?" Knuckles asks nervously, his eyes darting between us. Tornado shoves a finger back into Knuckles' ass harshly and the question is long forgotten for him.

"What about him?" I retort, raising a single brow. He swallows heavily and shakes his head, dropping the question. Deciding that I don't want to answer it anyway, I move away from Prez.

"When you're ready to listen, let me know. I might let you fuck my ass." Shrugging, I stand and make my way over to the night stand. A small bottle of lube is there, so I grab it and make my way over to the two men on the bed. I can't let Knuckles get fucked without proper preparation. Saliva works fine for fingers but not for bigger inserts like a cock.

Crawling over to the men, I swivel around and plant my pussy in Knuckles face. He doesn't wait for me to command him, instead circling my hips with his arms and devouring me. Pressure starts to build in my lower stomach, but I ignore it by popping the cap on the lube, squirting a generous amount onto Tornado, and fisting him in my hand. Tugging on his length, he seems to have a hard time focusing on prepping Knuckles.

"Are you ready?" I whisper, brushing my lips against his. He nods, lining his thick cock up to Knuckles tight hole.

"You will wait until I tell you," I say, leveling him. He nods. Just as I'm about to cum, I rip myself away from Knuckles face and turn myself around. Putting my ass against Tornado's abs, he grabs my ass and squeezes. "Guide him into me." I feel him moving around then Knuckles body jerks as I'm slammed onto his thick length.

"Yes!" I shout, my eyes rolling into my head from the burning stretch. No one can convince me that the first few moments of being widened aren't the best. The friction is the most important part, and even though I'm soaked, it's still perfect. "Fuck him." I can't see Tornado, but I force my eyes open to watch Knuckles reaction. Prez is shouting from the bed post and very apparently aching to be touching us. Sucks that he couldn't listen.

"Shit," Tornado hisses behind me, stretching the word out as far as it would go. Knuckles jerks upward from below me, bumping the special spot inside of me. Reaching down, I carefully wrap my hand around his throat and press the sides. He doesn't even stop me, instead embarrassing the lack of blood flow as he jerks around below me from Tornado ramming into him.

"Too bad you weren't here to please me," I gasp, looking over my shoulder at Prez. He quickly jerks, and the belt snaps in half. I would say I'm surprised but...I'm not. He marches over to me, his tall frame towering over the three of us as he angrily climbs onto the bed. Removing myself from Knuckles cock, I plant my pussy back in his face, except this time I lean down to swallow his cock inside my mouth.

Prez doesn't hesitate to slam into me from behind, his hands gripping my ass harshly as he takes me relentlessly. I can't even pretend to be upset with him. Each pump of his cock inside of me has him bumping against my G-spot.

All of us curse as we get closer to the edge together. Knuckles swirls his tongue over my clit at the same time Prez snaps against my G-spot, and I detonate.

Screaming, I chant. "Shit, fuck, fuck!" Over and over again in pure bliss around Knuckles cock.

"Please let me cum."

"I have to cum."

"Fuck, I gotta cum." They all rapid fire at me. I wail my approval before ropes of cum slam into my mouth. They are bitter, but I'm not a spitter nor a quitter, so I shove him down my throat and let him go. Warmth fills my pussy as Prez fills me to the brim with his own release. Tornado's abs clench tightly while I watch the base of his cock twitch with his own release.

"Holy shit," Prez gasps, pulling out of me slowly. I untangle myself from Knuckles while Tornado gently removes himself. We all collapse in a heap on the bed, gasping and smiling with pure satisfaction.

"I love you guys," I say softly, smiling widely to myself. They snuggle closer to me, their body heat like giant radiators on me.

Nothing could ruin this moment.

Chapter Fifty-One

PREZ

We must have fallen asleep because a loud knock jars me awake. Rubbing my eyes, I disentangle myself from the others and get halfway to the door before I realize I'm naked. Looking at my watch, my eyes practically bug out of my head. Our flight is in less than two hours, and we haven't finished packing.

"Shit, guys, we have to go," I shout, shaking Knuckles knowing he's less likely to punch me for waking him up.

"Five more minutes," he grumbles sleepily, tucking himself tighter around Leather. Rolling my eyes, I snap my hand into his ass and he jolts awake. "What the fuck was that for?"

"We gotta go, we're late to the airport," I say, and that seems to get him into action. Jumping out of the bed, he races around the room to collect things for us. Leather and Tornado slowly rise, sluggishly moving around the room to get their shit packed. We don't have a lot, so thankfully it only takes a few minutes before we're walking out the door. Leather leads the way, tossing bags into the trunk of the car.

"Blaine," Daryn calls. I turn to look over my shoulder, and he's waving his hands around like a freaking maniac. As I predicted,

Leather's spine snaps straight and she's immediately on edge, not bothering to turn around and look at him.

"What did you just call me?" She questions, though the tone is one that is deathly quiet, like a snake ready to strike.

"Uhm, I called you by your name?" He asks, though he's not as confident as he was just a moment ago. "I didn't know I wasn't supposed to call you that."

"That's not true," I pipe up, stopping next to Leather. Leaning against the open hatch, I shrug a shoulder. "He already knows not to call you that name, he just refused to acknowledge it. Funnily enough, his road name is Nemo, but I suppose he failed to mention that."

"She's my sister, I don't have to call her by her damn road name!" He shouts. If he was a dragon, he would have smoke rolling from his nostrils.

"I stopped being your sister the day you decided to put my life in your hands," she whispers, taking a step away from the car. Continuing to grace him with her back, she steps aside while Knuckles and Tornado chuck their packs into the trunk. Both guys watch on warily but don't say anything.

"Blaine, come on-" he grabs her shoulder, and that's the end game. He didn't seem to read the audience. Leather is jumpy and will defend at the drop of a dime. If you touch her while she's on high alert without already making your presence known? Well, game over.

She reaches back quickly and grabs his wrist. Daryn barely gets the chance to register what's happening before Leather does a grab and spin, and sends him flying over her shoulder. He lands on the ground roughly, the air whooshing from his lungs as Leather grabs his arms and flips him onto his stomach. She pins him to the ground, leaning in closely.

"I am Leather now. Hop on the wagon, or fall off." She gets up off of him, storms over to the trunk and slams it shut. None of us say otherwise as we hop into the SUV. Tornado sidles up next to Leather by the window and whispers something in her ear. She smirks, nodding as her head leans against his shoulder. A few moments later, a wheezing Daryn gets into the passenger seat while one of the prospects drives us to their airport. Glancing at my watch, I hope that traffic isn't that bad. We can practically skip through security, so that's no problem, but if we don't get there with at least thirty minutes to spare, we'll have to delay until tomorrow. For everyone's sake, we better make that damn plane today.

The ride is silent beside the occasional giggle from Leather and the other two. From my seat next to Knuckles, I watch silently as he leans against the back of the seat in front of him to get as close as possible to Leather. Tornado sits next to her with his leg tucked into the seat, watching her with his own sense of fascination. Leather bounces between them easily, like a simple conversation being volleyed back and forth. None of the struggle to keep up with the perfect threesome. As if on cue, Leather glances past the two guys in front of her and smiles directly at me.

"So, did you at least enjoy the trip?" She asks playfull, her eyes full of mirth. Shaking my head with a smirk, I scoot to the edge of my seat and crook my finger at her. She wiggles toward me, lightly shoving Tornado out of the way. He moves easily with a chuckle, both hands raised in surrender and nods his head in understanding.

"If I didn't have to go save a little damsel in distress, I think it would have been worth it to sight see," I remark casually as if it's an everyday ordeal. "Sadly, the sight seeing had to be canceled, and I had to go rescue this pretty auburn haired woman that needed saving."

"Tell me more about this girl," Leather whispers, leaning her head against the seat back. My head lays down next to hers, though I'm from the back seat and she's from the front. Our faces are close, too close to keep my eyes open so they shut.

"Well, she's a stunning young woman, far out of my league if I do say so myself. She usually doesn't require any saving, but luck struck out, and I had the opportunity to win her over." I can't see her, but with the little puff of air that hits my face and the barely-there huff, I know she's smiling.

"What else?"

"She's exceptionally needy," I tease, earning a playful head bump from her. "She is also one of the most dedicated women I have ever met in this lifetime, and I hope she will make me the happiest man in the world by staying at my side through thick and thin." Leaning back, I open my eyes to see her stunned face. Tornado and Knuckles smirk, understanding where I'm going with this since they were also in on the plan.

"What?" The confusion in her tone is palpable, but she also looks happy. Very happy.

Sitting up, Tornado and Knuckles come closer to Leather and I. "We were going to wait to make this romantic, but nothing about the three of us screams romance," Knuckles jokes. "But when we lost you, it was enough for us to realize how much you truly meant to us."

"When I got back to the club, there was no hesitation. I jumped right in as soon as the doc gave me clearance. There was nothing to stop me from getting you back, even if it meant walking through gun fire to get you back," Tornado says with conviction.

"We know the journey hasn't been ideal. There wasn't romance nor flowers, this isn't even the conventional way of doing this, but when do we ever do things society says is necessary?" I quiz, raising a brow as she sniffles. Her eyes are bright, her face slightly red as she holds back, what I'm assuming are, happy tears.

"Never," she giggles, though the sound is watery.

"So, Leather," I start, reaching into my pocket to grab the small ring. It's a simple diamond band, elegant yet practical for our girl. "Will you make us the happiest men in the world and marry us?"

She nods frantically, her hand flying to her mouth as she lets out a shriek of joy. "Yes, yes!" She holds out her hand, and Knuckles plucks the ring from me to put it on our girl. Tears start streaking down her face with pure joy. Turning a bad memory into a good one is exactly what she needs. Our jobs are to make sure she's okay at all costs, and this was just step-one in doing that.

"How long has this been planned?" She whispers as she gazes at her new ring. It fit her perfectly, which we knew it would. The guys and I actually decided this right before we left for Vancour. We didn't want to miss an opportunity with her, and the ring has been in my pocket ever since as a sign of good will.

"A while," I wink, gripping her chin with my finger and thumb to bring her closer. She comes easily, kissing me as though the world around us doesn't exist.

"Congratulations, sister," Daryn says from the front. Leather's joy radiates from her, and even his presence doesn't seem to faze her. She doesn't exactly acknowledge him though.

Chapter Fifty-Two

KNUCKLES

Walking toward the clubhouse, we're all dead on our feet. Well, all of us except for Leather. She's hyper and excited while the rest of us can barely keep our eyes open. I'm so thankful that she's not mentally rehashing everything, yet I just want to snuggle with her and sleep for a week.

The music pounds loudly inside the building, and once she registers that, she tenses up. We still don't know what exactly happened while she was in there, but we're hoping to understand and help her work it out. I go in first, having them turn the music down for a minute to reintroduce Leather. She's bombarded with good wishes, hugs, and lots of ribbing from the guys. Like the perfect girl she is, she takes it all in stride. We watch from afar as she's welcomed back into her home by the members.

It wasn't just the three of us that were worried for her. Leather was a huge piece of our crazy puzzle. When she was gone, it was as if none of us could function. The guys relied heavily on her for their routines and safety measures, so when she was on her own, they were lost. Not only that, but she was the life of the party for them. Just the thought of her lit up a room, and that was apparent when we stepped foot inside the club. They wanted to crank the music right back up, but we explained that the four of us are exhausted and just want to have some peace. They took the explanation, though a few of the guys appeared skeptical. Leather was never one to turn down good music and a drink, but she's not the same girl we had before. The music is low, no sudden movement is allowed, and it's like walking on eggshells. I'm perfectly fine with it for now, but she will need tough love soon and that's something we're able to provide for her. Whatever treatment or therapy or whatever magic is required, the three of us will be there every step of the way.

After she makes her rounds and says her goodbyes, we go back upstairs. It's almost two in the morning, but the party is raging downstairs, especially after we leave and they crank the music back to full blast. It's subtle, yet I notice the tensing of her muscles when it's turned up. I can tell from her clenched fists at her sides that she wants to cover her ears. She refuses. I would bet my bike it's because she believes acting strong will make her strong. Little does she know, it doesn't always work like that.

"Who's room?" She asks, bouncing on her toes nervously. Tornado and Prez meet my gaze before briefly nodding.

"I think it would be a good idea for Knuckles to get some alone time with you right now," Prez says, stepping forward to her. He grabs her hand and kisses the back of it gently. Her nose crinkles, and she looks adorably confused at the current situation. "We don't want to overwhelm you, and now isn't the time for all three of us to be doing it. We gave you some of that power back, but you also need to have that quality time with each of us, even if it's just to sleep."

She nods, then shakes her head. "I won't be overwhelmed," she starts, conviction in her voice as she tries to keep herself together. Prez gives her an incredulous look that breaks down her mental barrier a bit. "I don't know if I can sleep right now," she finally admits. Turning her toward me, I grab her face in my hands and lean our heads together gently. Together, we take several deep breaths until hers match mine and her heartbeat isn't jumping from her throat.

"We will figure it out together. Tonight is you and me, even if I just get to hold you and thank whoever exists that you're mine." That seems to soothe a part of her because she's nodding and letting me lead her away. I can feel Tornado and Prez's eyes on our backs as we leave, and she fiddles with the hem of her shirt until I shut the door behind us.

"I don't think I will be able to sleep," she huffs, plopping herself down on the edge of the bed before falling backward. Her auburn hair splays around her, and I can't unsee the angelic look she gives off. She would say she's the devil in disguise, except I see her for what she truly is. Beautiful inside and out.

"Yes you will, come on." Even though it's pretty late, I think washing off the day and letting it go down the drain is cleansing for all of us. So, turning on the water, I strip her down completely and help comb out her hair. She doesn't stop me from fussing over her, which is good because she would earn a few good swats to the rear if she tried to stop me.

The shower is quick, not wanting to spend too long in there since I can feel the energy depleting at a much faster rate than before. Scrubbing her down, I make sure to service all the appropriate areas while not giving her the satisfaction of *touching* her.

She whines but doesn't beg, hoping I will cave. The attention she craves is something I will willingly give, but she has to ask. I don't care if it's nice, I will do it if she demands it from me.

On the other hand, we're both exhausted from the long day and the drama that's been draining from us both. Information has been dumped on her from all angles, so we're all sure that she's about to either break down or knock out hard. From the sounds she's making right now, I don't think she's going to sleep anytime soon.

Rinsing the soap from her entire body, I wrap my arms around her center while she tucks her arms into herself. I hold her tightly as she listens to my heart beating for her. I'm not sure how long we stand there, but after my legs start going numb I decide we're long overdue to be done. Shutting off the water quickly, I grab a fluffy towel and swaddle her in it. She huffs grumpily, but it's like a kitten being wrapped up in a little cocoon. We take our time getting dried off as I help her.

Walking over to the underwear drawer she groans, "nooo." I turn my head and look at her over my shoulder, brow raised in confusion. "I just want to lay with you."

"Naked?" I ask incredulously, knowing damn well if we aren't wearing clothes, we aren't going to sleep. "You need to rest, Leather. It's been a day, and you *are* exhausted whether you want to admit it or not."

She shakes her head adamantly, stomping her foot on the ground petulantly. I have to say the persona of a kitten is simply getting stronger. This side of her is one that I haven't seen very often, and I'm just hoping it's because she finally realizes that she can trust me. She can trust *us*.

Turning my body toward her fully, we stare down. Her lower lip juts out, her eyes rounding out, and her brows curving oddly. Holy shit. "Are you pouting?" I question while holding back a laugh. It's cute but another thing I have never seen from her.

"Duh," she scoffs. She seems to contemplate something for a moment before shrugging and yanking the towel off of her. My jaw drops as she stands there in all her tattooed glory.

"Leather-"

"There's too much energy bouncing around inside of me to sleep," she admits quietly. After a moment of me standing in shocked silence, she crosses her arms over her chest. "If you're not interested-"

"I am!" I say, walking toward her quickly. Bending down, I throw her over my shoulder and haul her toward the bed. She doesn't even have a chance to think before she's flying through the air, landing on the mattress. Landing with a solid *oomph*, she quickly leans on her elbows as I prowl toward her. She tries to escape my advances by shifting higher up the bed, yet I happen to move just a little bit faster. Capturing her ankles, I jerk her back down the bed. A sharp squeal comes from her as she laughs. It's far too contagious, so I start laughing with her. My chuckle grumbles over her sensitive flesh as I kiss my way to the apex of her thighs. Her hips twist, trying to get me to one specific spot.

Instead, I jump to her other thigh and nibble on the soft skin there. She's groaning but doesn't say anything to hurry my advances. She must know that it would only make things worse for her. I make out with her thighs, licking it the exact way I'm going to devour her pussy.

When her hand lands on my head, I shake it away and kiss further away from her desired spot with a smirk. There's no doubt that she knows exactly what I'm doing, yet again, she doesn't protest with words. Her hips and legs on the other hand try to make their move on me, doing their best to force me back up.

Sadly for her, I'm in charge right now.

"Keep doing that and you will have to serve me to sleep," I growl, biting harshly on her ankle. She doesn't yank away or jerk. Oh, no. She releases a heavy exhale, one that sounds exactly like relief with the hint of a moan.

Pain is the perfect combination with pleasure.

"What would I have to do?" She asks, gasping again when I nibble on the skin next to her knee.

"I haven't fully thought of it since this is *supposed* to be about you." Jumping to her other leg, I chomp down on the same spots and matching them to one another. After a moment, I sit back and admire my handiwork. They are pretty damn identical if you ask me. My eyes mosey from the red spots covering her legs to the liquid dripping from her pussy.

"Wow," I gasp in mock surprise. Taking a single finger, I scoop the cum and smear it along my other fingers. "Is this discharge or are you happy to see me?" I tease, bringing the digits to my mouth and greedily having a taste. She's everything my dreams are made of. Sweet and bitter mixed into one.

Exactly like her.

"You know damn well that I'm always happy to see you," she bites back playfully, attempting to slam her legs closed. Unfortunately for her, I'm faster. My arms snap out, hands clamping over her knees to keep them from shutting.

"*Tsk, tsk,*" I hiss, kissing my teeth in mock anger. "You're a naughty girl for trying to pull that little stunt," I reprimand with a shake of my head.

"I just want you to take me," she admits on a gasp as I insert my finger into her cunt quickly. She jerks up the bed, her eyes fluttering shut as her mouth drops open.

"We will do it on my own time," I scold. I quickly raise my hand and smack it down on the inside of her thigh. Her greedy pussy clenches around my single digit, and I have to use my imagination on what her pussy will feel like when it grips my cock. Unless she specifically asks, or more importantly begs, I will be keeping it contained to myself and my hand.

"Yes, sir," she whimpers, her back bowing off the bed as I shove another thick finger into her tight heat. Retreating my fingers slowly, I drive them upward, hitting the spot that has her crying out in pleasure and her pussy threatening to shoot liquid all over the place. She tries to push her hips downward, most likely in a normal bodily response, but that's too much movement from her. With rapid succession, I remove my fingers from her and smack the tips of my fingers on her clit.

Her palms slam down on the mattress and grip for anything, finally making purchase as I bury them back inside of her. Taking in her body, she's relaxed yet tense, holding herself off of the edge of an orgasm while still having the time of her life. She must feel me staring at her beautiful face because her eyes open, and the first thing I notice is her pupils blown wide in pleasure. Her forehead has a beading of sweat, and her jaw finally unhinges itself.

While keeping eye contact, I lean down and take a long slow lick up her cunt. I don't have to use words for her to keep her eyes open even though it appears to be a struggle. Focusing solely on her clit, I let my fingers take the lead. They rub her g-spot as I work her over from this side.

Her cunt tightens, her body snapping straight, and I pull back. Electricity ignites in her eyes when she realizes that I'm not going to let her finish. At least not yet. Once her pussy releases my fingers from its death grip, I slowly start moving them again. I purposefully avoid her g-spot, making sure that I'm not really hitting anything in particular as I go. The stretch is enough for now.

"Please," she rasps, her head flying from side to side. "Please let me cum. Fill me with your cock and let me cum." Quirking a brow at her, I smirk.

"If I give you my cock, you aren't allowed to cum," I retort, and there's no waiting for a response as she's already almost back on the verge of an orgasm.

"I want you to fill me and let me cum, please Knuckles, I need you inside of me."

"You didn't seem to need me a moment ago when you almost squirted on my fingers." My voice is raspy as it comes out, and I'm honestly just filling her head with empty threats. She said she couldn't sleep, and I'm trying to rectify that by wiping her out with an intense orgasm. If I start fucking her, I will be finishing long before she's had enough. Well, my opinion of her having enough is a few more edges.

Bending down, I don't give her the chance to respond before I'm back on her pussy. Devouring her from top to bottom, my fingers find that special spot once again and bring her closer and closer...

"Fuck!" She shouts as I pull away. Anger is palpable from her at this point, but she will quickly learn that I'm in charge right now.

"You want to try that again?" I ask deeply, staring down at her. Her throat bobs with a gulp and a shake of her head. "Good. You will thank me for letting you almost cum."

"Thank you for letting me almost cum," she parrots sassily. It's a work in progress, that's for sure. One day she will be trusting with us enough for all of us to play. I have always wanted to see what she would look like wrapped up tightly in black ropes. I bet Prez would look just as delicious when hanging next to her. Lowering my hand to my cock, a few gentle tugs have me hardening even further. The image mixed with the feeling are the perfect combinations.

That's a sight I have to see.

Working her back up to the brink a few more times, she has tears streaking down her cheeks and her chants for more are practically screams at this point.

"Please give me your cock and let me cum!" She sobs loudly, her fingers white-knuckling the sheets in what I assume is an attempt to keep from pushing herself over.

"Since you asked so nicely," I grunt, moving quickly and shoving myself inside of her. Previously she mentioned loving the feel of the quick stretch and limited lube. With the scream and smile lighting her face, it's safe to say she's loving it.

Shockwaves roll through my body as I relentlessly pound into her. Her fingers find my biceps and her nails puncture my skin as she holds on. The orgasm that rips through us must take us both by surprise, and I swear my vision turns bright white. I'm not even sure if I stayed awake for a moment and there's a high possibility that I just passed out because holy shit.

Holy. Shit.

My cock jerks inside of her as I leg go fully, my body filling with tremors as ecstasy overtakes me. I'm not even sure if she's breathing right now because all I hear is static. I can feel her nails inside of my skin, and that has to be the only thing keeping me grounded at this point.

I'm not even sure how long passes before we both relax, and I slump next to her, wrapping myself around her in a bear hug. She doesn't protest, simply curling further into my embrace.

Chapter Fifty-Three
TORNADO

"What do you think they are doing?" I ask, sitting down on the chair. Prez toes off his boots and flops down on the bed heavily, sighing in relief after a long day.

"What do you *think* they are doing?" He retorts sarcastically, his head tilting to the side with a flat look on his face. Smirking, I untie the laces for my own boots and tug them off. I place them next to the chair, watching as Prez stares at the ceiling above him.

"I mean, I know she wasn't exactly exhausted but that doesn't mean they are playing hacky sack," I deny. He snorts, not believing a word I said. Good thing for him because I don't believe a lick of what I said either. If she's not tired, she will somehow rope him into tiring her out. Better yet, knowing him, he will most likely offer his services to her.

"To be frank, I don't even care right now. I'm so damn tired that thinking too hard might put me into a self-induced coma," he yawns, positioning his arms behind his head. His eyes remain staring at the ceiling despite his words of exhaustion. Just as I stand, he quickly sits up and pats the bed next to him.

"Oh, now you want to talk?" I tease, stalking over to him and plunking down next to him. He wraps his arm over my shoulder, pulling me toward himself. We sit in silence for a while, simply enjoying each other and the closeness we share in this moment.

I can't even begin to explain the feelings I have developed for him. There wasn't a part of me that came here knowing I would find someone for me, let alone finding three people that seem to fit their pieces with mine just right. I was simply on a mission for self-preservation and to right a wrong. However, I preserved more than just my physical being. I sewed my emotional being back together with all three of these individuals by my side whether I realized it or not.

As far as righting the wronged, I learned my lesson on two sides to every story. The side which had more influence fed me lies and deceit. They used my neutral ground to try and gain a leg up. Unfortunately for him, I may have been impartial but I wasn't born yesterday. His first mistake was not thinking that I would gather my own information. He needed someone who knew what they were doing but didn't think of all the shit I would do on my own. Thankfully, it worked out in the long run.

If I hadn't come here, I don't think I would have ever met these guys. I would still be stuck there and trapped against my will. There was no escape for me unless I killed them, and I wouldn't have been able to do that without the help of others. Silent Renegade, or more specifically Prez, took me in and gave me hope. He kept me from wallowing in my own self-pity and instead gave me a reason to keep going. I can't explain how he helped me because I'm not even too sure myself. All I know is that he was there for me when I needed someone and hasn't let me go since.

Even Leather was skeptical of me, not that I blame her, but she made it very clear that I wasn't to be trusted. Her instincts were right on point, but she misplaced the reason for it. She didn't have any reason to trust me, and she sure didn't. I had three different agenda's when I came here and falling in love with her wasn't one of them.

"I can hear the cogs turning up there," Prez mumbles, his grip tightening on my shoulder. "You want to talk about it?"

"I'm just thinking about everything." He nods against my shoulder. "Isn't it weird how far we've come?"

"What do you mean?" He asks. Sitting up and turning toward me, he clasps our hands together in his lap. He doesn't push me to answer the question. He just sits there patiently with curiosity on his face.

"Just how everything has gone the way it has. How I came here scared and fearing for my own safety, searching for two different people in a world full of millions only to find them in one location, mixed inside one beautiful female," I reminisce, remembering the way her auburn hair looked on that stage the first time I saw her. How the dais lit up just a bit brighter when she walked out on it. It wasn't something I was anticipating, yet it seemed to only drive the appeal. When she handled him and made him obey her every command, I was pulled into a trance that I haven't come out of.

Quite frankly, I have no desire to come out of it. Even if this was a dream, I would live happily in my head.

"It's definitely crazy," he nods, staring at our joined hands. "When I met you, I remember feeling at ease. I couldn't explain the feeling, and I will admit I felt a little crazy. Who just looks at a guy and thinks they feel at home?" He chuckles and shakes his head.

We sit here silently for a few more moments. My eyes flicker around his face as he stares at our joined hands. He looks deep in thought, but I want him to be able to tell me what he's feeling with a clear head. So, I give him time.

"It's strange, feeling like I have known you my whole life. I only felt that with Leather and Knuckles, but those two have always been joined at the hip," he laughs, and I chuckle along with him. Those two are definitely inseparable. "With those two, I didn't read any more into it because I knew she was struggling. She doesn't need my advances, and Knuckles practically throws himself at her any chance he gets."

"Why didn't you make a move?" I ask softly, flipping his hands in mine. I trace the lines of his palm in gentle strokes.

"She absolutely friend-zoned us," he chuckles, bringing the back of my hand to his lips. "It didn't seem fair to her, so I never did. It worked out in the end, like it always will." Nodding my head, we stare at one another for a while. The silence isn't terrible. In reality, we're both the quiet types who don't feel the need to fill the voids.

"I'm sorry that she didn't notice you earlier," I mutter softly, the emotions and longevity of the day finally catching up to me.

"Don't be. She found me, that's all that matters." His hand cups my face, tilting it to look back up at his. I hadn't even realized I looked away. "I'm also glad I found you."

Leaning forward, his lips gently graze mine, almost experimentally. It quickly becomes all consuming as we devour one another. Hands grappling each other, we can't seem to get close enough to one another. The hole in my chest fills almost instantly, and I realize that it's him that I have been missing. I have had a connection with Leather and Knuckles, on both physical and emotional levels. Prez and I haven't gotten that opportunity.

Until now.

After a moment, I finally manage to best him and tackle him onto the mattress. My body lays flat over his, and I grind down onto him, his hard cock concealed by his jeans creating the perfect friction for my own. Groaning against his mouth, I rock harder against him as I shove him further into the mattress with my weight. He doesn't seem to mind since his large hands reach around me to grab my ass, kneading it through my jeans.

"Fuck," I grunt, tilting my hips against him. Sucking his bottom lip into my mouth, I bite down onto it before hoisting myself up and off of him. "Strip." I unhook the buckle on my belt and swiftly yank it from the loops.

"Make me," he retorts, quirking a brow at me. With quick movements, I grab his wrists and secure them in the belt like cuffs. He struggles briefly but not enough to stop me.

"You made that far too easy," I quip, shaking my head and taking a few steps back. Peeling my shirt off and over my head, his gazes working down the ridges of my chest and stomach. I flex just for him, and he watches as the muscles define even more. Smirking, I undo the button of my jeans. His eyes snap up to mine. They are filled with mirth and lust, a combination that I'm perfectly okay with. He trails back downward and notices that my jeans are barely hanging onto my hips.

"So, how am I supposed to follow your command if I can't even use my hands?" Assessing him fully, I tilt my head from side to side in fake contemplation.

"I guess you will have to get creative then, huh?" I shrug. Pushing my thumbs into the waistband of my pants, I shove them off.

"No panties?" He teases as he eyes my solid dick, and I have to restrain myself from helping him. Wrapping my hand around myself, he tracks my every move. My thumb swoops down to rub over the head, and I swipe through the beads of precum already dripping out.

"Didn't need them." Tightening just a bit more, Prez struggles half assed against the belt. "Now, are you going to listen, or do I need to just get myself off?"

"Depends," he shrugs, leaning against the bedpost. "I have no problems listening, but I prefer to have a bit of...incentive."

Clicking my tongue, I kick my pants off the rest of the way and sit on the bed. My fist twists along my shaft, squeezing as I get closer to the tip.

"How is this for an incentive?" I ask, slowing my strokes even more. "If you don't behave and listen, I guess you'll stay right there while I fuck my fist, then I'll untie you and we will go to bed. How does that sound?" I growl, rocking my hips into myself. I can tell that he's contemplating my words, and I hope the look on my face will tell him just how serious I'm being.

Several moments of contemplation later, his body relaxes a bit further.

"Fine," he huffs as his fidgeting quicks. I eye him up and down, trying to determine if he's just blowing smoke to attempt to overpower me or if it's genuine. "Fuck, I promise to listen to you," he grunts, eyes narrowing on me in irritation. I decide to let him sit for a moment longer, my cock jerking in my hand at the thought of having him tied up from the rafters, swinging as I impale him on my cock.

Once I feel like he has had enough of my eye fucking, I stand and spin him around. He moves easily, letting me remove the belt with ease. His wrists are slightly reddened from the leather material, but he doesn't seem to mind. Jerking my head upward at him, he rolls his eyes but raises his arms above his head. Being several inches taller than him has its advantages. Taking a few steps towards him, my fingers find the hem of his shirt and drag it up his body. I take my time and feel the rough ridges along my finger tips, pressing them into each ridge one by one. His breathing turns ragged as I go.

Our gazes connect, clashing with one another before his disappears behind the cloth as I yank it over his head.

Grabbing his shoulder, I twirl him back around, walk him backward several steps, then shove him onto the bed. He falls with ease and grace, not even a bit surprised by my small show of dominance. He doesn't wait for me to move his arms as he raises them above his head. It must be his way of showing me that he's willing to let me lead. Not that I had given him much of an option.

Smirking, I pop the button on his pants and watch as it gives his cock a little more room. Not much but enough. I dig my fingers into the waist of his jeans and shimmy them down his body. He lifts his hips to assist me but other than that, he doesn't move. Once they come off, I realize he's not wearing any other layers either.

"No panties?" I joke, throwing his words back at him. He shakes his head, raising his eyebrows repeatedly. We both laugh at the commonality, but his laugh is quickly choked off when I bend down and suck him into my mouth.

His large cock barely seems to fit inside my mouth as I work down his shaft slowly. He's salty and smooth, the mixture blasting my senses as I get more saliva to coat his length. I honestly have no idea what I'm doing, but I try to follow everything I've seen from women in the past as well as what I know feels good on me.

I back up a bit, barely holding the head of his cock inside of my mouth as I use the tip of my tongue to play with his slit. His hips jerk below me, and I glance up to see his entire body taunt.

"More," he gasps when I envelope him back into my mouth. Relaxing my throat and dropping down, he slides deeper than before. He grunts as he tilts upwards, probably unintentionally, but that's not what matters. I come up off of him, shaking my head and clicking my tongue.

"Please don't stop," he pants, his eyes wide with lust. Reaching over to the end table, I grab the tube of lube and set it next to us. I shove two fingers into his mouth while moving them around a bit.

"Suck." The command is gruff but it's enough to have him slurping them down quickly. His warm, hot mouth works my fingers over until they are dripping with his saliva. Yanking them out of his mouth, my hand smacks down on his cheek quickly, the saliva splashing off his skin while the rest of it trails down his tattooed throat. We both go still with shock, my mouth popping off his cock as my heart leaps into my throat while we process what I just did.

"Again," he rasps, gasping as his fingers trail over the spot I smacked. Something inside of me shifts, a possessive and aggressive beast that I didn't know existed. I push my fingers back into his mouth as I suck his cock back into mine. Bobbing over and over, his groans turn into moans, then his moans turn to shouts of pleasure as he gets closer and closer to climax. I move my fingers from his mouth and slam back down on his cheek, dragging them down his face onto his chest and wrapping them around his length as I move away.

Giving him a few rough tugs, I slip my hand lower and lower...

"Fuuuck," he groans out as I put pressure on his tight rim. I don't push in yet, just letting him get the feeling of it. His cock jerks between us as I push harder. "I want your cock in my mouth," he gasps when the tip of my finger breaches him fully. Pulling away, I climb onto the bed with him and position myself by his head. He doesn't waste any time in lifting his head and licking me like a lollipop. I shutter and grab the lube, squirting it on his cock and letting it drop down his asshole. His deep groan pushes vibrations up my shaft which in turn pushes them all the way up my spin.

Scooping up the lube, I use it to coat a few of my fingers before plunging my pointer finger into him. His whole body jerks up on the bed and relaxes when I remove it. I don't give him time to relax as I slam it back inside of him. The vibrations carried in his voice pull me closer to my own release. I yank myself from his mouth as I work on stretching him out, not wanting to cum before it's time.

Just thinking about shoving myself deeply inside his tight ass, how the heat would feel around my cock and swallow me deeper has me fighting to fuck my own fist. Working another finger in with the last, I slowly breach him again. This time, it's a tighter squeeze. He clamps down on my fingers as his hand slams against my thigh, digging his nails into my skin.

I pour more lube over my fingers in his ass then wrap my other hand around his thickness. With a twisting motion, I swirl around his cock. It gets him to relax and let me in for more.

"That feels so good," he croaks, eyes barely able to stay open as I work him faster and faster from both sides. Pressing my cock against his lips, he opens his mouth and starts flicking tongue over the head without sucking on it. I try not to focus on the feeling, concentrating more on getting him stretches and prepped for me to fuck his ass instead.

Curling my fingers upward, I find the perfect spot that has him choking.

"Fuck, don't stop," he snaps, eyes clamping shut as he tries to ride my fingers. I let him do it, watching with awe as he starts losing control over himself as he races toward the edge. "I need to cum!"

"Then do it," I agree, which seems to be enough for him. Tightening my hold, I pump him over and over again as ropes of white cum splatter across his stomach as he cries out, the euphoria evident on his face as his brows crease, mouth drops, and eyes rolling back.

I take the opportunity to add another finger, but he doesn't make it easy while he grips my other two tightly. I have to force the third on in. With the groan of pleasure that he lets out, I take it that he's perfectly okay with it.

"That's right, take my fucking fingers," I growl down at him, shoving my cock back into his mouth as he screams with pleasure.

He sucks me with fervor, not pausing until I practically ring him dry.

Once his body sags and lets me in with ease, I slow down and remove them gently. Moving back to down, I step off the bed and shove his legs wider. His ass cheeks spread and ass pulsates with the stretch with ease.

"You still want me?" I ask quietly, smirking up at him when he scoffs.

"You shoved your fucking fist up my ass, better make it worth it for both of us." Nodding, I grab the lube again and fully saturate myself in the liquid. I'm already sensitive as fuck, and I have no doubt that I'm not going to last too long with his tight ass squeezing me tightly.

Grabbing his hip with one hand and my cock with the other, I line myself up with his entrance. We stare at each other for a few more moments, and with a subtle nod from him, I slowly start pressing inside of him.

I can't compare it to the feeling of a woman because they're completely different, but I have to say. I definitely think this will become a favorite of mine. His hands white knuckle the sheets, jaw clenched tightly as I try to press inside of him as gently as possible.

"Split me in half, why don't you?" He gasps, his head dropping coming up only to drop back down with another few movements from me.

"Do you want to stop?" I whisper, leaning down and over his body to bring us face to face. His eyes are wide, pupils blown with pleasure. I can guarantee there's pain mixed in there, but it's not evident in his eyes. I was right in thinking he would make me blow my load quickly. I'm not even half-way into him and I'm ready to detonate. I can't have him thinking I'm a two pump chump, though.

"No," he barks, his eyes snapping open. "Don't you dare fucking stop, Alec!" I'm taken back for a moment at his use of my name, yet he doesn't even seem to realize he said it. I put a bit more lube on before slamming home. His whole body flies off the bed, a loud shout echoing through the room as he grips the sheets.

"Like that?" I grunt, pulling out and burying myself to the hilt again. He nods rapidly, shouting loudly in pleasure.

"Yes, yes! Just like that!" The feeling of his tight ass wrapped around me is intoxicating. I'm nearly overwhelmed with the amount of pleasure that I'm feeling. It's like nothing I have experienced before. I mean, it was similar with Knuckles and Leather when we did our thing, but with him? I can't explain it. Just he and I making this memory together. The connection we share feels validated while I make him mine.

My fist grabs his cock roughly, tugging it back to full mass as I plow into him. My brain blanks, body jerks as I fight to keep from blowing.

"I want you to mark my ass and make it yours," he commands, grabbing my other hand and laying it on his throat. I press into the sides and use the base of his throat as a handle to fuck into him faster and harder. Skin slapping is like music to my ears as I writhe above him. I can't hold it back anymore, and I explode inside of him.

Ecstasy ripples through my body as my own vision turns white, my body barely able to support me as I continue to own his ass and make it mine. I don't stop until he's screaming beneath me. Another stream of hot cum flies from his cock, and I waste no time in cleaning his chest while slowly coming back from riding my own wave of pleasure.

Leaning forward over his body, I push his body back into the mattress with mine. His arms wrap around me, his legs moving further to accommodate my side.

"I'm not that flexible, man. I can't stay like this without getting a charlie horse," he chuckles. Pecking his lips, I hoist myself up and off of him.

"I love you, you know," I admit, plopping down next to him. He rolls toward me, his leg lifting over my hip and pulling closer to me.

"I love you too, you know," he says back, cupping my cheek and leaning forward for a kiss.

"Do you still think they're fucking?" I ask him, laughing quietly.

"Probably. Knowing those two, they're probably going to be fucking for the rest of their lives like rabbits."

"The rest of our lives?" I parrot, looking down into his eyes. He nods, smiling tenderly up at me.

"You know you're stuck with us, so I guess you better buckle up for the ride."

"Motorcycles don't have seatbelts," he retorts. We laugh together, kissing one another softly. "I hope you know that happily ever after doesn't exist for people like us."

"I guess we're made for one another because we're a group of assholes. We'll be fine," I yawn, wrapping my arm around his waist and pulling him even closer.

"Forever?" He mumbles against my chest. I nod quietly, kissing the top of his head.

"Fuck yeah," I mutter, barely able to keep my eyes open. "Forever."

Epilogue

LEATHER

TWO YEARS LATER

"Are you sure you want to do this?" Prez asks me, his rough knuckles grazing against my cheek. I feel entirely too exposed, but it's all a part of growing. The trauma I endured no longer has existence in my life and I want to show my men that I will not entertain it any longer.

"I'm positive," I mutter, leaning further into his touch. Another set of calloused hands land on my shoulders. They massage gently as the kinks and knots disappear from my tensed upper body.

"Relax, Leather." Knuckles whispers in my ear, pulling my hair back and away from my face. Closing my eyes, I lean against him. He holds my weight easily while soothing my overactive nerves.

"I don't want to be nervous," I confess. Blinking my eyes open, I'm met with adoration. Affection. Admiration. Strength. With a deep inhale and heavy exhale, I straighten. Tornado is behind

Prez, his body bent down to Prez's height and whispering away. Knuckles works quickly to braid my hair as I watch a deep blush bloom on Prez's face that I never would have put there without a bit of coaxing. Tornado and Prez have a special bond, similarly like Knuckles and I.

"You can be nervous, beautiful," Tornado assures as he sweeps Prez out of the way. His arms band around my waist and hoists me up. I don't hesitate to wrap my legs around his trim waist as I hang on for dear life. "There is strength in submission. You of all people should know that."

"I just don't know if I'm ready," I whisper. Staring into his electric blues, he doesn't even appear hesitant. There's no deception in his tone nor eyes. He's serious, and I appreciate he's willing to be my rock in this.

"You will still have Knuckles to dominate," he teases, earning a huff from the man behind us. The small giggle escapes from me as I picture being dominated while ruling Knuckle's body.

"I do, don't I?" Leaning down, I plant my lips on his. Sparks immediately fly, my brain short circuiting as I slowly start to rock my hips against him. With a growl, Tornado detaches us and sets me heavily on my feet.

"Show time, baby." Prez grabs the metal ring from the leather collar around my neck and guides me into him. He smashes into me, his lips landing heavily as his tongue evades my mouth. We kiss frantically, my fingers raking into his hair and holding on tightly.

Tugging, he releases my death grip and steps back with the leash in hand. I didn't even realize he clipped it on.

"No fair," Knuckles grumbles. Another laugh rings through the group as I pad my way over to him. Standing on my tiptoes, he instinctively lowers himself to my height. I waste no time in claiming his lips too. His fingers dance to my uncovered core, playing in my already wet folds. A different hand smacks Knuckles away from me.

Prez gives my leash a solid tug. Narrowing my eyes, I silently warn him to behave. With the look of marveled joy, I know my warning will not be heeded. That is entirely okay as I plan to have him tied up and taught a lesson. It may not be today, but I will ensure sometime in the near future.

Knuckles trails behind me on his hands and knees, licking the back of my heels with each step. It's a sign of worship, the point that he literally worships the ground I walk on. I can feel myself getting wet from the idea of having this insanely strong male on his knees for me, his ass in the air and waiting for a good whooping.

Strutting onto the dais, Tornado turns me toward the crowd. It's silent, the lights too blinding for me to see outward.

My breasts are cupped with wire, the leather bodice cutting into me in all of the perfect places. There's plenty of skin on show while maintaining a level of covering to keep my scars hidden. This was part of the compromise, not that I'm complaining.

"They are watching you, my love," Tornado whispers in the shell of my ear, dragging his fingers from the bottom of my ribcage to just under my swollen nipple. Instead of stroking over it, he goes around it, teasing me away from the temptation of pleasure. "So many admirers...all for you." Prez does the same trail on my other side and goose bumps erupt over my skin. Knuckles still kneels on the floor in front of me, his tongue swiping happily over the leather heels.

"Open," Prez demands, and I drop my jaw for him to shove two fingers in. "Suck." Immediately I begin working his thick digits over. Both men rock their groins into my side as my pussy aches for them.

"Are you wet, mistress?" Knuckles asks from below me, his face right between my thighs but not quite touching me. Glancing down at him, I'm sure my smirk is anything but innocent.

"Not enough," I tease and look at the men over my shoulder. Both of them seem to bristle at the answer as if I have slighted them in some way. Maybe I have since their mere bodies are not enough to get me drooling for them all.

Who am I lying to? Just thinking about these men without their clothes has me wanting to jump their bones.

Gesturing to Tornado, I quickly kick my leg upward and he barely manages to catch under my knee. His growl rings into my ear, vibrating through my entire body and right to my clit. Reaching down to grab Knuckles hair, I fist his dirty blonde locks to guide him to where I need him. "You're going to eat this pussy like you've never before. If I don't cum in the next minute, you will not like it. Do you understand?"

Knuckles immediately dives in. It takes everything in my body not to buckle under the instant pleasure. Prez wraps my hair around his fist and tugs. My head snaps backward forcing me to stare at the ceiling instead of at Knuckles.

"You will cum when I say," Prez growls, his teeth sinking into my throat. Swallowing thickly, he licks over my pulse point with a groan. "Tornado will decide when that is. For now, Knuckles will simply bring you to your highest point..." A finger is suddenly pushed inside of me, rubbing that special spot. My hips jerk forward in surprise, my moans ringing louder as I get closer and closer to the edge.

"Enough!" Tornado commands and Knuckles removes himself from me with an audible *pop*. I have to gulp down the urge to growl at them for taking away my pleasure, though I know I will relish in their punishments if I do not listen...

Before I have time to catch my breath, they're forcing my knees to buckle underneath me. Crashing not-so-gracefully onto the wooden dias, both men stare down at me with heat in their eyes and their hard cocks pressing against the zipper of their jeans. Knuckles makes a choking sound from behind me, and I can absolutely relate to the feeling. Nothing has really happened, yet it's pure fucking torture just waiting for them to make their move.

Tornado and Prez smirk at me, both of their hands dropping to their jeans and quickly undoing the zipper. A hand quickly wraps itself in my braid then jerks my head backward. The two dominating men in front of me aren't close enough to do it, so I can easily deduce who it is.

"You better be careful," I sing-song while I'm forced to stare at my two other beautiful men. Their smirks are nearly identical. Full of mischief, lust, and danger. Lots and lots of danger. Not to mention the overall promise for pain.

My favorite.

"Or else, what?" Knuckles questions, his grip tightening as my hair pulls on the roots. Grimacing, I can't help but shut my mouth to obey.

He will absolutely be getting his ass blistered after this. I may not have full control right now, but mark my words...it's coming for him.

Something is heavily placed on my lips and forcing my mouth open. I let it in, knowing if I don't, I'll be the one with cream rubbed into my ass. Which, I may still end up that way. Knuckles keep me in place as Prez moves my mouth around the silicone O-ring gag. It stretches my jaw to full capacity, and I'm ninety-nine percent sure my jaw will be locked once it comes out. Once they have it secured, both men step away from me, staring down and seemingly admiring their handiwork.

Movement from behind me startles me, and I nearly faceplant into the dais. Thankfully Tornado was able to catch me before I did.

"Perfect segway," he rumbles as he lowers me to the ground. The angle I was going to fall keeps my ass in the air. Hands immediately start grabbing at me, and my eyes slam shut as distant memories threaten to evade me.

"I'm here, Blaine," Prez mutters, petting the hair away from my face. "Open your eyes. Now." The command is swift and not for argument. Popping them open, he stares at me as the deep sounds of buzzing take over.

"You have been such a good girl already, Leather." Knuckles's voice is sweet as honey, but I know it's nothing more than a lure. One that I'm willing to be hung up on. "Let's see if you can keep it up."

"Oh!" I gasp as the cold, vibrating head is placed directly onto my clit. Jolting my hips away, I try to escape the intense feeling. Saliva drips from my mouth onto the floor and I nearly put my cheek in it. "Oh hy hod!" I shriek past the gag, doing my best to wiggle away from the immense pleasure. It's far too strong for so little preparation. It almost hurts.

Multiple tendrils of leather smack down on my ass, forcing another surprised sound from me. This time, my face slides easily with the rest of my body as I fight the feelings. Two hands land on dips of my thighs and force me back to having my ass in the air. Another set of hands grab each of my arms, shoving them between my thighs and holding me face down and helpless. Metal clanking, locks clicking, cold metal is placed on my wrists and ankles.

Once the hands let go, I test my limits only to realize I'm bound in this position. All three men have backed up, their cocks protruding from their jeans as they tug their lengths in my direction.

"Isn't she just sexy?" Tornado asks, his head tilting to where Prez stands beside him.

Prez hums. "She definitely does. Though, her fighting attitude will get her ass blistered if she's not careful, don't you think?" Prez turns to look at Knuckles, who simply stares at me with a look of wonder.

"If she's not careful, our names will be carved into her flesh as a sign of submission. Though, hers would be on us as well."

They talk about me as though I'm just an object instead of a hearing, seeing being. And while I'm internally complaining, my traitor of a vagina is fluttering in flattery as she waits for a cock to fill her. Rolling my eyes at the stupid thought, it seems to catch their attention.

"Five," Tornado growls as he holds out his hand. His entire body is protruding veins as if he's been stopping himself from moving. That may be true as they all stared at me like a piece of meat. I'm sure my side profile doesn't do it justice.

Knuckles laughs as he grabs the flogger and gives it to Tornado. I want to swallow, but with the current predicament my mouth is in, dripping on the floor will have to do.

Prez, with a smirk on his face, slowly walks out of my line of sight while keeping his cock in hand. Tornado doesn't hesitate to come near me and enact the punishment.

"You will count as I go or you will start again, do you understand?" Nodding my head frantically, he swats it down on my exposed ass. "I said: do you understand?" He growls, kneeling down next to me and running his calloused hand over the red welts he made.

As I have no plans for getting into more trouble, I mumble, "ess err," barely able to make out the words from around the ring in my mouth. The failed attempt seems to satisfy him enough as he brings it down harder than the first time. I swear I can feel each piece of leather making contact with my ass as he goes.

"Uhn," I try. His next ones are rapid, far too fast for me to be able to count and digest at the same time. No doubt that was his plan all along, though.

"Start again, Leather," Prez announces, suddenly dropping to his knees in front of my face. His thick cock rests on my cheek as I wait for the eventual strike to come. My body tenses, bracing for the worst. "Stick out your tongue and taste me." The demand is swift, and I stretch it out as far as I can to reach his tip. The need to taste the salty pre-cum slowly overpowering my other needs, such as my weeping cunt.

Screaming, I push my hips toward Tornado as the strike comes down, only to impale myself on his positioned cock. He doesn't move me as he smacks the material back down again. I stupidly count again and again, rocking myself on his cock until we reach five perfect whoopings.

"I will never understand how you are always this tight," Tornado grunts from behind me, tossing the flogger away from us. "You take all three of us, and yet you still manage to feel like a virgin."

My cheeks burn brightly at the statement, embarrassment heating my core.

Pulling away from me, Tornado barely keeps himself lodged inside as Prez positions his cock at the ring of my gag and presses inward.

"I'm going to fuck this pretty throat while he destroys your pussy," Prez grunts as he slams forward. He immediately hits the back of my throat the same time Tornado pounds back into me. The sensations are overbearing, but it's not quite enough for me to go over the edge. He buries himself to the hilt each time, my stomach rolling in pleasure with each stroke. I admit I don't get much satisfaction from a throat fucking, but hearing and seeing Prez enjoying himself has me growing wetter for them all together.

A third figure probs at my ass, the sensitization not foreign yet surprising every time I feel it. I'm given no time to adjust as Tornado continues his fast pace while my tight asshole is quickly stretched out. Thankfully they worked me over earlier to prepare for this, but nothing is ever ready when it comes to anal. There will always be some level of preparation when it's time, as evidenced by right now.

Eyes screwing shut, Knuckles thick cock stretches its way inside of me. One hand grips my hair while another set quickly undoes the straps from around my head. Once it comes off, the cuffs to my wrists also come undone. Feeling like a new woman, I quickly jerk myself to my elbows and suck Prez back into my mouth. The groan of satisfaction curbs my insanity, the feeling of being far too stretched almost taking over my senses.

Knuckles takes care in not forcing himself too quickly, but with a level of irritation, I slam back onto them. Pain rings through my entire body as more tears stream from my eyes, yet it's pain that I relish in. Prez's cock jumps inside my mouth. Glancing up at him from under my watery lashes, there's no doubt in my mind that he's enjoying my pain almost as much as I am.

His fingers dig into my scalp as he forces his cock further into my throat, his balls hitting the underside of my chin as I take him without complaint. On cue, Knuckles and Tornado set a perfect rhythm of slamming inside of me, never leaving me without a cock and always feeling full.

The sensations quickly build, their united front against my g-spot has me hurling toward the finish line.

Popping off Prez's cock, Knuckles grabs my shoulders and uses them for further leverage.

"I need to cum, please let me cum," I beg, shouting with pleasure as I force myself to stay on the edge. Tilting my hips slightly is the only thing I can do to stop from having one of the best orgasms of my life.

"Prez cums first, then you can cum like the good, dirty whore that you are."

Taking that as a challenge, I don't hesitate to shove him down my throat. The men like to think they use me, but I am definitely using them. Knuckles jerks me backward onto his cock then forces me to swallow Prez. All of their sounds mixed with the sounds of others enjoying the show has me cumming without permission.

Stars dance behind my eyes while my cunt spasms over the two pounding dicks inside of me. I'm pretty sure I black out, yet when I come to, they're still using me as their own personal sex toy.

"You're fucking lucky we love you," Knuckles growls in my ear as my upper body decides to fail me. "You better be grateful Prez finished mere seconds before you."

A tired giggle escapes as they split me open, my moans still echoing around the room as another, fluttering orgasm suddenly strikes.

"Oh God," I cry, my fingers digging into anything. Finally making purchase on Prez, he grips mine tightly in his as I ride the wave with Knuckles and Tornado.

"You are ours!" Tornado roars, slamming home and stilling. Knuckles follows quickly behind him, both of them pressed so damn deep I swear they're in my throat.

I can't move. My entire body is one giant jelly. Prez doesn't waste a second in scooping me up into his arms and carrying me away in all of our partially naked glory. My eyes start to drift closed, the pressure of today's events enough to tire me out, let alone the actual act of it.

"You did so good," he mutters into my hair as we walk.

"You prove every day that you are perfect for us." Knuckles agrees, his hand gently gripping my ankle. That's one thing that hasn't changed. Knuckles and I still tend to be attached at the hip, though now we're attached to the groin instead.

"We are so proud of you, love," Tornado assures as a door gently shuts behind us. I don't open my eyes, though I muster a half smile.

"I love you," I murmur sleepily, letting my body relax and settle into utter darkness.

Acknowledgments

Thank you to my amazing husband for supporting my craziness through and through!

A *massive* thank you to the wonderful Megan Henry! She has been with me since the beginning and has been a major support in all things, including my Twilight addiction! You're amazing, and I love you so much! <3

To my amazing Alpha & Beta teams as well as the ARC team, y'all help me put this badboy into reality, and I couldn't be more thankful for the honesty you've provided through the process.

I also want to thank the WONDERFUL Danielle Piper. She kept my sanity from going out of the window more times than either of us can count! Not only that, but she kept me on track with minimal whipping (unfortunately)!

To my lovely PA Chardonae Davis for helping me get everything promoted for this amazing new read!

Lastly, but most importantly, I want to thank YOU. Thank you for taking the time to read this piece of my art and sharing it with the world. Thank you for giving this small town author a chance to experience new heights. Without you, I wouldn't exist.

Crisis Hotlines

If you or someone you love are in need of emergency assistance, do not hesitate to call your local emergency number. Professionals are there to assist you as needed. All hotlines are FREE.

National Sexual Assault Hotline/Support Lines:

Australia: 1800 737 723

Canada: 604-255-6344

Germany: 08000116016

USA: 1-800-656-4673 or 877-995–5247

UK: 0808 500 2222

Suicide and Crisis Hotlines:

Australia: 13 11 14

Canada: 519-416-486-2242

Germany: 0800-181-0721

UK: 08457-90-90-90

USA: (800) 723-8255 or Dial 988

Crisis Textline:

Canada: Text HOME to 686868 for Self-Harm Help

USA: Text CONNECT to 741741 for Self-Harm Help

UK: Text SHOUT to 85258 for Self-Harm Help

About the Author

Lexi Gray is an Alaskan-Based author with several years of freelance editing under her belt. Ms. Gray has also dabbled in narrating, which can be found on Audible. She's had a passion for writing at an early age; however, started out in helping authors develop their writing skills and bringing languid movement and passion to their works. Her unique voice shines through her works, using emotion-based writing and hitting subjects that may present as taboo. Ms. Gray utilizes critical thinking and good, dirty and dark humor to get through it all.

Ms. Gray herself enjoys reading dark romance, but also loves to dive into a dirty RomCom or two. From her own past experiences, she hopes to use her books as a sense of learning for those who read it, even if they end up only holding it with one hand along the way...IYKYK.

You can check out updates along the way on her Instagram: @AuthorLexiGray or on her website at AuthorLexiGray.com

Also By

Satan on Wheels by Lexi Gray is a slow-burn, enemies to loves, motorcycle club thriller that you don't want to miss! Action packed full of fan-favorite tropes and triggers! Don't forget, smut starts on page one! It's book one of the Rubber Down Duology.

Satan's Naughty List is book two of the Rubber Down Duology. Another action packed motorcycle club story, featuring your favorite duo from book one! This is an RH, MM/MMF love story. HEA guaranteed. Again, smut starts in chapter one!

Devil's Sweetheart is in case you're looking for something a little softer, sweeter, and full of friends to lovers. If so, then this is for you. Shibari love, new to bondage play, but it's Valentines day sweet. Book 2 releases June 2024.

Made in United States
Troutdale, OR
06/13/2024

20526959R00239